Southwestern Shifters

Rescued
Relentless
Reckless
Rendered
Resilience

I0542427

Reverence
Revolution
Revenge

Southern Spirits

A Subtle Breeze
When the Dead Speak
All of the Voices
Wait Until Dawn
Aftermath
What Remains
Ascension
Whirlwind
Reluctance

Love in Xxchange

Rory's Last Chance
Miles to Go
Bend
What Matters Most
Ex's and O's
A Bit of Me
A Bit of You
In My Arms Tonight
Where There's A Will

Leopard's Spots

Levi
Oscar
Timothy
Isaiah
Gilbert
Esau
Sullivan

Wesley
Nischal
Justice
Sabin
Cliff

Mossy Glenn Ranch
Chaps and Hope
Ropes and Dreams
Saddles and Memories
Fences and Freedom
Riding and Regrets

Yes, Forever
Yes, Forever: Part One
Yes, Forever: Part Two
Yes, Forever: Part Three
Yes, Forever: Part Four
Yes, Forever: Part Five

Spotless
Hide
Hunt

Breaking the Devil
Unexpected Places
Dark Nights and Headlights

DARK NIGHTS AND HEADLIGHTS

BAILEY BRADFORD

Dark Nights and Headlights
ISBN # 978-1-78430-140-8
©Copyright Bailey Bradford 2014
Cover Art by Posh Gosh ©Copyright July 2014
Interior text design by Claire Siemaszkiewicz
Totally Bound Publishing

Published in 2014 by Totally Bound Publishing, Newland House, The Point, Weaver Road, Lincoln, LN6 3QN, United Kingdom.

Totally Bound Publishing is an imprint of Total-E-Ntwined Limited.

DARK NIGHTS
AND
HEADLIGHTS

Dedication

Strength comes in surprising packages.

Chapter One

One of the good things about owning your own fairly decent-sized ranch was that you had a certain amount of freedom other people didn't. You could walk around bare-assed naked in most places on it, let the grass grow crazy and not landscape for shit. You could have a pile, or piles, of rusty old equipment and trash that ought to be hauled off, buildings crumbling and in various states of disrepair, and you could do shit like what Joban 'Joe' Jacek was doing tonight— driving back across his property from his brother's trailer, a little stoned and buzzed.

Joe didn't have the piles of trash or the crumbling buildings, and being butt naked outside was just asking to be mosquito bait. He did allow himself to get a bit loose sometimes. He knew the dirt road going from Trent's place to his like he knew his own dick. Joe was on pretty damn great terms with his dick. They'd been best friends for going on two decades now.

It wasn't the first time Joe had made the drive in a somewhat altered state. Living on a ranch in the middle of Uvalde, Texas, Joe took his relaxation wherever he could get it. It was just him and Trent running the ranch, and at a little over a thousand acres, they were kept busy enough from morning until evening.

And there wasn't Joe's preferred kind of fun anywhere around. Sure, the creation of Grindr had helped some, and Craigslist—well, that one just scared the shit out of him as often as the pics loaded to it made him horny. But even Grindr couldn't plop a choice of gay men down real close to the ranch, and Craigslist… Joe would just take a pass on that one. He'd seen the news stories about people using that media source to find victims and all. Plus, with his luck, he'd wind up having to pay whoever he met up with. Or he'd get mugged, beaten—something like that.

So he was feeling pretty good, tired and relaxed in a way he didn't experience often. The truck bumped along down the road, and Joe figured he should maybe grate it again and try to smooth the ruts out of the dirt. It'd mean scheduling a day just for that, so he'd need to talk to Trent about it, see when Trent could take over his chores for the most part.

"Probably shoulda thought of that before I left his place," Joe muttered to himself. He snorted. Trent was messed up and wouldn't have been able to plan anything. He'd added tequila shots to his beer drinking and the pot smoking. Joe would be surprised if Trent wasn't puking sick half the day tomorrow.

Joe just felt *good.* Calm and mellow and relaxed. It was almost as good a feeling as the sleepy, melty sensation following a fantastic orgasm.

As he drove slowly down the road, Joe was awed by the land at night. The moon was high in the dark sky.

Stars sparkled overhead like millions of hopes and dreams just waiting to come to earth. The moon was incredible, big and so bright it almost made his eyes ache.

Joe wondered just how bright it was. Curious, he turned off his headlights. Then he braked, and blinked as white spots danced before his eyes. Once his vision had cleared, or mostly, he looked out of the windshield.

"Well, shit. It's dark out." And he was a genius. Joe snickered and narrowed his eyes as he leaned against the steering wheel. A little concentration and he could make out the road. Not very far, but yeah, a few feet or so in front of the truck.

He drove along like that, hunched over the wheel. His beater truck was too old to have airbags, so that was a worry he didn't have. Joe concentrated as well as he could, trying to see the road. As familiar as he was with the land, he'd have said he could drive home blindfolded. Thirty-eight years he'd spent on the place—his whole life. Trent had gone away to college since their dad had said one of them needed a degree, but he'd come home as soon as he'd graduated.

Both of the Jacek boys had ranching in their blood. Both of them were gay, too, something that would have killed their daddy had he not already been dead when Joe'd started to accept his own sexuality.

Joe's chest ached and he took a hand off the wheel, slowed down some more and rubbed at the spot. "Hope I'm not having a heart attack like Dad." He blinked, because surely he had something weird going on with his eyes. There was no way something was moving out there in front of the truck. "What the—?"

His first thought was that one of the cows had gotten loose, except it wasn't big enough to be a cow. Plus, its eyes were glowing yellowish in the dark.

A chill shot down Joe's spine. He hit the brakes too hard even though he had been poking along, and the impact of his chest against the steering wheel knocked the breath out of him.

Or maybe that was fear, because those glowing eyes were getting damned closer to the truck.

Joe didn't know why he was so scared. He was in his truck—he hit the door lock. Unfortunately, the passenger door had to be locked manually, and he dove to the right, reaching for the little knob by the passenger window.

And he missed, falling over halfway while his foot slipped off the brake.

"Shiiiit!" Joe flung himself upright and stomped on the brake. The truck shot forward. "Fuck! Gas! Brake!" His head spun as his pulse accelerated at a speed much faster than the truck.

Joe slammed on the brakes and hit the steering wheel again. He shoved the truck into park and reached for the knob to turn on the lights again. His hand was shaking so bad it took two tries, but he managed finally to get the headlights back on. He watched as those glowing eyes faded some, but they still seemed unnaturally colored when Joe saw the critter they were attached to.

"A—" He frowned and leaned so far forward his head almost touched the windshield. "Coyote?" If so, it was a big one. The thing was almost as tall as the truck. Joe was certain its pointy ears reached the top of the grille, at least. "You ain't no coyote."

He felt instant relief when it dawned on him that he must be looking at someone's German Shepherd. A big German Shepherd, sure, but it wasn't a coyote and the markings were similar to a German Shepherd he'd seen ages ago.

"Someone must have dumped you, huh, buddy?" Joe chuckled and leaned back in the seat. "Damn, boy. Or girl. You about scared a decade off me."

For one fleeting second, he wondered if it was a wolf, but Joe discounted the idea. Once there'd been red wolves in the area, but they'd been extinct for a long time. At least they had been from Texas. He vaguely remembered hearing something on a TV show about them having been raised in captivity and freed elsewhere.

As far as he knew, there weren't any other wolves native to the area, so that had to be a dog, he reasoned.

It walked out to stand in front of the truck. Joe shivered as he looked into the dog's yellow eyes.

"Ah, hell, I must be more messed up than I thought." Joe rubbed at his eyes before giving the dog another look. His stomach did a weird flip. "German Shepherds have some red on them, don't they?" He racked his brain trying to recall, but all he came up with was a black and tan dog.

"That's it. I'm totally wasted and seeing things." What else could it be when that dog was grinning at him? It was, too, he was sure of it.

Normally, a few tokes and a few beers didn't do much more than make him relax. "Guess I got some good stuff, or bad stuff, or something. Bad beer. Shoulda checked the expiration…date…" he trailed off, because that dog put first one big ol' front paw then the second on the hood so that the critter was staring straight at him. "Oh, shit."

Joe slapped at the horn, remembering too late that it had quit working weeks ago. "Those are some fuckin' freaky eyes, dog." They were *really* yellow. "Aw, now what're you doing?" he asked, whining just a little when the dog leaped and there it was, the big burly maybe-not-a-dog after all, pushing its nose against the outside of the windshield.

"No, no, no, don't do that, you're getting the glass all slimy." He gawped as he got a look at the long, sharp canines. "Uh, okay. You just lick until you're all licked out, bud."

Something kept him from putting the truck in gear and driving off. One, it went against Joe's nature to hurt anything, except for flies and mosquitoes. Those were such nuisances that he could get over his embarrassingly squeamish and okay, soft-heartedness, and off the little bastards.

But anything else? Trent had to handle it when any of the cattle needed to be put down, or when there was butchering done for their own freezers. Joe just didn't want to mess with that part of it all.

And there was a reason he didn't have a dog. Once Roscoe had died, his heeler he'd had throughout most of his childhood and into early adulthood, Joe hadn't been willing to have his heart broken like that again.

So he didn't want to hurt whatever the hell was on his truck, dog or hallucination or some coyote or extinct wolf. "Besides, it ain't real. Probably."

But Joe did flick on the windshield wipers, knocking them into the spray position.

It might have been funny had the dog not yelped like it'd been hurt. Joe felt like an asshole as the animal scrabbled on the hood before sliding or jumping off, he couldn't tell with the wipers and the water going.

He couldn't see where the critter had gone, either, and after a couple of minutes, he began to worry. "What if it broke a bone, or...or hit its head on the bumper and died?" The thoughts raced around in his head until finally Joe risked opening his door. Slowly. Very, very slowly, in case he'd pissed the dog off and it was just waiting to rip out his throat.

There was nothing out there on his side of the truck except dirt and scrub. Joe almost took the rifle off the gun rack, but he didn't want to shoot anything. He'd just have to hope, if the animal tried to attack him, that he could run back to the truck and get away.

So he was really going to do it, get out and see where the dog had ended up. Joe was a little quivery inside, and his head was still spinny from the beer and pot. He was beginning to question whether maybe Trent had laced either of those things with something stronger, because the night was turning out to be so freaking bizarre.

The ground crunched under his boots when he slid out of the truck and made contact with the dirt. Maybe he wasn't loud, but it sure seemed like it in the quiet of the night. Even the purr of the engine had an almost animalistic sound to it, as if the old thing belonged out there, one of Mother Nature's beasts.

But Joe's boots on the dirt didn't fit in at all. *So much for being stealthy. Shit.* He held onto the door handle with one hand and the left side of the frame with the other. His arms burned from the tension and strength of his grip.

The door was in the way, so he had to scoot out and around it. That meant letting go of his two supports, which turned out to be harder than he'd have thought.

Joe's concentration was split between letting go and watching for a vicious killer dog. Every canine horror movie he'd ever seen ran through is head — which meant *Cujo* was on a loop upstairs.

Joe got his fingers to cooperate and he flattened himself against the truck as he slid to the left. The rear passenger door handle jabbed him in the back and he hissed.

And froze as a low, rumbling growl came from down low, way too close to him. Joe gulped and looked down.

"Fuck," he yelped as he froze in place. The head of that big, snarly dog-thing was between Joe's calves, the ornery beast having gotten under the truck. Joe's heart tried to pop right out of his chest and he damn near swooned, something he'd thought only women in old romance books did.

He wasn't telling how he had come to that idea.

The critter growled again and Joe tried to judge whether or not he could dive for the interior of the truck without getting bitten. Those were some big-ass teeth in that mouth, and those yellow eyes gleamed up at him as if the animal was already imagining how Joe would taste gutted and spread out.

Fuck it. I got thick boots and he's under the truck mostly. Joe dove —

And yelped when his right ankle was caught in a vise. It was the dog's muzzle, he knew it. Joe was jerked by that leg, hard to the left. It completely threw him off balance, and since he was a little — or more — stoned in the first place, his attempts at keeping upright only ended with him clawing uselessly at the truck as he went down.

He wheezed, his throat too constricted by fear to let out even a peep. Joe smacked the back of his head on the truck and saw a brilliant array of stars, brighter than those in the sky, as he hit the ground.

He didn't lie still. Joe kicked and immediately began pushing himself up on his elbows. And wished he hadn't because… *That's a big fuckin' wolf coming at me!*

And it was a wolf, Joe suddenly had no doubt. There was a feral, primeval feel to the beast.

Maybe I'm just about to shit myself in terror. Joe scrambled for an explanation as the wolf let go of him and began stalking its way up his legs. *Those eyes are just…* He shuddered and it broke something free in him. "Git! Go on, you damned—" Joe waved his hands as he yelled, but one snarly, snappy show of teeth had him gripping his own throat, hoping to keep from having it torn out.

"Fuck you," he spat back at the wolf. Joe's vision went wonky, going dark around the edges. *Oh, no.* He was not going to pass out.

Except that darkness kept cloaking his vision and the wolf was a blur as it placed huge paws on his stomach.

His determination not to pass out wavered. That pissed him off. He wasn't like one of those cute little fainting goats that dropped unconscious when they were spooked. He was a man, damn it all, not a freakin' goat!

Plus, if he lost consciousness, his hands would probably slip and that would be the end of him.

Joe stopped being a passive Patsy and kicked his legs as hard as he could while he bucked up at the same time. It was really a whole body convulsion, with him trying to shake off the wolf.

It got him a back paw to the balls and that darkness he'd been fighting pulled him right down into it. Joe didn't even have a chance to panic about dying.

Chapter Two

Diego sat back on his haunches and eyed the man. He smelled of beer and pot, though not a lot of either. Diego had been watching the human—Joe, he'd heard him called—for a while now. Why Joe had caught his attention so thoroughly was a mystery. The guy was attractive in that weathered cowboy sort of way, but Diego had seen better-looking men. He'd also seen worse.

If Diego had to try to pinpoint it, he'd have said it was because of the time he'd seen Joe sitting astride a big chestnut horse, shortly before sunset. It had been the second time Diego had seen him. There had just been something about the way Joe had sat in that saddle, all loose and sure of himself at the same time, as if he knew he belonged right where he was. Diego had tried to imagine what that kind of sense of self must have felt like, and had failed. Joe had watched the sunset and Diego had watched Joe.

Maybe it was a dumb reason to waste two weeks in the area, but it was the reason Diego had hung around all the same. It was why he hadn't been able to keep from finally approaching him, though that hadn't worked out so well.

He hadn't figured Joe would turn the damned windshield wipers on him. That had scared the shit out of Diego. Actually, Joe was lucky Diego hadn't pissed all over the hood when he'd slid off.

Diego still might mark a tire or two, because he did have his pride, after all.

Joe's breathing was fine, and while it was cute the way he'd tried to cover his throat, passing out had rendered that attempt useless. Not that it would have saved Joe had Diego been intent on ripping his throat out. It was easy enough to tear through fingers. They crunched like tortilla chips with as much jaw pressure as Diego had.

Killing Joe hadn't been the plan anyway. Diego had just wanted to see him up a little closer. He'd been concerned when Joe had turned off the headlights. That was a dumb thing for a human to do. They didn't have excellent night vision like shifters did.

So Diego had crept closer, thinking how it'd be a shame if something happened to Joe since he was so comfortable in his own skin. Diego envied that, but not in such a way that he'd wish any ill on someone who had that confidence.

Joe had spotted him, and Diego had figured it was a sign of sorts. He scolded himself for the thoughts he didn't want to give way to. Romantic thoughts — stupid, fanciful, ridiculous thoughts.

Like the one murmuring in Diego's head about how Joe was messed up and shouldn't have been able to see him with those headlights off. The moon was out, sure, but it wasn't like the moon acted as a giant flashlight or disco ball. Unless the rays were right on a spot, it was kind of dark, especially for a human.

Joe had seen him anyways. Diego supposed he could have gotten too close to the truck, could have lost track of how careful he was supposed to be since he'd been worried about Joe.

Then he'd just had to mess with the man, because he'd picked up on the tang of Joe's fear. Even with him in the truck, Diego had scented it. He'd thought being a little goofy might set Joe at ease, but all it had done was almost give Diego a damned heart attack.

Diego was going to give Joe another minute or so. If he didn't wake up on his own by then, shifting would be necessary. Diego considered licking Joe's face but discarded the idea even as he salivated a bit at the idea of tasting the man. Joe would sure as shit freak out if he woke up with Diego in wolf form slobbering all over him.

He probably wouldn't react much better to finding a naked man by him, but whatever. It seemed the lesser of two evils. Diego counted Joe's breath for thirty seconds. After that, he watched the fluttering pulse point at the base of Joe's neck.

A minute passed, then another. Diego tore his gaze away and focused on the moon. *Help me, Goddess.* It was the first time Diego had prayed since he'd been a kid.

He tried to shrug it off. There was no rhyme or reason for him having done it. There didn't have to be any reason for him to stress over it, either. It was just a thought to a deity that didn't even exist. Or if She did exist, didn't care about Her worshipers.

Diego felt the prickling under his skin, like a million hot needles just barely pressing into him. It was followed by fiery hits in his joints as they snapped into new forms. His muscles and tendons were next. For one split second, he was lost, then Diego was on his hands and knees, panting, sweating, as he tried to draw in a breath.

Always during that blink of an eye when he went through the last of his transformation, Diego panicked. Whether other shifters felt the same momentary sensation of being lost, he couldn't say. It wasn't something they discussed.

Conversations about anything more than what and where to hunt weren't all that common amongst them, in Diego's experience. Even then, most pack members didn't have a say in jack shit. The alpha male and female ruled the pack.

Diego put his past behind him, where he wished it'd fucking well stay. He didn't know why his hand was shaking badly as he reached out to feel that fluttering pulse.

It could have been exhaustion, the heat or loneliness—there was no one thing he could pinpoint that had changed. He supposed he could just be tired of being on his own. As a pack animal, it seemed unnatural, and Joe called to Diego deep in his core. The way Joe was obviously the alpha of the two brothers on the ranch also appealed to Diego's nature.

Diego brushed over the warm, sweaty skin. The shaking spread up his arm and all the way through him. He snatched his hand back, gasping and tipping onto his ass.

Joe groaned and mumbled something about never trusting his brother again. Diego had no idea what that was about. As far as he'd observed, Joe and his brother got along okay. The brother wasn't as attractive as Joe.

Tall and rangy, with broad shoulders and a tight-looking little butt, Joe stirred Diego's blood like no man had in far too long. Normally Diego had sex with dark-haired shifters with soulless brown eyes. That could be another reason for his attraction to Joe.

Joe was blond as could be, his hair almost white. There were no shifters Diego knew of with such fair hair or eyes. Joe had pale blue-green eyes that always seemed to be conveying amusement at the world around him.

Except for that one time, when Joe had watched the sunset. Then he'd seemed at peace instead of on the verge of snickering.

Trent was shorter, had a stocky build, and darker blond hair. His eyes might have been green. Diego couldn't honestly say, because it was always Joe who'd captivated him.

And now he was getting stupid and melodramatic. He was out of his element, almost being the aggressor — well, he supposed he *was* at this point. The whole situation was so absurd. No one in his pack would believe how he was acting, nor would they have allowed it had Diego tried to exert any control. He'd been the pack's property to use at will, and they sure had done so.

Thinking back to them and the reason he'd left wasn't doing him any good. Who knew when he'd get another chance to touch Joe, see him this close, watch the movement of his eyes behind such thin lids?

Joe distracted Diego from the hell inside his head, from memories he didn't want. As long as he concentrated on Joe, everything was better, brighter, and Diego's body was definitely interested, his dick hard and ass throbbing for what Joe could give him.

He'd never take without being given, though. Diego waited until he had his body under control, dick going soft because he wasn't an asshole. It didn't take long once he'd put his mind to it. Diego had long ago learned to get a rein on his body or suffer the consequences.

Plus, he wanted to see what Joe would do when he woke up to a naked man straddling him.

Diego did just that, sliding one leg over Joe's waist and kneeling above him. It was tempting to lower himself down and rub a little. He wasn't quite that immoral, so he held himself back.

He did lean forward onto one hand and use the other to touch Joe's neck again. As much self-control as he had, it wasn't enough to keep him from shivering. His cock tried to perk up, but Diego refused to give in to that bodily reaction. A hard-on was a little bit more than he wanted Joe to wake up and see.

Joe groaned again. Diego repeated the touch, and Joe flinched, his eyeballs moving even more rapidly behind his closed lids. His mouth pursed, pushing his lips out into a mock-kiss. On impulse, Diego dipped his head down and met those lips with his, giving Joe an innocent buss.

Lust hit him like an electrical current, jolting Diego so that he would have pulled back, much as he'd done when he'd first touched Joe's hand. The only thing that kept him from doing so again was the rapid reaction on Joe's part, enfolding Diego in strong arms before he got more than an inch away.

Diego hissed as he was pulled down fully onto Joe's body. Where were his quick reflexes and fighting skills? He was so stunned that he didn't even realize he was being flipped over until his back hit the ground.

He gasped, the breath knocked out of him. He had a second to look into amused blue-green eyes, then Joe's mouth was on his, Joe's tongue pushing in demandingly.

Diego melted like butter on a Texas summer day. His muscles went lax and he couldn't do much more than moan and tangle tongues with Joe. The man tasted kind of addictive, the beer and weed an odd combination that Diego had never experienced before. Neither substance affected his kind at all, so the heat that surged from his mouth to his dick had to be solely because of Joe.

It'd been too long since Diego had been taken, that was all there was to it.

Diego's liquid bones firmed up enough that he was able to wrap his arms around Joe. His legs parted more on their own since Joe wiggled his way between them. Diego hitched them up and swallowed a whimper when Joe ground his denim-covered groin against Diego's bare dick and balls.

Joe kissed him harder, their teeth clacking together as Diego tried to angle his head for better oral penetration. Kissing wasn't something he'd done much of, and never like this, raw and burning, a claiming as Joe pushed his tongue in deeper to access Diego in places no one else ever had.

And all Diego could do was try to keep up, move his tongue alongside of Joe's and revel in the taste of the man. Joe nipped his tongue, sucked on his bottom lip, and Diego's brain just shorted out. He became a thing, a body in need, not a man or shifter capable of thought. Diego dug his heels into Joe's ass and tried to fuck him through the clothes the man wore.

Joe retaliated by biting his lower lip, sucking on it hard enough to bring up blood, and thrusting almost painfully against Diego. He also grabbed a handful of Diego's hair and framed his face with the other hand. Both things caused an ache to ricochet through Diego, a mix of pain and pleasure so intense he could hardly stand it.

He damn sure couldn't process it. Diego whined, the sound swallowed by Joe right before Joe sucked on Diego's lower lip. Joe rumbled into his mouth and began rutting with more force and speed. The friction from the denim was uncomfortable, and yet Diego craved it, driving his hips up eagerly. The rough rubbing burned, made his dick ache, but shifters like him always did need that helping of hurt with their sex.

Joe pulled at his hair and tightened his hold on Diego's jaw. Diego gasped, which got him more tongue and teeth. He clutched at Joe's shoulders, curling his fingers against the firm muscles there. Joe fucked on him like he was trying to drive Diego into the ground.

And Diego came so hard he couldn't even get a breath to scream. He turned his head aside, tried to, only to find that Joe held him firmly in place. That knowledge spiked Diego's orgasm out of the stratosphere, shooting it right past pleasurable and trampling all over ecstasy. It was more than that, more than Diego had ever known was possible from a climax. He came in spurts almost painful, they were so intense.

Joe shuddered and humped on him. Diego was just coming back to earth from his release when Joe threw his head back. His lips parted, a long, drawn-out sound coming up from Joe's core.

It went right to Diego's, settling deep inside him, imprinting the sound into his very being. It was surreal and scary and fascinating.

Joe thrust a few more times, the scent of his spunk mingling with then overpowering Diego's. "Aw,

God," he mumbled, tugging harder on Diego's hair. "What a dream."

Everything good about what he'd just felt dissipated as Diego realized Joe was too messed up to comprehend that what had happened was reality, not, as he'd said, a dream. It turned Diego's blood cold, made him shiver as if he were buried in a foot of snow instead of pinned between the warm body above him and heated ground below him.

Diego didn't want to be a dream or a nightmare. He shoved at Joe, then got his hands beneath Joe's chest and pushed harder. Joe opened one eye and grimaced. "You're fucking up my dirty dream."

Diego scowled at him and put a bit more power in his attempt. It would have been nice if Joe had let go of his hair quickly, but Joe didn't. When Diego threw him off, Joe probably took some of Diego's hair with him.

"Oomph!" Joe hit the ground hard.

Diego didn't care. His ass and back hurt now that he wasn't trying to get off, and his dick and balls were raw. He scrambled to his feet as Joe groaned and flopped an arm over his eyes. How had he not seen that Joe was so fucked up on his drugs and booze?

Joe's eyes rolled back in his head and Diego's temper was doused as fear clutched at his gut. Joe didn't smell like a brewery or a heavy pot smoker. Diego was back at his side, kneeling in a heartbeat as he began looking for a reason for Joe passing out again.

He found it on the back of Joe's head, a lump the size of a hen's egg. Diego's heartbeat tripled. *When did Joe hit his head? How do I help him? What kind of sick bastard am I to not even have noticed – ?*

Diego cut off the self-recriminations. Now wasn't the time for them. He felt Joe's pulse, watched him breathe again. Both were normal, as far as he could tell. Diego bit his lip as he considered what to do. He couldn't leave Joe outside. There were snakes and other creatures that could hurt him. The truck wasn't much of an option, since Diego didn't know how to drive.

Then again, it was an option of sorts. Diego got an arm behind Joe's shoulders and one under his legs. The smell of Joe's cum was making Diego's dick twitch, but he ignored the reaction. He stood, picking Joe up. Diego was a good foot shorter than Joe, but he was strong despite his thin build.

Diego had him back to the truck in no time at all. Joe was all floppy man and unwieldy body parts as Diego tried to get him settled somewhat comfortably in the seat. When he had Joe in there to the best of his abilities, Diego considered his next action. He needed to get Trent over to Joe. Diego knew Joe had a cellphone, but that wasn't a good option for Diego since he couldn't read more than a few words, either. Schooling wasn't a priority or even a possibility in the pack he'd been raised in. He knew what a T looked like, but there was always the possibility that Trent's name wasn't under Trent. Could have been brother or some nickname Diego wouldn't know.

Besides all of that, Joe had a password on his phone. Diego had heard Trent teasing Joe about it a few days back, telling Joe he'd hack into the phone, whatever that meant.

Joe moaned and Diego decided, fuck it, he'd humiliated himself already with Joe, what was the point in trying to hang onto any pride now?

And so he shut the truck door then shifted. That done, Diego took off running toward Trent's trailer, barking as much as he could in the hopes of drawing

Trent outside. Diego just hoped like hell Trent didn't step out and shoot him, though with the way his night was going, that would probably be just what happened.

Chapter Three

Jesus, the sun was crashing down on him, right into his damned brain. His left eyeball was going to fry first. "Fuck," he rasped, trying to close his eyelid. Something was holding it open.

So I'm being tortured then. What the hell did I do? It didn't make any sense.

"Come on, wake up," a familiar voice growled at him. "You don't get your ass up, I'm gonna have to haul you on over to the urgent care clinic in town, and you know damn well how good they are at their jobs."

Joe groaned as Trent let go of his eyelid. The brightness was still lingering in the form of a jillion white starbursts. Joe's head throbbed and his mouth was so dry he'd swear someone had stuffed it with cotton.

"Bro, did you…? Did you piss yourself or…?" Trent poked at Joe's groin.

And at least one memory came flying back to Joe. A thin, sleek body, almost too thin, full lips, a narrow, slightly hooked nose, large eyes that gleamed yellow then amber, a thick pelt of hair— "What the fuck happened?"

Trent cackled and it made Joe's brain throb. Not that Trent seemed to notice. "Looks like you shot in your jeans, dork. What were you doing? Rubbing off on the truck? You got one of those weird fixations on it?"

Joe managed to get his eyes open. It was dark, which threw him off his bearings even more.

"Hey," Trent said softly, seriously, which concerned Joe more than his own confusion did. Trent was always a sarcastic little shit, poking and prodding and picking until sometimes Joe wanted to throttle him.

"Joe." Trent shined a light in his direction, but not, thankfully, right in his eyes.

"'M right here." Joe recognized the interior of his truck. When he blinked, he saw those yellow eyes staring at him through the windshield. Joe sat up so quickly his head spun. There was nothing outside looking in at him.

"Joe? Come on, you're scaring me," Trent pleaded. He took Joe by the shoulder and shook him. "What's wrong? Why do you have that—?" Trent shined the light on Joe's crotch. "There?"

Joe followed the beam down to his groin. There was a cool wet patch he knew wasn't piss.

Trent continued with the questions. "Did you pass out from the beer? You drank more than that Friday night, bub. Are you sick? But why'd you come in your britches?"

"Trent, please—shut up." Joe was going to puke, his stomach going all swirly on him like he'd swallowed a mini tornado. His head was pounding. Joe reached back to rub it and yelped. "Ow!"

Trent shrieked and fell out of the truck. That was awful hard not to laugh at, too hard for Joe to resist.

When he did guffaw, his head hurt even worse, so he shut up and tried to breathe through the pain.

Trent clambered back to his feet, cussing up a blue streak. "Think that's funny, huh?"

Joe pointed at him. "You shine that flashlight in my face one more time, and I will purely whip your ass."

"Uh-huh." Trent didn't put the beam on him, though, instead shining it on the seat. "Why'd you holler like that? You about made me piss myself. Guess then we'd kinda look like twins."

They weren't ever going to look like twins, but Joe got the gist of it. "Gotta knot back here that might explain why I was passed out." Slowly, the pieces were coming together. Except for the spunky jeans part—that just didn't make sense. There couldn't have been a sinfully sexy man beneath him, holding onto Joe like he was that man's lifeline.

And the sounds Joe kept imagining he had made, little whimpers that fed right into Joe's mouth, because Joe hadn't been able to stop kissing him, to stop taking and owning those lips. Jesus, God, he didn't ever have fantasies that hot. Imagination wasn't Joe's strong suit at all.

"Let me check it out. Might have to take you to that clinic after all." Trent put a foot up on the truck's running boards.

Joe glared at him. "You ain't taking me nowhere, and especially not there. They'd probably want to castrate me or cut off my foot."

Trent cackled. They both knew that clinic was only good to go to if you knew yourself what was wrong and what the cure was.

"There's the hospital, then, but it's farther away," Trent suggested. He raised the flashlight up until it was illuminating most of the interior. "How many fingers am I holding up?"

"You got the damned flashlight in one hand and I can't see past that to your other, moron," Joe sniped. Sometimes his brother was a real pain in the ass. Of course, Joe took his turn tormenting Trent in return. Not that he was going to admit it. "And it's just a bump. I've had worse. Ain't even my first concussion. Remember when you dared me to ride Ol' Rigs?"

That set off another round of laughter from Trent.

Joe didn't mind it. He'd been young and dumb and had thought he could ride any critter. An old bull like Ol' Rigs? No problem. Except that bull had tossed him off so quickly and so hard that Joe'd been lucky to only have a concussion and a broken arm. If his daddy hadn't seen Joe and come running when he got on the bull in the arena chute, Joe might have even been stomped to death.

Well, if Ol' Rigs hadn't stood over me all but snickering.

"That bull was laughing at you," Trent said, speaking Joe's thoughts. "He just stood there snorting and pawing the ground by you while Daddy screamed and hollered his head off."

The memory was a good one, oddly enough. Daddy had never been one given to shows of emotions or loving words. Seeing the fear in his daddy's eyes and hearing it in his voice had been reassuring to an insecure boy not sure where he stood in life. "If I hadn't broken my arm, Daddy would have taken a belt to my backside, sure as the world."

"You know it," Trent agreed. "But I got your spanking and mine. Had bruises on my ass for a week over that one." He didn't sound bitter, merely matter-of-fact. They'd grown up in a different time, before all the political correctness had kicked in. Plus, in small towns, a cop was more likely to come watch and make sure you spanked your kid for misbehaving than they were to arrest you for it. Add to that, their daddy had been best friends with the sheriff, and claims of abuse had never been a threat.

Joe sighed and gingerly touched the bump again. "Damn, it hurts. I don't think there's any blood." He brought his fingers around front and Trent shined the light on them. Joe didn't see any blood. "Nope. I'll be fine."

Trent snickered. "Or back to your usual self, you mean." He leaned against the doorframe and looked at Joe. "I miss the old man, you know? Even though he wouldn't have approved of either of us. Not for being gay, and not for having a few beers or a joint now and then."

"Just because he was different from us don't mean we can't and shouldn't love him," Joe said. Thinking of him made Joe ache with a longing that hit him at the strangest times. "Who knows? Maybe he wouldn't have hated us, not forever. He ranted about queers and Democrats, everyone who wasn't an evangelical Christian. Can't say for sure he wouldn't have changed some had he lived longer and known both his boys were gay."

"I guess. I just always feel like he was disappointed in me." Trent cleared his throat, a sign he was done with that particular discussion. "So what happened here?"

Joe was glad of the topic change. It had been getting a bit deep for both of them. "I don't know. I was driving—"

"I told you ya oughta crash at my place, but do you listen? No." Trent had to be smirking at him. Joe could hear the smugness in his voice.

"I've driven this road over a thousand times, Trent," Joe pointed out. He leaned over and felt around, and was relieved to find his keys still in the ignition. At least he hadn't dropped them outside— *No, that was all a hallucination. Had to be.* One hot enough to make him come in his pants. "Ain't like it's changed in the almost thirty years I been driving it back when Uncle Mike lived down at the end of it."

Trent didn't argue. On a ranch, driving while underage was pretty common and Trent had done it too. Joe had fond memories of being about ten or so and nervously trying to impress his daddy with his driving. Of course, he realized now the old man had always kept him away from anything dangerous, just let him drive on the open areas of the ranch. Worst Joe could have done was hit a cactus.

"Yeah, well, obviously something happened here." Trent shined that damned light in his face. "You have a stroke or a heart attack?"

"Trent! Put that goddamned light down!" Oh, shit. Yelling just made Joe's head throb like one giant, raw, exposed nerve. He grabbed the sides of his noggin and closed his eyes. "Fuck, fuck, fuck."

"Jesus, bro. That's it. I'm taking you to the doctor somewhere." Trent grabbed him by the elbow. "Scooch on over."

There was no way Joe was going anywhere but back to his place. He took a few deep breaths while Trent kept trying to shove him over. "Trent," he finally growled. "Cut it out before I swat you."

Trent snorted at that. "Yeah, you may be taller, but I'm faster and can hit harder."

Both were, unfortunately for Joe, true. "Whatever, I ain't going nowhere besides home."

"You sound more like a hick every second that goes by," Trent muttered. "Mom would have thumped your ear for that sentence."

Joe suddenly felt so tired and worn clear to his bones that he couldn't bother sniping with Trent anymore. "Yeah, she would have. Look, I want to go home. I don't know what happened exactly except that I was stupid and turned the headlights off so I could drive by the moonlight. Didn't work so well. Then I saw something off to the side and I hit my brakes. Must have hit my head somehow, too."

"Right," Trent dragged out. "So you hit the back of your head on the windshield, because it couldn't have been the headrest that left that knot. And while you were busy getting that concussion, you spooged yourself." Trent pushed at him again. "You don't want to tell me you were beating off or whatever, that's fine. Maybe you did see something, though."

Joe was so surprised by Trent's acceptance of at least part of his explanation that he could only stare at his brother.

"Scooch. Over." Trent shoved him with enough strength that Joe had to slide or topple, and he'd already had enough of the latter for the night. "What do you mean?" He moved over to the passenger side. "And I ain't going to no — to a doctor."

"Good save, I guess," Trent told him. He got into the truck and shut the door. "I was almost in bed when I heard a ruckus outside on the porch. Lots of barking, and you know we don't have a dog, so that was weird enough."

"D'you spike the beer?" Joe asked, remembering that bit of suspicion from earlier.

"Don't be a dumbass," Trent snarked. "Oh wait, too late. You opened your own beers, bub, and we grow our own smoke so don't even go there."

Joe closed his eyes. His head hurt too much to deal with everything. "Okay. So maybe I was just extra worn out. I only got two hours' sleep last night with those two cows birthing." And it'd been a bitch of a birth for one of them, with the calf being breech and Joe trying to keep the cow and calf alive. It sucked only having two vets on call when it was calving season too. Fortunately, Joe had enough experience and luck, last night at least, to get both animals through the experience alive.

"So this dog was barking away on the porch," Trent said as he closed the truck door.

Joe immediately had a flash vision of yellow eyes, long sharp teeth and a beast on his hood. "A dog? Did it have yellow eyes?"

Trent started the truck up. "I honestly couldn't say. I came out the door with a rifle and only saw the back end of the dog. Fucker was wagging its tail like crazy and bouncing all over. I wanted to ask you about keeping it, but as soon as I saw your truck, the thing took off." Trent glanced at him. "Weird, that. Some dog shows up outta nowhere and leads me to my unconscious, wounded brother."

Fear and something very much like excitement shot through Joe. "Yeah. Weird." Now he wondered if he was wrong, and he hadn't hallucinated after all.

Which would mean there really was a naked, horny man I rubbed off on. Pretty sure he got off, too. Joe's eyes popped open and he almost asked Trent for the flashlight. Fortunately his sense kicked in and he just felt down the front of his shirt instead. There was no cause for Trent to know what he was checking on since there wouldn't be anything there. His heart and head couldn't take it if he…found cold, wet stickiness.

"Oh fuck," Joe whispered.

It was all Diego could do to hide in the darkness and watch the two brothers. He felt a pang of longing as he listened to them banter and pick at each other. What he wouldn't give to have that kind of closeness with any of his siblings. Such wasn't the way of his kind, though.

But why couldn't it be? The question refused to go away as he observed the two. Diego had been certain he was going to get shot when Trent came outside with the gun. He was lucky that Trent wasn't one of the kinds of people who shot first then tried to figure things out. Acting like a happy, hyper dog had seemed the best way to keep from getting his head blown off. That, and hiding his eyes. Diego was aware that they were remarkably different from a dog's. *Shifter eyes* – they glowed like a firefly's ass-end.

It wasn't much better in human form. Every wolf shifter Diego had ever seen had the same light, amber-colored eyes. Verging on yellow, no contact lens could match them or replicate the color exactly. It was one way to tell a shifter from a pure human.

Of course, they could sniff each other out. Like recognized like and all. Diego knew when he was around another wolf, and whether it was just a wolf or a shifter like himself. He'd not encountered either creature in the part of Texas he was in, and that was another reason why he'd hung around.

Trent got in the truck and shut the door. Diego sat up and whined so quietly even he barely heard it.

It looked like Trent was going to take Joe home. The headlights came on and Diego scurried back, frantically trying to ensure that he was out of the damning beam. When Trent began driving down the road rather than getting out or turning the truck in his direction, Diego sagged with relief. He wasn't willing to be spotted and perused as a pet.

Leaving was probably the best thing to do, but as Trent drove toward Joe's house, Diego found himself slinking along behind them, following the taillights on a path he knew well.

Chapter Four

The events of a week ago, combined with the feeling of being watched, were enough to make Joe think he was losing his mind. Not all of it, maybe, but some of it.

He couldn't convince himself that he hadn't had a naked man come on him. Kind of hard to deny it when there'd been spunk on his shirt. For all he knew, he could have come twice, once with his dick out, once with it in his jeans. There was also the unexplainable strands of reddish hair, or what looked like it, that Joe had found stuck to one hand with a mixture of cum acting as the glue. Trying to figure that mystery out caused an odd chill to skate down his spine, so Joe was content—mostly—to put that down as a weird fluke. Besides, the coming twice theory was kinda making him out to be studly.

Okay, not likely for a man nearing forty. Joe could admit it. Then again, it was probably more of a possibility than a man appearing out of nowhere, naked and horny. A man with almost yellow eyes.

Eyes that reminded Joe of a creature that he wanted to believe he'd hallucinated.

He had a dim memory of turning on the windshield wipers in a moment of daring or, more likely, stupidity.

And he hadn't so much as toked or had more than a single beer since that night.

Joe was so wound up he felt like he'd snap in two if one more problem popped up, or anything bizarre happened.

Every night, he woke up panting, sweating no matter how cold he set the AC, visions of a dog-wolf-man all tangling in his mind. It worried him bad for the first few days, enough so that he'd even seriously considered going and getting his brain checked out.

He couldn't imagine explaining to the doctor that he was having weird-ass dreams and, even more embarrassing, wet dreams like he was fifteen all over again.

Every night. *Every goddamned night.* And Joe fucking hated doing laundry! Between the sheets and waking up stuck to them or with his dick all but glued to his underwear, Joe was cranky and, surprisingly, horny. Often. More than he thought a man his age should be.

The chances of him telling a doctor any of that? Zilch.

So he was dealing with wet dreams and daytime fantasies that kept creeping into his head. There was nothing quite like birthing a calf while trying to battle aside filthy visions of yourself fucking a tight, round ass or getting sucked off by a pair of plump lips while being watched by pretty amber eyes.

If sometimes during those sex daydreams, those eyes turned bright yellow, Joe no longer recoiled. He just kept imagining thrusting until he came so hard his eyeballs rolled back in his skull.

Joe pushed his cowboy hat forward and rubbed at the shrinking knot. He wished he knew what had happened that night. Yellow eyes gleamed in his memory. "Or maybe not," he mumbled.

The back screen door's hinges squeaked just as Trent called out to him. "Hey, you cooking dinner tonight or are we gonna starve?"

Joe turned on the bathroom sink. He'd scrubbed his hands and arms outside to get the mud and blood and other fluids off that even gloves never seemed to completely protect him from during birthing. "It's your turn to cook, Trent."

"I don't have anything left at the trailer," Trent said as he stopped in the bathroom entrance. Joe hadn't bothered closing the door since he was in his own home.

"You can make spaghetti, got the stuff in the kitchen cabinets, and some of that greasy garlic bread in the freezer." Joe couldn't get irritated at his brother. They'd both been working hard and running on too little sleep. "Won't take but fifteen minutes if you use that skinny spaghetti instead of the regular one."

Trent nodded and stretched, his back popping loudly. "Ow, fuck. How come a thirty-three-year-old man can feel so fucking old? That ain't right."

"Ranching," Joe offered, scrubbing at his arms with the soap. He set to getting every fleck of goop out from under his nails next. "Wears a body out sometimes."

"Yeah it does," Trent agreed. "I can't believe we haven't seen that dog again. I found tracks, faint ones, but they're fresh, so I know he's still around here."

"Why're you so sure that dog's a he?" Joe asked. He finished rinsing the soap away then turned the faucet off. "You keep saying that."

Trent shrugged and tossed him a hand towel. "Because I am. Think I saw balls when he turned and ran off. I could be wrong, since I was going by the porch light. Maybe it was something else flopping back there."

Joe laughed as his brother explained his reasoning. "Well all right then." He didn't know why hearing Trent's argument made him get all warm and fluttery inside. It was almost like he was aroused, which was well beyond stupid because Trent was talking about a dog and Joe wasn't a pervert.

"I swear to God, bub, that dog didn't touch any of the dog food I left out all week." Trent took a couple of steps back into the hallway then waited for Joe to join him. Once he did, they strode to the kitchen, Trent chattering along the way. "Figures he'd take the steak, right? I mean, I sure as shit wouldn't want to eat dog food. I bought that healthy kind and it smells awful, like something already ate it and pooped it back out. Maybe I should get the cheaper brand that looks like meat chunks. You think that's like the canine version of junk food?"

Joe had an epiphany. "Trent, you want a dog?" he asked, stopping and pulling Trent to a halt in the kitchen.

Trent turned and his cheeks colored as he rolled his lips in.

Joe knew that look. It made him feel like an asshole, too, because obviously the answer to that question was yes and why hadn't he seen that sooner? "You never said." It wasn't quite an accusation, but close to one. "You could have told me, Trent. Hell, we've been living on this ranch all our lives. Well, you got off to College Station for four years, but you've been back here for a decade. Don't tell me you've been wanting a dog that long and been scared to ask."

Trent's blush deepened and he got that stubborn tilt to his chin. "I'm not scared, it's just that…"

Joe got it. Their daddy had shot any stray that showed up on the property. The cats he'd been okay with, since they'd had to be ratters if they'd wanted to eat.

"I've thought about it for a while now, but not the whole time I've been back, no," Trent explained. "Part of me thinks I shouldn't get one, or I don't deserve one since I never raised a hand to stop him from shooting the strays."

"He'd have whipped your ass until it was raw if you'd tried. Wasn't anything either of us could do to stop him." Joe knew, because he'd found out from experience. And he'd been slow to take to heart his dad's first no on the subject. Trent didn't need to know about that. "Dad out and out hated dogs. Never did learn why." Joe remembered the burn of his dad's belt welting his backside. "No reason to think you don't deserve a dog. You want one, you get it. Might want to wait until calving's done. Get you a pup, if that's what you want." What was he saying? A puppy? That'd be a lot of work.

But Trent's eyes lit up and he gave Joe a broad smile that made him look a decade younger. "You're sure? You can take some time to think about it, I won't get mad."

"Jesus, Trent, this is your home too. You shouldn't feel like you have to ask me anything like that." Joe really did feel like an asshole. He patted Trent's back and went over to the cabinet to get out the makings for dinner.

"Thanks, whether you want to hear it or not," Trent said from behind him. "And I'm supposed to be cooking."

"Sit down. I got this." Joe needed to keep busy. Between his weird fantasies and thinking about Trent being too scared to ask about getting a dog, or whatever his reasons were, Joe's mood was plummeting quicker than a comet. He'd learned long ago not to sit and brood, to work instead. The moving around helped burn off anger and energy, at least it did when it came to him.

"I'll cook the next two nights." Trent took the bread out of the freezer. "Actually, I was going to try to make it to Uvalde tomorrow and pick up some of that special feed the doc told us about for the weaker calves. I could bring back pizza if you want."

Joe's mouth watered. He nodded while he filled a pot halfway with water. "You do that, plan on it, and I'll handle things here. Get enough to last a couple days, and maybe some wings, too. That way all we have to do to eat is zap it in the microwave." Joe turned the faucet off. He set the pot on the stovetop and turned the burner on high. "I'm not changing my mind about the dog, either, Trent. You get you one when you want, though I do think it'd be best to wait until calving's done. Get you a couple, hell, get a pack for all I care. Just pick up their shit if it's in my yard is all I ask."

"What if I catch that dog?"

Joe peered over his shoulder in time to see that Trent had the bread on a cookie sheet. Joe flicked the switch for the oven and set the temp around four hundred. "Forgot to get the oven going, so it's gonna take the bread a little longer. Give me time to warm up some meatballs."

Trent opened the oven door and slid the bread in. "Is that a no, then?"

Joe cocked his head at Trent. Why did Trent always think he needed Joe's permission on stuff like this? Joe didn't ask. Trent was pretty independent when it came to everything but the ranch—which should have, by all rights, been theirs, fifty-fifty.

It wasn't. The old man had only left Trent the acre his trailer was on and one of the pickup trucks. Joe didn't know why, and his attorney had said the will was iron-clad. Joe couldn't give his brother half the ranch, or sell it to him. If he did, the will was void and the property went to support the political party Joe and Trent both disliked.

Made Joe wonder if his dad had suspected something about Trent that Joe hadn't at the time. Joe had been so busy burying his own secrets from his dad, he hadn't noticed if his little brother was struggling with his sexuality.

And Joe had tried for years, dating women, having sex with them just to keep his dad from getting suspicious. It was lousy of him, but he'd been up front with every one of them about not wanting anything long term.

"I don't care what was in the will, this place will always be just as much yours as mine," Joe said, not for the first time.

Trent ducked his head and wouldn't meet his eyes.

"Trent." Joe closed the distance between them and waited, knowing Trent would eventually raise his head. When he did, when he let his gaze rise up to Joe's, Joe continued, "I loved Dad as much as any kid could love their parent, but he wasn't an easy man, and he wasn't always nice. I don't know what he was thinking with the will." Joe couldn't even claim it was outdated, because their dad had gone and had his attorney draw up a new will a couple of years before he passed on. "Whatever his reason for it, he was all kinds of wrong, and this is always going to be your home, just like it is mine. You could move in here, I'll give you the main bedroom." Joe would do it in a heartbeat, had offered before.

Trent sighed and took off his cowboy hat. He ran his fingers through his hair, disheveling the hat-hair even more. "Nah, you've offered before and I know you mean it, Joe. It just—you'd think it wouldn't hurt after all these years. I loved him, too. He was my daddy, how could I not? With Mama gone so early on, he was all I had, him and you. I can't help but think he must have figured me out."

"Neither of us should have had to hide it," Joe told him. "He would have come around." Joe had to believe that, and he wanted Trent to believe it, too. "He was stubborn and mean sometimes, but he wasn't a total fool."

Trent settled his hat back on his head and a goofy grin slipped into place. "Well, that's debatable, since he liked you best."

Joe didn't poke back. Trent was making fun, but it was also the truth. Seemed like it was most of the time, though every now and then Joe would think back to the harsh whippings he'd gotten as a boy. Trent hadn't fared nearly so badly with those, not that he'd been spared often. Part of Joe figured his dad had been trying to toughen him up, maybe, help make him into a real cowboy. *Silly way to think nowadays, but it'd been common enough a theory once upon a time.*

The conversation had been too serious, and so were Joe's thoughts. "Tell me about what kind of dog or dogs you're interested in, besides the one you can't catch." Joe sort of hoped Trent caught the dog that was likely still on the property. But if it had yellow eyes… Joe shook his head and listened to his brother yammer on. It was good to hear Trent so excited about something, and while he started out almost timidly, by the time dinner was eaten and the dishes were washed, Joe had almost had his ear talked off.

"You coming down for a couple of beers? I didn't see any in your fridge." Trent looked at him expectantly after the last dish was dried and put away. "You haven't had anything since you bonked your head. Might be a better idea to wait a couple more days."

Joe yawned until his jaw ached. He was worn out. It seemed like he'd never be able to get enough sleep to feel rested. "Nah, I think I'll pass. I'm dead on my feet."

Trent nodded and gave his arm a pat. "Okay then. I'm going to kick back on the porch and have a couple. See you in the morning."

After Trent left, Joe moseyed over to the kitchen window. He watched his brother drive off until the red taillights had faded out of sight. The moon wasn't very generous tonight, hiding most of her light as she'd shrunk down to a sliver. Soon she'd play hide-n-seek with the clouds.

Joe snorted at his silly description and started to walk away from the window when he found himself staring at two bright yellow eyes. Fear and anticipation made Joe's body flush hot and cold. He didn't know what he was anticipating, what he feared.

"Jesus, those eyes ain't natural." No animal had ones like it. He'd Googled. Some critters had glowy eyes if a light was shined on them somewhat. That wasn't the case here. Even the moon sliver was hiding behind a cloud now.

Joe blinked. He judged the distance between him and whatever was watching him to be about thirty feet. There was no reason for him to be spooked. He was inside, safe— "Shit." And he hadn't locked the doors.

Should I lock 'em or stand here and keep this stare-off going? If that's the dog Trent wants, maybe I could catch him. Then again, could be that ain't ever been an animal at all and it's just some smart-ass kids having fun at my expense. It'd be a bit of a drive if that were the case, but there wasn't a lot of other shit for the local teens to do than cause a little harmless trouble.

"Seems like either way leads to me going out there," Joe mused to himself. He stood a little straighter and took a step to the left. As far as he could tell, those eyes followed him. "Could be my imagination." Joe tipped his head down and pointed out of the window. "You wait right there. I'm coming for you."

Chapter Five

He'd meant to leave. He really had. Diego didn't hang around one place too long for good reason. To his knowledge, he hadn't been tracked to Texas, or at least not this part of it.

Doesn't mean it's safe to tempt fate. Yet he couldn't help but hope that Joe would come searching for him, really search for him and find him. Diego had fantasies about it—Joe running him to ground, cornering him and forcing Diego to admit who and what he was, what they'd done. He wanted Joe to want him that badly, and it was that need that held Diego in place there on the ranch.

Even so, he fought it. Every morning, he told himself it would be the last day he spent watching Joe. It sucked that the Texas dirt felt so good beneath his paws, and even the heat soothed the aches in his bones that acted up now and then. Diego liked to find a nice, sunny spot to curl up in, or stretch out in, depending on his mood and where Joe was. As much as Diego would have loved to sneak closer when Joe was alone, he never dared. Even his fantasies weren't powerful enough to give him that kind of courage.

Until night-time, when Joe was settled into bed. Diego was becoming quite the voyeur, since Joe left the curtains open. He wondered whether Joe had always done so or had only started since their encounter a week ago.

Did Joe look out at the stars? What if he searched for Diego in the darkness? Joe had been asleep every night by the time Diego had allowed himself to get closer to the window so he hadn't been seen. He'd been playing it safe so that if Joe *had* been searching for him in the night, he'd never have been able to spot Diego.

Tonight was an exception. Diego was determined to leave and give up on the senseless yearning he had for a human. He still smarted from knowing Joe believed their encounter to be a dream. Diego wanted to be memorable, not that he'd ever been before.

He had to get moving, and couldn't hang around, eating shitty dog food or fantastic steaks, mooning over Joe. It was a stupid waste of time, not that he had a schedule to follow or any goals other than survival, honestly. If he hung around the ranch or any place for too long, even that goal would be cut short.

But he was so tired of being afraid. He yearned for Joe, and having had that small taste of the man before only made him ache for Joe more.

It was stupid, dangerous, a risk he shouldn't have taken then and shouldn't take again. But he did.

When he dared to step out of the shadows and peer back at Joe through the kitchen window, Diego quivered inside and out with a need he couldn't define. Joe stared back at him. Diego saw his mouth moving, understood that he was being pointed at.

What he didn't comprehend was that Joe was coming outside, for him, until it happened.

The front door opened and Joe stepped out onto the wrap-around porch. He had his gaze trained to Diego's almost from the instant he left the house. Joe didn't stand still, either. Diego's paws were glued to the ground by his inability to have more than one functioning brain cell.

He wanted Joe to come to him. Diego realized it in that moment, as he stood still as a stump. It was stupid, a stupid thing to want. Diego was going to leave. Nothing good could come of Joe getting any closer.

Yet Diego remained where he'd been, his focus all on Joe, but his gaze dipping down to Joe's boot-clad feet, each step bringing him closer. The boots and earth sounded like they were battling each other, rocks crunching, leather soles slapping at the dirt. Joe took long, steady strides even though his pulse was fluttering again and his breathing was choppy.

"Come here, boy," Joe crooned. "Come here and prove that I ain't crazy. Come here." Joe whistled and Diego cringed.

He took a half-step back then. Whistling the way Joe had done it had always hurt his ears.

"Aw, now don't go doing that." Joe slowed his approach. He made kissy sounds that Diego was sure were meant to be enticing or interesting instead of just silly.

He hadn't known it was possible to get goosebumps while in wolf form, but it was. Diego was scared and hopeful all at once. Joe was making goofy noises to try to encourage him closer. Had he been in human form, he'd have laughed his ass off or run like hell.

Joe was a dozen feet away when he extended his hand. "Man, this ought to be Trent's job since he's the one wanting a dog. I don't even know if I should be approaching you or waiting for you to approach me." He smirked. "Maybe if I apologize for turning the windshield wipers on you, huh?"

Did he want Joe to come closer or to leave him alone? Diego couldn't decide. There was no logic to the turmoil inside him. He should have run, yet he remained as if his paws were glued to the ground.

"That was really you, wasn't it?" Joe continued, still coming closer albeit at an even slower speed. "You know what happened that night. I keep having these dreams that—" Joe stopped talking long enough to snort. "See, there was this... I had... So I— Why the hell am I talking to you, and why is it so hard to say?" Joe narrowed his eyes. "Are you even an animal, or are you some kid pranking me? If you are, I'll put you over my knee and paddle your ass, fuck what society says about spanking."

Heat pooled in Diego's groin. His dick slipped from its sheath as he was aroused by Joe's words. Diego liked the idea of the man dominating him, holding him down, doing things to him Diego wouldn't have wanted from anyone else.

"Was that a real growl?" Joe asked. "You gonna bite me?"

Diego hadn't realized he'd made a sound.

Joe's voice dropped to a lower register as he continued speaking. "What's with those eyes? I can't find any animal on this planet with eyes that color. I'd think I was crazy, but I'm pretty sure you're really out here with me. If I didn't hallucinate you, then maybe I didn't hallucinate what came after. There was all that cum on my shirt."

There would have been. Diego had fled the scene so quickly it hadn't occurred to him that he'd left any physical evidence of their quick coupling behind. Well, other than Joe's own wet pants.

"Some strands of red hair, too."

Shit! Diego remembered thinking Joe might have yanked out some of his hair, but he hadn't really worried about it.

Joe stopped five feet away, an expression on his face like he'd just thought of something brilliant. "Hey, you could belong to the guy, the naked, hot little fucker that I thought I'd made up. But you're here, and he's—I don't know if he's real. I want to think he is, and he had odd eyes too. Could have been me bumping my head made me see things weird."

Diego squirmed, contemplating bolting. He didn't, yet again. Shifting into human form was probably what he should do. If Joe really thought he was a 'hot little fucker', then maybe they'd have sex if he changed from a wolf.

Of course, his eyes would still be an 'odd' amber color. In the dark, they tended to glow just as his wolf eyes did.

If we were inside, in the light, they'd just be a strange, pale amber, they wouldn't glow.

And if I got lucky, really lucky, Joe might touch me again.

Diego wanted that, very much.

"Are you going to let me touch you?" Joe asked.

The question so mimicked Diego's thoughts that he jolted as if he'd been avoiding a rattlesnake strike.

The movement must have been obvious despite the cover of night, because Joe cried out, "You *are* out here!"

Diego's entire body strained toward the man. Why bother holding back? He could possibly have a little time with Joe before he left for good. In order for that to happen, he needed to shift. Joe was too close for Diego to do so now.

Diego dug his back paws into the dirt and leaped. He heard Joe's startled exclamation as he soared past the man.

"Shit!" was followed by, "Where're you going? Shit!"

Diego's heart beat faster than his paws on the dirt as he ran for the back of the house. He had to shift, and knew Joe was going to follow him. Joe was a hell of a lot slower than a wolf shifter, though. Diego had a plan—lead him around back, shift before Joe got to him, then haul ass around to the front and into the house. He hoped Joe would look for him in the back instead of catching on that Diego was going to run to the side of the house where a small shed was.

The backyard had plenty of good hiding places, and maybe Joe would spend some time looking in them. Diego only needed a few seconds...

He could hear Joe, his footfalls and heaving breaths, muttered curses. Diego was excited in ways he hadn't been before, and probably shouldn't be. This was chase, a game of pursuit and it wasn't a child's game at all. There was a very real chance that Joe would do something to him. Fuck him, yell at him, hit him. Diego thought of that spanking and stumbled over his own paws. Fortunately he was at the side of the house, and he was certain he'd been fast enough that Joe hadn't seen him turn the corner of it.

Diego skidded to a stop behind the shed. He paused and listened to make sure Joe hadn't followed. When he was certain Joe was in the backyard hunting for him and in no danger of finding his hiding spot, Diego let himself shift.

That disorienting sensation of being lost made him shiver once he'd changed forms. Diego pushed to his feet and peeked around the side of the shed. He didn't see anyone. He sniffed— *No Joe*. Diego ran for the front door, not caring when his feet slapped against the wood loudly. He wanted Joe to hear him now, to find him and fuck him.

The screen door popped the doorframe, the sound like the crack of a rifle to Diego. Once inside, he froze, uncertain of his next move. His eyes burned from the change in lighting, and the complete saturation of his senses by everything about Joe held him as immobile as his own confusion did.

Then the sound of Joe's approach registered. Diego spun around just as Joe flung the screen door open. Diego had one second or less to register the shock on Joe's face before he was tackled.

"Gotcha!" Joe hollered, his arms wrapping around Diego like steel bands.

Diego could have fought, could have kicked and hit and bit. Joe felt too good against him, Joe's clothed body landing hard on Diego, pinning him to the floor. Diego was saved from a head injury by Joe's hand cupping his skull, but his lungs were compressed to almost nothing as the air whooshed out of them.

"I'm not crazy," Joe mumbled while Diego was trying to inhale.

It'd have helped if Joe had lifted some of his weight up, but he didn't. Diego gasped, lips parting as his vision swam. Joe's crotch was pressed firmly against Diego's, and the rough grit of the denim against his dick was bringing back searing memories of their coupling last week.

Joe fisted one hand in Diego's hair and pulled. Diego arched his neck, chasing the sting of his scalp, still trying to get a breath. He squirmed, ready to fight if he needed to. Panic was right beneath the surface of his skin, partially from being caught even though he'd wanted it, but mostly from the lack of air.

"Be still," Joe ordered. He peered down at Diego with those pretty eyes. "My God, I can't even figure this out."

Diego was clueless as to what Joe meant. He just needed to get a good breath or two before he flipped out. The little bit he was able to get into his lungs wasn't doing anything but making his brain shriek that it wasn't enough and he would never get more.

Just as Diego was about to give in and let the flight part of his senses take over, Joe levered himself up onto one elbow. He didn't let go of Diego's hair.

Diego took one deep breath, then another. Joe's hand tightened in his hair.

"You're going to tell me what's going on," Joe rumbled. He moved his other hand around to cup Diego's neck. Joe's thumb pressed lightly against his Adam's apple.

Diego wasn't sure if it was a threat or not. He wasn't worried. Now that he wasn't on the verge of flipping out over the lack of oxygen, Diego could think rationally. He could have Joe on his back and broken in no time at all if Joe tried to seriously hurt him. Joe moved his thumb, caressing Diego in such a way that Diego trembled.

"I get the feeling you're a wild thing," Joe mused. He kept up the stroking as he watched Diego. "You've got eyes like I've never seen before. Remind me of a dog that was outside, except yours are darker, more an amber color than that bright yellow. What do you want to tell me about that, hmm?"

Diego gulped. His dick was hard and his pulse was aiming for some record speed. He couldn't think with Joe looking at him like that.

Like he wanted to eat Diego up in one big bite.

"I remember, I think," Joe said right before dipping his head and licking Diego's lips.

Diego just managed to hold back a plea for more.

Joe did it again. "Oh, yeah, it happened. I'm not crazy. I don't know who you are or why you're here, but I know this" — another lick — "about you. Open for me."

Diego had forgotten to struggle, not that he wanted to escape. He parted his lips when Joe slid his tongue over them. Diego struggled to keep his eyes open, wanting to see everything, each expression on Joe's face. Even when his vision went blurry with Joe so close, Diego didn't let his eyes close.

Joe could have overpowered Diego with the kiss, shoved his tongue in and made it a brutal taking, but he didn't. Instead he took his time, nibbling at Diego's lips, sucking on them, lapping at them with something close to tenderness. Maybe it wasn't, but Diego wouldn't have known the difference. He'd never been treated as anything other than a nuisance fuck at best, and kissing? No one had ever bothered to do more than slobber across his face in a mockery of the act itself.

So Diego melted a little inside, emotions he didn't understand springing to life while his body went from tense to soft and yielding beneath Joe's. Joe moaned into his mouth then, slicking his tongue over Diego's lips.

Diego was ready to beg for a deeper kiss. He spread his legs, parting them widely so that Joe fit better against his groin. At the same time, he dared to put his arms around Joe, as far as he could reach them. With Joe up on his elbows now, Diego was able to rest his hands on Joe's shoulder blades as Joe finally gave him the kiss he was craving.

The way Joe handled him, hand in hair, tongue and lips staking ownership of him, the commanding drive of Joe's hips against his—it was altogether more gentleness in any situation than Diego had known in a very long time. His eyes burned and he feared for one horrific moment that he was about to start bawling like a baby. Joe chose that instant to scrape his teeth over Diego's tongue. While it didn't hurt, it did provide him with an anchor against the emotions trying to overwhelm him.

Diego pressed his fingers along Joe's shoulders, wishing he could mark him. It wasn't that he wanted to hurt Joe, but to see him wearing Diego's scratches would be something. It'd mean he was Diego's, at least for a short while.

Joe kissed him fiercely then, more pressure and teeth to it. He gripped Diego's hair tighter and rutted roughly. Diego's dick throbbed, his balls drawing up. If Joe kept manhandling him, he was going to come all over the place in seconds.

The tenderness had been something, touching a part of Diego he hadn't known craved it. It had scattered Diego's senses, made a mess of him inside.

But rough, near-violent sex, it was what he knew, what his body was familiar with, and Diego's body knew an orgasm wasn't far behind. He hadn't come since the night with Joe, hadn't wanted to because his own hand on his dick seemed a pathetic substitute for the man above him now.

Joe laid a string of nibbles and kisses down Diego's jaw. Diego's eyelids won the battle then, because no one had ever bothered doing the things to him Joe was doing. He turned his head, offering Joe more skin, making himself vulnerable to a human, something he'd never have imagined doing in his life.

Joe sucked at a spot just below Diego's ear that pulled an embarrassing mewling sound from him.

"That's nice," Joe rumbled right before taking Diego's earlobe between his teeth.

Diego was going to shake right apart into a billion pieces. There were too many sensations going on, too many points of pleasure. His cock, balls, everywhere Joe touched him — it was all so good, so much.

"Please," Diego got out as he tried to rut up against Joe. His own voice sounded hoarse, stripped to the bare necessities needed to make noise.

"Please what?" Joe asked him, warm breath wafting over Diego's ear.

Joe raised his head and Diego opened his eyes after a minute of silence and no more kissing. He found Joe peering down at him, a confused look on Joe's face.

Diego's gut clenched and sweat broke out on his brow. He had the distinct feeling the sex was about to come to an end.

Chapter Six

"What am I doing?" Joe asked, the question slipping out regardless of whether or not he might have wanted to keep it to himself. He had a sexy, horny stranger beneath him, one who was obviously willing to let Joe do whatever he wanted to him. And what did Joe do? *Stop. Because I'm a fucking moron.* "Who are you?" He couldn't keep that question back either. He was certifiably crazy is what he was.

Here he had the hottest piece of ass ever, ready and willing to go. The man had reddish brown hair that looked as fine as silk splayed out on the floor. It had to be at least shoulder-length. Large eyes were framed in sandy tipped lashes.

Well, those eyes were odd enough to give Joe pause. They were almost the same color as the man's hair. "What's your name?" Joe demanded, his heart pounding. He wasn't sure if it was fear or anger causing the adrenaline to slam through him.

Those eyes went wide, conveying, oddly enough, an innocence that was surprising. "D-Diego."

Joe darted a glance down past the pert freckled nose to the full lips he'd been kissing. They were a darker color, going well with the man's dusky skin tone. "Diego," Joe repeated, bringing his gaze back to the man's eyes. "Diego what?"

Diego shook his head what little he could. Joe realized then he was still gripping the man's hair. He didn't let go. It wasn't like him to be so animalistic, so brutal when it came to sex. Usually he was just grateful to be hooking up with someone and getting off with them.

But Diego wasn't fighting him, and had been making all the arousing noises that signified he'd very much been enjoying the rough way Joe had been handling him.

And that turned Joe on deeper than he'd ever been turned on before.

"Diego what?" he demanded again, testing Diego and himself by pulling on Diego's hair a little. He liked doing it, and if Diego's stuttered moan was anything to go on, he enjoyed it too.

"Just... Just Diego," Diego answered breathily. He wiggled under Joe. "Gods, don't stop."

It sounded like a plea, and Joe liked hearing it. Still, there was that one word —

"Gods?" Joe repeated questioningly. It wasn't what he usually heard. "As in, plural?"

Diego nodded. He wrapped his ankles over Joe's and thrust up. Diego's eyes rolled and his lids fluttered shut. "Gods, Goddess, whatever. Just f-fuck me. I'll beg. Whatever you want."

Joe's dick couldn't possibly get any harder. He'd never had someone want him so badly. It made him think he was going to do something really stupid, because when might he ever get a chance to be the focus of someone's intense desire again? *Probably never*. He was almost forty, not a catch by any means in the looks or brains department, and he didn't have money. Didn't know many ranchers who did, except for the ones that had sold mineral rights to the oil companies.

"So what if it's...?" Joe trailed off. He didn't have words for what it was, finding a naked man in his home, a naked man that was familiar to him because he was pretty damned sure they'd gotten off together before.

A naked, sexy man with eyes that weren't quite human. Joe couldn't shake the thought, and he sure as hell didn't want to dwell on it.

Diego tensed beneath him, and Joe got the impression the man was going to try to flee then, because Joe had hesitated too long. That couldn't happen.

Joe pulled harder on Diego's hair, forcing him to arch his neck. His Adam's apple bobbed enticingly. Joe brushed his lips over it, getting a gasp from Diego before Joe lifted his head again.

Diego's lips parted, and Joe took his mouth then, kissing him with a need that threatened to become all-consuming. There was an earthy, wild taste to Diego that matched the raw scent of his skin Joe had been cruising on a few minutes ago.

There was no cologne in the world that could match the way a man smelled naturally, not to Joe's way of thinking. And Diego's aroma was addictive. Joe wanted to coat himself in it.

But for now, he plundered Diego's mouth, aware that the rougher he got with his grip and kiss, the more delicious sounds Diego made, and the more he undulated.

Diego was short and thin, maybe too thin, but his dick was fat and long as he thrust it over Joe's. If they kept that up, he'd spurt in his jeans again.

Joe didn't want that. He wanted more, and Diego did too. Joe sucked on Diego's bottom lip until he tasted the coppery tang of blood then he released it. Diego whimpered and tried to pull him back down. For a small guy, Diego was strong. Joe growled and jerked back, and it made little difference.

"I want—" Diego began, his voice cracking. He opened his eyes, greeting Joe with that amber stare. He had a dazed look on his face. Diego licked his swollen lips, the movement of his tongue catching Joe's attention. "I want you to fuck me, please."

That request had Joe's gaze back on Diego's. "I don't even know you."

Diego frowned, a little line appearing between his bushy eyebrows. "So? What does that have to do with anything?"

What does it have to do with anything? He's a stranger, there's something weird going on with him and he's been hanging around my ranch, apparently.

But he's also a man. He's an adult, and he's coherent—and he wants me. Why make it more complicated than that?

Joe took another bruising kiss, this one making his own lips ache. Diego loosed another sweet sound and clung to him. Joe pulled back and came up on his knees. He'd be feeling that tomorrow, no doubt walking stiff-legged and having to snack on ibuprofen all day. It'd be worth it, though.

Diego started to sit up. Joe pushed him back down. "Stay there. Let me look."

"I want you to fuck me," Diego protested, though he didn't get up.

Joe cocked his head. He knew about the games some people liked to play, he just hadn't ever thought he'd be doing the same, or that he'd like it. Turned out, he believed he did. "Then you'd best mind me, hadn't you?"

He knew it was the right thing to say when Diego flushed darker with arousal, the pink running down from his face to his chest. Joe followed it with his eyes, saw the taut little brown nipples poking up and begging for a touch. He also saw scars, and those made him feel kind of queasy because they weren't all very old. Some were deep, some were long. Others weren't either. Despite them, Diego was obviously able and willing to have sex with him.

Joe didn't ask about the scars, nor did he ask why he could see every one of Diego's ribs. A man had his pride, after all, and Diego had to know Joe saw him, all of him. Besides, Joe would feed the man well after seeing to him. And he'd wash that red hair, work out the knots he could see now.

Diego's chest heaved with every breath. If Joe was going to take care of him, he was going to start with what Diego kept asking him for. Joe cupped Diego's cheek. He let go of Diego's hair and used that hand to stroke down his neck. Diego's eyes went wide with something that looked a lot like wonder. Joe thought maybe no one had ever been gentle with him, which made those scars all the more awful.

Diego flapped his hands, as if he didn't know what to do with them.

Joe began caressing — neck, shoulders, chest. Those prominent ribs. "Put your hands behind your head."

Diego did so promptly, which reaffirmed Joe's notion that the smaller man wanted to be told what to do. God knew Trent told Joe he was a bossy bastard plenty of times. Joe could hand out orders, sure enough.

Joe cupped Diego's slight pecs. He watched for a second or two as he kneaded them then he looked up at Diego's face. Diego seemed stunned, stunned and needy. Joe liked that combination a lot. He rubbed his thumbs over Diego's nipples.

"Oh," Diego said on an exhalation, though he was so quiet with it Joe wasn't certain he'd even spoken at first. Then Diego said it again, just the one word as his eyes rolled back and his lids slid down.

Joe gave those little tits more friction, watching Diego's face the whole time. There was nothing hidden in the man's reactions. Diego's enjoyment, his need was right there for Joe to see in the way his mouth went slack, his nostrils flared and his eyelids cracked open just enough that Joe could see his eyes moving.

And the sounds he made — susurrations Joe couldn't quite parse out, but that was okay. When he went from rubbing to pinching, he understood Diego easily enough.

"Fuck!" Diego yelped, but he didn't move his hands, just pushed that thin chest up for more.

"Like that?" Joe asked. He wanted to hear it from Diego. Joe twisted Diego's nipples and Diego hissed. "Better tell me if you do, otherwise I'll stop."

Diego opened one eye and Joe thought he was trying to glare. Joe pinched those tits harder.

"Yes, I like it, I like it," Diego babbled, arching for him again. "Don't stop. Do it harder."

"When I'm ready," Joe told him. He wasn't willing to give over control now that he'd figured out he liked having it. "And that ain't happening yet." He pushed the nipples down, as if he could press them into the areolae and smooth the whole plane of Diego's chest out.

Diego nodded jerkily and licked his lips. Joe let his nipples pop up and gave them a sharp pinch.

Diego's shout was followed by a spurt of cum splattering his chest. A second and third volley followed as Diego gasped, opening his eyes with a look of terror mixed with pleasure.

Joe assumed he was flipping out over going off like a geyser from tit play. "Perfect," he informed Diego, gaze locked with that amber one. "Nothing like a man who's so responsive." He flicked Diego's nipples again.

Diego gulped loudly. When he licked his lips, Joe couldn't hold back a moan of his own.

"Open," he demanded while unfastening his belt. He'd have to wait to fuck Diego's ass.

Diego let loose a hungry sound and opened his mouth as if he were yawning. The man was eager for what Joe was going to give him. Joe got his belt and pants open. He rolled over onto his butt, unable to move his legs much with his jeans pulled down his thighs. He'd have taken them off, but his boots were still on too and that was all just more work than he had patience for then.

"Over here," he said, taking hold of Diego's arms. "Come over here and suck me. Show me you want my dick."

Diego scrambled up and kneeled over Joe, facing away from him, knees on either side of Joe's chest. He went down on Joe like a dream, ass up, head in Joe's lap. Joe held his cock at the base and Diego sucked the tip right in.

"Shit," Joe rasped, fiery need ricocheting from nerve ending to nerve ending.

Diego sucked hard, all the way down until his lips touched Joe's hand. Joe let go, wondering if Diego could take him all.

He did, the crown of Joe's dick slipping into Diego's throat. "Jesus Christ, Diego," Joe gritted out, his jaw aching as he tried to keep from just fucking away at Diego's face. With shaking hands, he cupped Diego's hips. "Jesus." He couldn't seem to get anything else out then as Diego swallowed. The man must not have ever had a gag reflex.

Diego came back up and pushed his tongue against Joe's slit. Joe was torn between watching Diego's head bob or his ass wiggle. For a scrawny guy, Diego had a nice little bubble butt, and his cheeks parted every time he went down, as if he were begging to be fucked. Joe had to thrust, so he pushed his dick deeper into Diego's mouth and that, in turn, infused him with so much pleasure his head swam.

He got his hands on that ass, though, grabbing both cheeks and squeezing. Diego's moan around Joe's dick almost did him in. Joe slapped one cheek and Diego moaned again, this time the vibrations even stronger as he let Joe know he liked the swat.

So Joe did it again, and again, turning that honey-colored skin red. Spanking Diego distracted him from the blow job enough that Joe managed not to come in the first few minutes. Diego worked his shaft perfectly, sucking and licking better than anyone else ever had.

It was just that Joe wanted to do so much to Diego, and really, Joe was probably going to be done for a few hours after he came. Pretty much the norm for a man his age.

But if Diego still wants to play, I'd have plenty of time to get to know his body. Maybe even get to know him. Just focus on him...

Joe quit holding back. He cupped Diego's ass hard, burying his fingers in Diego's crack and using the hold to pull him forward. Joe humped up, too, taking as much as Diego would let him, fucking that pretty mouth of his.

Diego didn't draw a line anywhere. Joe grunted and slipped a dry finger against his asshole. Diego pushed his butt back, at the same time coming up to really suck on Joe's cockhead. When he did so, Joe pushed that finger in deep. Between the heated grip of Diego's ass and the wet suction of his mouth, Joe was done for. He bucked up hard and fast, lost in his release.

When he was able to breathe again, his finger was still in that snug grip. Joe wiggled his digit around and that got him a rumbling sound from Diego. Joe felt it to his core since Diego still had his dick in his mouth.

"Stop," Joe wheezed shortly thereafter, his shaft too sensitive for any more. He added a slap to Diego's ass for emphasis.

Diego released his length and pressed his face to Joe's pubes. The mewling sound he made told of his need. So did the rumbling of his stomach.

Joe blinked and realized he could see Diego's ribs along his back as well as the knobby ridges of his spine. There were more scars, too, some that looked like he'd been mauled by a wild beast. Those ran on both sides of his back in uneven, fading pink trails. Diego rotated his hips, obviously wanting more from Joe.

But Joe was sated and now he could think beyond the need to come. He remembered the way Diego had tensed beneath him earlier, when he'd taken too long to answer. There was a good chance Diego would run off if they weren't having sex. Joe felt it in his gut.

He fingered Diego's ass and thought about his options. Diego's stomach growled and when Diego didn't even seem to care about it, or for all Joe knew, he wasn't aware of it—that just disturbed Joe. He imagined Diego hungry and so used to starvation being a fact of his life that he didn't believe it could be any different.

Maybe he was casting his own imaginings on Diego, but Joe couldn't help it. The man was hungry, and clearly hadn't been getting enough food. There were scars all over his body, and he wasn't used to a gentle touch. If he was homeless, he was clean somehow. There was no body odor that wasn't enticing, and Joe hadn't spotted dirt or anything like open wounds on the man. Plus, Diego's face was clean-shaven. Diego could have been bathing in the river or one of numerous ponds, except his scent was off for either of those options.

The man was a puzzle, and Joe was a curious sort.

And he was going to feed Diego.

Joe slapped his ass again hard enough to get a gasp from Diego. "You want more than this?" Joe asked, curling his finger and searching for Diego's gland. He didn't touch it, but Diego sure appreciated the attempt, rolling his hips eagerly. "Well, you can have more. Takes me a little while to get ready to go again, though."

Diego stilled. Joe waited and slowly, Diego tilted his head enough to one side that he was looking at Joe through a curtain of hair. Joe couldn't tell if that was hope or what in the man's expression.

"Yup, it's true enough. My dick's still soft, and if anything could entice me into getting hard again, it'd be you all willing and wanting." Joe nodded. "So here's what's gonna happen." He was going to boss Diego around, that's what was going to happen, and he'd just hope it would keep the man from running off.

"You're going to get up, and walk to my bathroom. We'll shower." After all, he really didn't know where Diego had been. "You'll answer two questions. Just two," Joe reiterated when Diego jerked back as if to escape. Joe caught him by one hip and he still had a finger up Diego's butt. "I'll answer as many questions as you want to ask me."

"I just want to fuck." Diego didn't look at him, instead turning his face away. His voice was still wrecked, as if he didn't really speak much.

Joe moved his finger, playing with Diego's ass. He kept at it until Diego's breath hitched. "We'll get to it. Ain't any reason to rush. I want to take my time, and maybe I want someone to talk to besides my brother." He rubbed the outer rim of Diego's hole while doing the same to the inner side of it. Part of him was astounded by his own behavior, being so controlling and forward.

Still, it wasn't as if he found himself in this position every day. Or ever, until now, so he was going to enjoy the fuck out of it. If he could find out more about Diego along the way, then that would be a bonus.

"You're going to stay, and we'll shower. You'll answer two questions, and you're going to eat." Joe pushed the tip of a second finger into Diego, getting a soft hissing sound from the man. "You'll need your strength."

Diego shivered and rocked back onto Joe's fingers. Joe pulled his fingers free, then clutched both of Diego's ass cheeks in his hands. He spread them as far apart as he could, knowing that'd place pressure on Diego's pucker, stretching it open.

He didn't wait for an answer, either. "You're going to get up and march this ass into my bathroom. It's down the hall past the kitchen. You'll get the water going and get in. Then you just wait for me." He let go of Diego's cheeks and popped them both at the same time. "Get on it."

Diego hesitated for an instant then sprang to his feet. His cock was wet-tipped and so hard the crown was purple.

"Don't touch yourself, either," Joe instructed. He cupped Diego's balls. "You save it all for me." And squeezed them as much as he dared, watching Diego's face to judge how far to go with that particular act. Diego never even flinched. Joe would have. He didn't want to hurt Diego, not really, so he let go of his nuts. "Now. Move it."

Joe got a nice view of Diego's pinked ass when the man spun around and jogged to the bathroom. Joe grinned. He could definitely get used to this.

Just as quickly as he had thought it, worry set in. He'd let a stranger into his house, had tackled the guy and got off with him, not even considering safety or if someone else was in the house.

He wasn't acting like himself at all. Joe rubbed his forehead. He got up and tucked his dick away before removing his boots. It was kind of stupid to do now, but he still went silently from room to room, looking for anyone else, any strangers that might be waiting naked for him.

And he felt foolish for it. Joe snorted softly and shook his head. Diego was odd, and had a bad past, that was obvious to anyone with eyeballs. Joe doubted he was dangerous, and if he did try anything, Joe had him by a good seventy-five pounds and several inches.

Joe did a gut check. His instincts weren't always something he paid attention to, because he feared losing his temper or doing something else foolish. All he could feel in regards to Diego was want, and a need to take care of him, help him out if possible. How he'd do that was something Joe would have to decide depending on how the night played out. Maybe he could get Diego to hang around a little longer, a few days or something. Trent would probably flip out, but he'd get over it.

Decisions made, or mostly, Joe locked up the house then headed for the bathroom.

Chapter Seven

What am I doing? Diego quivered as he stood in the shower. He'd meant to demand that Joe fuck him and leave if he didn't. Or let Joe fuck him then leave. Either way, a shower, questions and food hadn't been part of the plan—then again, neither had letting the man dominate him. Somehow Joe had seen into his soul and known what Diego needed. Yet Joe was different about it than the others who had tried to control Diego.

For one thing, Joe wasn't trying to hurt him just for the fun of it. Diego liked the pain, but he didn't like the intentions behind most people's deliverance of the pain. Nor did he like being hurt beyond his ability to endure it. Diego really hated that.

He stepped under the fall of water and sighed. It did feel good. Everything Joe had done to him did, but this especially was a luxury. Diego hadn't had a shower in weeks. As a shifter, he was saved from the normal stink of an unwashed body by shifting. When his particles and parts were rearranged, the dirt on his form had no place to cling to. At least, he thought that was how it worked.

That didn't mean he didn't enjoy showers or baths. He just wasn't able to get them very often. Maybe that was why he'd given in. Diego snorted. He wanted Joe to fuck him, that's the reason he was still there.

Showering, in a bathroom painted sky blue, with pictures of starfish hanging on the walls. It was so bizarre as to be unrealistic. Diego even had to wonder for a moment if he'd passed out and was dreaming. Trent had put out some disgusting dog food and the one yummy steak, but that was hardly enough for Diego to survive on.

He'd had shit luck hunting for food on the ranch and nearby properties. It was just another reason he needed to move on. If he didn't, desperation might make him take down a calf, and he'd be even more hated and hunted.

A meal might not be a bad thing, really. Diego put a hand against the cool blue tile and let his head droop. He was so tired, and worn in a way that had nothing to do with lack of sleep.

He could do it, stay for a few hours. Answer two questions—nothing he'd seen of Joe over the past weeks gave any inclination that Joe wouldn't keep his word. Two questions, then food, real human food, maybe even some of that spaghetti he'd smelled when he'd dashed by the kitchen. Diego's stomach rumbled and ached. How much longer would Joe make him wait?

Turning his head slightly, he could just make out Joe's shadow on the floor in front of the bathroom. The man himself appeared seconds later. Diego watched him through the glass shower door. Joe had undressed before coming to the room, so there was no teasing strip show. Joe stared back at him before looking Diego up and down. Then without a word, he turned and picked up a razor off the countertop where the sink was.

Diego crept over to the shower door. He pushed it open, wanting a clear view of Joe as he shaved. Shifters didn't have facial hair, and most didn't have much body hair at all. The few who did were regarded as oddities in the packs.

Diego realized he was touching his own face as Joe rubbed on shaving cream. Joe looked at him via the mirror and Diego's cheeks flared hot with embarrassment.

"It's okay. I like you watching me." Joe took the razor and slowly ran it down from his sideburns to his jaw line. The raspy sound it made was discernible over the noise of the shower. Diego couldn't look away as Joe continued shaving.

The scent of the foam he used made Diego's nose tingle, like he was on the verge of a giant sneeze. It remained just out of reach, a frustrating feeling. Diego rubbed at his nose.

"Don't like the smell?" Joe asked. He started shaving his neck.

"Tickles." Diego blinked and realized his answer likely made no sense. "It tickles my nose. I have a sensitive one." Then he dared to grin, delighted at how easy the request Joe had made of him would be. "That was a question."

Joe, to his credit, didn't argue. "Yup, I reckon it was. I'll have to be careful with the next one."

Diego ducked his head. He shouldn't be a jerk. What would it hurt to let Joe ask him two more questions, ones he really meant? Joe wouldn't know to ask him anything about being a shifter, though he'd probably ask about the scars. The two were tied together. Diego could still answer those kinds of question without giving away what he was.

"Stop frowning so hard. You'll give yourself a headache."

Diego glanced at Joe and saw him rinse off the razor then set it down. He splashed water on his face, removing the remainder of the shaving cream. Diego moved back to allow room for Joe to join him.

"Glad this ain't one of those tiny showers," Joe said after he stepped into it. "Used to be little, but a few years back, I got a wild hair and a little time. I don't think I did a half bad job on it."

Diego looked around the shower. The tiles were a pretty blue, not dark but not a powdery shade, either. All of them were evenly applied, and the grout between them was as white as possible. The soap bar, towel rod and shelf in the shower were all burnished silver, as was the large showerhead. "It's nice. You did all of this?"

"All of the bathroom." Joe picked up a fluffy scrubber and a bar of soap. "It was getting run-down and the toilet leaked like a mother no matter what I did to it. I figured, I'm gonna live my whole life here. Why not fix the house up like I want it? I'd let it be my dad's for too long. Made a lot of changes here since then. I've redone half the house. Still have two bedrooms and a second bath to go."

Diego hadn't lived anywhere long enough to consider a place home, not even when he'd been with a pack. Being a shifter wasn't an easy way of life. "You can ask me two questions still," he said, completely out of context with the conversation. His mind did odd things in cooperation with his mouth sometimes.

Joe gestured at him. "Gonna wash you now." He didn't say anything about Diego's offer.

Diego didn't know what to think about the man. He didn't know what to think about everything that had happened since he'd laid eyes on Joe, either.

"Step out of the water."

Diego moved at Joe's command. Joe grunted what might have been approval and began scrubbing Diego's back. "You been hungry a long time?"

That was Joe's first intentional question. Diego saw no harm in answering it, except his pride would take a hit. Wasn't the first time. "All my life," he admitted roughly. Being the runt of the pack meant he'd been last to be allowed to eat. Once he'd left, it'd been better at some times, worse others, but generally the same overall.

Joe didn't speak. Diego wanted to look at him. He didn't. Letting Joe know that his reaction mattered — and it did — seemed unwise. Vulnerability was deadly to those weaker than most. All runts knew that fact, learned it early and harshly.

"You got a lot of scars," Joe remarked after he'd moved on to washing Diego's arms. "That ain't a question, either. Just a fact."

"Yes. I was —" Diego stopped. How to explain his world to a human? It'd be abuse for a human child to be treated as Diego had been. In a pack, it wasn't. He was the runt, he could die or not, it didn't matter to the alpha or anyone else. His sire and dam put out a litter every two years. Like all shifters, less than half of the litters survived. Of those pups that did, another half at the very least ended up dead before adulthood. There were many, many ways wolf cubs could die.

"Unlucky," he settled for. He didn't owe Joe an explanation anyway. "Things are different where I was raised." Yet his damned mouth kept spewing shit out.

"You don't have to say any more unless you want to," Joe murmured. "I can tell some of these scars are old, and you ain't my age yet. That tells me plenty."

Diego would just bet it did. Joe wasn't stupid. He'd know Diego had been hurt from the time he was a child on upwards to a few months ago. "I'm twenty-seven, I think."

Joe turned him around with a gentle tug on his shoulder. Diego wanted to keep his head down. Would have, if Joe hadn't tucked a couple of fingers under his chin and pushed. "You think. You don't know."

It wasn't a question—Joe stated the words as plainly as Diego had. Still, Diego shrugged. Looking at Joe was impossible just then. "I don't. There aren't any papers on me." Human papers, dog papers, wolves weren't registered with anyone unless they'd been caught and tagged by human scientists.

Joe applied a little pressure, more of a questioning touch than a demand.

Diego raised his head. It took him longer to raise his gaze to Joe's, but he got there eventually. There was no pity in Joe's eyes, which helped Diego to retain a smidgen of dignity.

"I know a little about getting hurt by the people who ought to be kinder." Joe trailed those fingers up the side of Diego's face until he was cupping it. "Nothing like what you went through, I'll admit. Still, I loved my dad something fierce, and every time he took a belt to me and bruised my ass and legs, he'd tell me he was doing it for my own good. Can't help but think now that wasn't the case. It takes a lot of anger to leave marks on a kid, don't it? Rhetorical question, there."

Diego was surprised by the confession. As normal as Joe and Trent seemed to him, he'd have thought they were raised up with parents that loved them. Something must have shown in his expression, because Joe nodded.

"Yeah, our folks loved us. Well, Dad did. Mama took off for parts unknown back when Trent was in sixth grade. Can't say as I blame her now, looking back on it. Dad didn't take any backtalk from her either. He'd tell her to mind her mouth just like he would us kids." Joe made a disgusted sound and shook his head. "Never saw him lay a hand on her, but once I was older, I learned there's other kinds of abuse, other ways to hurt that maybe leave lasting scars unlike the bruises I had on my backside. I don't know for sure what happened between them, but Dad could be very judgmental and, well, mean, I reckon. No wonder to me Mama took off."

Joe surprised Diego, slipping an arm around him and pulling him into a wet embrace. "People can be pretty awful, you know. He wasn't all bad. It's hard to see that, especially for those who didn't know Dad. I just hope whoever did this to you, they were kind at times, too." Joe stroked down Diego's spine.

Diego clumsily hugged Joe and buried his face in the man's chest. He was glad they'd gotten back into the spray. It hid the tears that Diego couldn't keep from falling.

He hadn't cried since he'd been set upon by the pack the first time. After that horrifying experience, tears had seemed futile. Now he knew they could be a little bit therapeutic, too. *But they won't solve a goddamned thing.*

Joe murmured wordlessly, more humming than anything else while he held Diego. It was comforting.

Diego almost felt safe, even. If he let himself, he could be lulled into believing he fit perfectly right there in Joe's arms for a reason.

But if he stayed for much longer, leaving would be harder than it already was proving to be — and Diego couldn't stay without risking the life of the one man he cared for.

Joe had a scar here and there, and he did have one smaller spot on his hip where his dad's belt buckle had caught him. Usually his dad had made sure the leather was what smacked Joe, but he'd been particularly mad that day, and Joe had smarted off. The belt buckle had done some damage to him, but nothing like what had been done to Diego.

If Joe wasn't totally off, Diego was crying quietly in his arms. It would have been awkward if Diego had made a noise, sobbing and boo-hooing like woe is me and all, but he didn't. That made it all the more heartbreaking.

Joe understood the need for dignity and privacy. He just kept holding Diego and touching him — and thinking. The scenarios he came up with were all probably wrong. He mostly was leaning toward Diego having been raised in some weird-ass cult. There were sure as shit too many of them in existence.

Diego was different from anyone Joe had ever met. Something was off about the man, and Joe couldn't pinpoint it. Not in a psychotic sort of way — he hoped. More like Diego hadn't been around a lot of people, maybe, and was innocent in some things.

Or Joe could be making all sorts of shit up in his head because he really liked the way Diego felt in his arms. He liked the way Diego looked, too, all fine-boned and tough at the same time.

Hell, he just liked Diego, period, from what he'd experienced of the man so far.

Joe held him until Diego tensed a little, then he released him and went back to washing the lean limbs without giving Diego a chance to protest. "You don't have a lot of body hair," Joe noted, rubbing over the scant leg hair on Diego's calf. "It's gold."

"We're not very hairy like—" Diego snapped his mouth shut with an audible clacking of teeth.

Joe nodded and kept touching him, trailing fingers up to the start of Diego's pubes at thigh and groin. "Not too bushy here, either." He slipped his fingers back and hefted Diego's balls. They were a nice handful, not huge but plump. "Smooth here, too. Do you shave?"

"No," Diego said rather breathlessly.

Joe's own breath stuttered when he saw the scars on Diego's nuts and inner thighs. It was a real struggle to keep himself from cursing and reacting to those reminders of Diego's abuse. Joe imagined it'd make Diego feel worse if he acknowledged them, so he settled for running his thumb over one then reaching farther back.

Diego's asshole was devoid of the usual swirl of hair Joe's partners had had back there. Joe found that he liked the smooth skin. He hadn't noticed earlier when he'd been playing with Diego's ass. "I like this," he said, glancing up at Diego. There was no reason not to try to build the man up considering it looked like someone had spent years tearing him down. "Soft, smooth. Bet you taste like heaven."

Diego's eyes widened to the point of it looking painful.

Joe took that to mean no one had ever bothered licking his ass until he came. He was going to have to find a way to keep Diego there for a few days. Maybe feed him and get him looking healthier and show him how good sex could be.

Diego closed his eyes and moaned softly.

"Yeah, I bet you do." Joe slipped the tip of one finger into Diego's hole. He was glad Diego wasn't watching him anymore, because he was close to panicking. Why was he thinking about trying to keep Diego there, and the right person and—?

Skinny as Diego was, what if there was a reason other than being hungry for it? Diego could have something wrong, be ill—Joe silently cursed his stupidity and removed his finger from Diego's ass. They were going to turn into prunes if they didn't get out soon, and he needed to feed Diego since the man's stomach kept growling.

As for sex, he'd see how things went after they got done in the shower. If he could talk Diego into hanging around for a while, then he'd broach the subject of illnesses and safety.

It was definitely something they'd discuss before they had any more sex. Joe was as clean as an angel. He'd been tested twice since his last hook-up, and he'd never fucked without a condom.

Joe caressed Diego from his ass to the tip of his dick as he came to his feet. "You're something, Diego. You probably have no idea of the things I want to do to you."

"Can I wash you, too?" Diego asked in a shy manner that charmed Joe to no end.

Joe pushed the wet hair off Diego's brow so it didn't hide his eyes. There was a pink blush to his cheeks. "Let me do your hair, then yeah, but we ain't fooling around in here. I have plans to take care of that later."

Diego licked his lips. Joe followed the tip of his tongue visually, his dick reacting to the sight. Joe ignored his erection and reached for the shampoo instead. "Tip your head back and get your hair good and wet."

"Okay." Diego turned and did as directed. Joe appreciated the arch of his neck and back, the plump mounds of his ass. Diego's cock was half erect, the foreskin just beginning to allow the head to peek out. It took every bit of restraint Joe had not to tug Diego off then.

Joe opened the shampoo then poured a good amount into his hand. Diego's hair was a lot longer than his own collar-length strands. In fact, under the shower fall, Diego's hair reached a couple of inches past his shoulders. It was a dark red now rather than the sandy red it was when dry.

Diego stepped out of the water and faced Joe. His dick brushed Joe's thigh when he moved closer so he could suds up Diego's hair. "Close your eyes," Joe advised. "Not real tight, 'cause that makes the soap head right for 'em. Just normal-like."

Why he was telling a grown man how to avoid soap in his eyes was beyond him. Joe would have laughed at himself had he not been so fascinated by the way Diego did as he was told. There was a blissful look to Diego's expression when he followed Joe's orders, too, and Joe was going to get addicted to it right quick if he wasn't careful.

Next, Joe conditioned Diego's hair. He didn't bother with his own half the time—the conditioner was in there more for jack-off shower sessions than anything else. Diego, however, had matted hair that Joe patiently worked loose. By the time he was done, the water was chilly and he had Diego get out.

"Get a towel and dry yourself off. Have one ready for me when I'm done in about a minute." It took longer, but not much. Cold showers were only enjoyable when it got hotter than the devil's dick outside. Joe took the towel from Diego. "You can show me how much you know about cooking." He'd nearly asked, but had caught himself at the last moment.

"Er, no." Diego shuffled his feet.

Joe was learning that he could discover a lot about Diego without questioning him. He just had to pay attention to everything Diego said and did. Like now, he could tell that Diego was nervous, perhaps afraid of disappointing him.

Diego had the towel wrapped around his waist, the surplus of it gripped in one hand. He sucked on his bottom lip and tipped his head down before answering. "I mean, not much? I could probably boil water and…and put stuff in it."

"That's good enough." Joe hung up his towel and gestured for Diego to do the same. "Just put it by mine so it can dry. Come into my bedroom and I'll find you something to put on. Wouldn't want you to burn yourself while we're cooking."

Joe tried not to grin when he walked past Diego. The man's cock was hard and he was ogling Joe's shaft in return. Felt like he was looking at Joe's ass, too, when he started following.

Joe liked it. He wondered what would happen if he could convince Diego to stay for more than a few hours. A couple of days would be nice, just to have some company at night.

And sex. Lots of sex.

Trent would have questions, but Joe would handle that. One of the bonuses of having a brother was getting to aggravate him, and Joe could be pretty vague when he wanted to. It irked Trent to no end when he did that.

Trent would flip out over Diego being there, especially if he found out how Joe had found him — naked and having broken into Joe's house. Joe just thought Diego was starving, and maybe he fascinated Diego for some reason. *Whatever got him here.*

He'd worry about Trent if and when the time came. For now, he had a horny, handsome man accompanying him to his bedroom. There were better things Joe could be doing than fretting about the future.

Chapter Eight

Diego opened his eyes, confusion being the first thing he experienced upon waking up. He blinked into the darkness. There were no stars overhead, which was odd enough to have fear flooding his system. Add to it he was lying on a soft, warm bed, and someone else was in it with him, and he was quickly on the edge of outright panic.

There was a snuffling sound beside him, with warm breath caressing the back of his neck. Diego's skin broke out in goosebumps almost instantly. The artificially cooled air wasn't something he was used to any more than the rest of the situation he found himself in.

He wasn't so close to freaking out once he heard the exhalation and caught the scent of the man it came from. *Joe.*

Diego was wrapped in his arms. He liked it, too. He closed his eyes again. It wouldn't hurt to lie there for a few minutes longer. As he did so, Diego reviewed the happenings of the night before—which hadn't gone according to his plan at all.

Short and sweet, when he'd thought to have a rough fuck instead. But no, he'd helped Joe make more spaghetti and sauce, along with some bread and a pitcher of sweet tea. It'd been fun, really, and Joe hadn't ever asked him that second question. In fact, Joe hadn't prodded him to talk much at all.

He'd gotten an admission from Diego in regards to his health. Joe had said he was 'clean', and Diego had asked what, specifically, that meant. Once he'd understood, he'd done what he could to reassure Joe that he was 'clean' as well. Shifters had no such diseases as the humans did. They died by old age in very rare instances, but most of them met a violent end long before they could ever hope to attain elder status.

After that bit of conversation, minus the shifter history, talking had slackened off. They'd cooked, eaten, washed the dishes, and that was where it had all gone wrong.

Not bad wrong, just wrong. Joe had led him to the living room, they'd sat on the couch. Joe had turned on the TV and pulled Diego close to him. The food, the comfort offered, it'd all proved too much, he guessed, because unless he'd slept through it, there'd been no sex. Diego remembered snuggling beside Joe on the couch—then he'd opened his eyes and was in bed, with Joe, in the dark.

The arms around him tightened. "Stop thinking so hard," Joe huffed in his ear. "Sleep."

Diego opened his mouth to argue and instead loosed a jaw-cracking yawn.

The next thing he knew, the barest hint of sunlight was slipping into the room through the window Joe had left open. That, and Joe was pressing a thick erection to Diego's backside.

"Morning," Joe rasped.

Diego didn't even get to reply before he was pushed onto his belly and covered by Joe.

"Wanna fuck you," Joe said. He nipped at Diego's ear. "Think you'd like that, me sliding this—" He pushed his cockhead against Diego's asshole. "Right in here?"

Diego couldn't nod fast enough. His throat was too dry with want to get any words past it.

Joe rumbled happily, almost a laugh. Diego didn't mind. He knew it was a sign of Joe's pleasure with his response, and making Joe happy was what Diego wanted to do as often as possible for what little time they had left together.

Diego parted his legs and tried to push his butt up. Joe's weight on him prevented Diego from being successful. That was okay—he liked the way Joe felt holding him down.

Joe stretched over him. Diego saw him pluck a condom from the stand by the bed. He wished Joe wouldn't use one, but there was no compelling argument against it that Diego could use without revealing his true nature. Since admitting he wasn't a human would likely end up with him not getting fucked, there was no way he was going to protest the condom.

"This is gonna be quick and nasty," Joe promised.

Diego whimpered, shivering with anticipation.

Joe sat up and squeezed Diego's ass hard enough to leave marks. Diego closed his eyes. His breathing was too fast, too shallow. He wanted Joe so bad it hurt to wait.

There was the tearing of the package then a sound that Diego knew had to be Joe rolling the condom on. The bed shifted as Joe leaned over him. "Lube," Joe said. "Lots and lots of it, because I need in you too bad to stretch you for long. Unless you need it. You tell me if you do."

"No," Diego got out. He'd take any pain Joe gave him. It'd help keep the memory of what they did together stronger in his mind.

Once Joe had poured out lube, he began rubbing slick fingers over Diego's hole. Diego mewled when Joe pushed two into him without warning. The burn was quickly melted away and surpassed by pleasure. Diego's dick leaked pre-cum and he rubbed his shaft against the sheets.

"Nuh-uh," Joe scolded. He swatted Diego's ass. "No getting off until I'm pounded into you. You come before I do, you're just gonna have to take it until I shoot."

Gods. Oh, Gods, he's perfect...

Diego shut that train of thought off. Joe was a human, and he was a very temporary lover. *Just a fuck, not a lover.* Diego didn't have lovers.

Joe fingered him roughly, occasionally glancing over his prostate. Every time he did, Diego made the most embarrassingly needy sounds. He couldn't help it or keep them back. Joe drove them out of him with soft touches over his gland.

"Enough," Joe rumbled. Contrary to his words, he pushed a third finger in.

Diego started to come up onto his elbows, ready to go ass up, but Joe planted a hand between his shoulder blades and forced him back down. "No."

No explanation, just that one word and the pressure demanding that Diego follow.

Diego did, lying flat on his belly again. Joe rewarded him with a long, sensuous massage of his gland that left Diego shaking and keening, so close to coming he couldn't think.

Then those fingers were gone and Joe was covering him again. The hot prod of his dick at Diego's ass was threatening to push the spunk right up from Diego's balls.

Joe planted his elbows beside Diego's shoulders. "Now," he murmured gruffly. At the same time, he thrust. Joe's cock was definitely thicker than the three fingers he'd used. The broad head spread Diego's hole achingly wide.

Diego's eyes opened, but he saw nothing as he was filled in one long, forceful stroke. Joe panted once he was seated. He held still while Diego processed the sudden invasion. It wasn't a new experience — Diego had been fucked with much less care before.

But Joe *did* care. He wasn't out to hurt Diego, but to bring them both pleasure. Otherwise, he'd not have bothered prepping Diego at all, or holding still while Diego's ass adjusted to his length.

Diego clenched around that shaft, wishing he could keep Joe there with him like that forever. He closed his eyes and curled his fingers into the sheets, needing to hang onto something.

And Joe began to move, undulating slightly against Diego's ass. "You're so tight," he mumbled. "Gripping me so hard I can't—" Joe moaned. "Jesus, I can't— I don't want to hurt you, honey."

Diego didn't know why that made his eyes and nose burn, or his throat so clogged he felt like he was choking on something. Joe pulled back a little then.

"Yeah, so sweet." He moved one hand to touch Diego's face. The other he used to lever himself up just a bit before thrusting in sharply. "Uhn."

And from there on, the conversation ceased. Joe rested his head against the side of Diego's as he began fucking Diego like they both needed him to.

Deep, long strokes that filled Diego repeatedly, short, hard ones that jarred him, stirring moves of hips that set to fire every nerve in Diego's ass. Joe fucked him with a care that may not have been apparent to anyone watching, but to Diego, who was being driven out of his mind with a pleasure he'd never felt before, it was clear that he'd never truly been fucked before. Used, many times, but never had his own needs been seen to in such a fine manner.

Joe grunted every time he thrust. He raised up some and nibbled on Diego's nape, then his cheek. Diego tried to turn his head more, wanting a kiss on the lips. He got one, all messy and wet and perfect.

"Fuck," Joe whispered brokenly. He shoved both arms under Diego and held him. "Can't—" Joe didn't finish whatever he'd been about to say. He pounded away at Diego's ass while Diego's head went light and spinny with ecstasy that spread up from his ass to his balls. It encompassed all of him from there on, and at some point he came, more rapturous bliss filling him and spilling out in equal measures.

Sounds came from him that he'd never heard before. They mingled with Joe's, tangling in the air and in Diego's mind, where he locked them away to remember always. Joe tightened his hold on Diego and shoved his cock in deep. He thrust rapidly then, already encased fully in Diego's body. When he went still, it was only for a second, followed by a mighty shudder and the throb of his dick in Diego's ass.

Diego felt it, the pulse of release, the warmth of Joe's spunk in the condom. He wanted the barrier gone, wanted to carry Joe's seed in him for as long as he could. Never before had he wanted to have another man's scent in him, and it was ironic that the one time he did, was the one time a barrier prevented it.

Joe gasped then dropped down on him with a final thrust. He panted heavily, and while Diego could hardly breathe, he didn't care. If he died, he'd be content to do so. At least he'd been given a gift from Joe first, whether Joe ever knew that was how Diego viewed what they'd just done or not.

It probably meant nothing more than getting off to Joe. That was okay. Diego didn't hold his own notions to the man.

Joe snuffled and pushed himself up a little, giving Diego some breathing room. He kept his groin pressed to Diego's backside, though, so his softening dick didn't slide out.

Then he proceeded to kiss Diego's skin and suck on it in places that made Diego's insides warm and quivery.

He was losing himself in the sensual experience when Joe brought his lips to Diego's ear. "Want to keep you, honey. Stay for a few days. Please."

Was it a question? Diego was too stunned to even think of anything else.

"Don't get all tight on me like you're wanting to run." Joe suckled on Diego's earlobe before moving down to bring up a purple mark beneath it on his neck. He was trying really hard not to demand that Diego stay, not to demand explanations and words and promises he had no right to.

What he wasn't trying to do was understand his own actions and request. If he examined them, he might start doubting himself—and Diego, well, Diego needed someone. For some possibly insane reason, Joe wanted that person to be him.

I don't even know what I want with him. I just don't want him to leave yet. And it was more than sex. They hadn't even done anything sexual last night. Diego had curled up beside him on the couch and had promptly fallen asleep. The trust that implied had touched Joe. He supposed Diego could simply have been worn out, but even so, Diego had turned into his side and rubbed his cheek over Joe's chest. He'd made contented little sighs when he exhaled. He hadn't just passed out and snored away, oblivious to Joe.

Maybe that was why Joe wanted him to hang around. Diego made him feel ten feet tall and invincible. Stupid, sure, yet it was the truth. Joe liked feeling as if he were needed.

"Stay, just a few days," he said again when Diego failed to agree. "I'm not asking for forever. Just rest, eat, help me and Trent if you think you have to." He understood about pride and not wanting to be a charity case. There might be a better chance of Diego hanging around if he believed he was pulling his weight. "It's busy this time of year on a ranch."

Diego swallowed loudly. He finally opened one eye and looked up through strands of hair at Joe. "Why should I stay?" he got out in a sandpapery voice.

Joe didn't have anything but the truth for him. "Because I want you to."

Diego squirmed and Joe regretfully pushed up to his knees. He was careful when it came to pulling out of Diego's ass. The man might be sore, as tight as he was, and Joe also didn't want the condom to slip off. He did that part himself, tying the rubber up before tossing it toward the trash can. Joe missed and cringed at the splat he heard. He'd be cleaning it up shortly.

Diego still hadn't agreed and was watching Joe like he was a puzzle to be visually put together.

Joe moved to lie beside him. He propped up on one elbow, head resting on his hand as he used his other to brush the hair away from Diego's brow. "Here's the second question." And it was probably stupid to waste it on what he was going to ask, but if Diego was going to run off on him, then what did it matter? "Why not?"

Diego rolled off his belly and onto his back. He sat up and kept his head bent, his red hair acting as a shield for his features.

Joe leaned over and tucked it behind Diego's ear. "No hiding from me."

Diego snorted at that. He raised his legs up until his knees were almost to his chest, then wrapped his arms around them and rested his chin on his kneecaps. "I could not answer you."

"You could," Joe agreed, forcing himself not to tense up. He wasn't entirely sure he wouldn't tackle Diego if he tried it.

Diego slanted him a knowing look. "That would be…dishonest, and you've been nice to me."

"Nice," Joe repeated. "Not sure fucking you hard and spanking your ass were nice things to do."

Diego's half-smile caught at Joe's heart. "Those were better than nice. I meant feeding me, letting me shower and sleep in your bed. Everything else was—" Diego huffed. "I don't even have words. Never had sex like that, like I mattered." He untucked his hair and fanned it out beside his face.

Joe itched to move it again, but Diego surprised him by flipping it around to the other side of his head. "Sorry. This is—it's uncomfortable," Diego finished.

Joe was also battling with a surprising well of anger Diego's confession about sex brought up in him. He was out of questions, allowed ones, anyway. That just meant he'd need to be more demanding for the moment. "I don't know what kind of idiots you had sex with before, but they all deserve to be whipped if they never saw to your needs."

Diego actually laughed at that, and the sound bruised Joe's soul almost as much as Diego's next words.

"Why would they do that? I didn't matter. I've never mattered and that isn't self-pity, it's a fact and the way of the pa—" Diego coughed. "Um. It's the way of the people I was raised up around."

Joe sat up then, trying his best not to look horrified. "Your family—"

"No," Diego barked, sitting up straight and eyes going wide. "Gods, no! They didn't care what was done to me, and some of these scars are from them, but not the sex! We aren't that screwed up of a pack!" He slapped both hands over his mouth so hard Joe expected he'd busted his lips.

Joe frowned. What had Diego said that he regretted? The last word had been 'pack', which was admittedly weird, but people nowadays had bizarre names for everything.

There was very real, powerful fear in Diego's eyes. Seeing it, Joe couldn't dismiss the slip as something simple. He sat up and tugged Diego's hands away from his mouth. Sure enough, the bottom lip was smeared with blood.

"What do you mean by a pack?" Joe asked before he could think better of it.

And he knew, his heart dipping down to his belly, that Diego was going to run.

Diego had been scared many times in his life, but nothing like he was the moment he'd screwed up with Joe. The one absolute rule all shifters lived by was to never tell a human about their existence. Shifters had chosen death before fucking over their own species. The stories of their bravery had been handed down for generations, and Diego had gone and nearly made it all for naught.

He knew Joe could see his intentions, yet Diego couldn't stop himself. As if to egg him on, Trent hollered from the other room, calling for Joe.

It was too much for Diego. He bolted, shooting up off the bed.

Joe grabbed him by the legs, knocking him back onto the bed.

Diego lost it. Wild with fear, panic and guilt, he fought Joe, hitting, scratching, a part of him no longer human as he tried to escape. He didn't shift, didn't dare, but he let his animalistic nature rise to the surface.

Joe struggled to keep a hold of him. He caught Diego's wrists and used his greater weight to hold Diego down. Diego used his wolf to get free, letting the beast rule his actions otherwise.

"Jesus, fuck," Joe yelped, his grip loosening.

Diego didn't even know what he'd done to the man. He hit at Joe, shoving and clawing, kicking and squirming.

The scent of blood reached him. Diego knew he'd busted his lips seconds ago, but it wasn't his blood he smelled. Guilt tried to creep in, but his wolf was having none of it. Diego pushed at Joe with all his strength, and Joe was gone, tossed off him like a sheet being kicked aside.

"Joe? Joe!" Trent yelled from outside the bedroom.

Diego's heart raced. Trent's presence was adding to his panic. Diego glanced at Joe and wanted to weep. The hurt in his eyes was too great a burden to bear.

The bedroom door was thrown open. "Joe! What the—?"

Diego hit the open window at full speed. He threw himself out of it, rolling when he landed. He was on his feet and running an instant later, the sound of Trent's curses singeing the air.

He couldn't think about what he'd just done. He'd hurt someone who'd been *good* to him. For all the abuse that Diego had taken, he'd never meted any out to an innocent. He'd never done more than fight back at first. Later on, he'd been so used to the abuse he didn't even bother. He took it and never harmed anyone in return.

Until today. Today he'd surely lost what was left of his soul. Diego shifted, unable to stand himself as a man, and let his wolf run.

Chapter Nine

Joe had never seen anything like the way Diego had turned on him. No, that wasn't right. It was his own fault for tackling the man. He should have let Diego go. After all, Joe had seen all the scars Diego bore. What must he have thought when he'd been forcefully taken down? No wonder he'd fought like a cornered animal. Fear caused a man to revert back to his primitive nature, and Joe was awash with shame for having pushed Diego to that point.

"What the fuck happened?" Trent demanded. "You're bleeding!"

Joe glanced away from the window. His cheek throbbed and his chest burned in several places where Diego had raked his nails down it. A quick check told him he'd live. "I'm fine. Been cut worse working the fences. When'd you get here?" He hadn't even heard Trent come in.

Trent rolled his eyes. "God damn, I been hollering for the past minute, banging on your front door five minutes before that! You locked the damned thing, and I had to find the spare key. You didn't show up with breakfast at the barn and I figured you overslept—" He hissed. "Fuck that! What happened? Who was in here?" Trent looked him over thoroughly. "You're naked, it smells like ass and cum in here, there's a used rubber on the floor! Seriously, what the hell?" He bounded up and loped to the window. "Whoever he is, he hauled his bony ass off already."

"You saw him?" Joe asked, heart fluttering. His legs might give out on him, but he was going to get up off the floor. He'd have a bruised ass and back, and another lump on his head, owing to his own stupidity.

"Yeah, I saw him. Skinny little twerp with a nice ass. Went out the window like he was a pro at it." Trent scowled when he turned back to Joe. "Where'd you find him? Did you slip off last night? Or were you fucking around with Craigslist?"

Joe rubbed his throbbing head and ass. Both were aching. "Neither." Lying to his brother didn't occur to him. "He's been hanging around on the property, I think. Hiding, maybe. He spooked easy."

Trent's eyes bugged. "You fucked a homeless guy?"

Joe's temper snapped. "You gonna be a judgmental cunt?"

"Yeah I am," Trent yelled. "And fuck you. At least I'm not a stupid cunt!"

Joe arched a brow. Trent came at him, fists flying.

Two fights in one morning was a record for Joe, and he didn't fare so well against his little brother. Joe barely made it to his feet before he was trying to dodge Trent's punches.

He wasn't very effective. Trent took him down with a right to the jaw that had Joe seeing stars.

"That was too easy," Trent snarled as Joe lay sprawled on the floor. "Get up."

Joe snorted and cradled his jaw. He'd been stupid enough for one day. For a lifetime, actually. "Get over your fit," he advised. He closed his eyes and breathed through the worst of the pain.

A few minutes later, there was a soft thud beside him that Joe knew was Trent sitting down on the floor. "Shit," Trent whispered. "I'm an asshole."

"Sure are," Joe agreed. "So'm I. Scared Diego off."

Trent nudged him. "Diego? Was he an illegal?"

Joe opened his eyes. "Can you not be an asshole for five minutes?"

"Maybe." Trent looked toward the window. "He's been hanging around the ranch?"

"I think so." Joe groaned as he sat up. "He's got scars all over, Trent. Someone hurt him bad, many times."

Not surprisingly, that got Trent's attention. "I didn't see scars, but he was halfway out the window when I came in. What kind of scars? You need to start explaining things here, bro."

So Joe did, cheeks burning when he came to the part about finding Diego in his house.

"He didn't try to kill you that time you jumped him," Trent pointed out. He raked Joe over with a considering look. "I mean, dude. You're all bruised and scratched, and that might be a bite mark on your shoulder."

Joe glanced at the spot in question. "It is. He was terrified, and that was my fault. I don't know what the difference was this time. He said something he didn't want to is all I can figure, and it scared him, though I can't for the life of me understand why."

"I probably didn't help, hollering like a fuckhead." Trent scratched his chin as he spoke. "Well, so you went out to see if the dog was there, and it was. You chased it, lost it, came in and found a naked guy with funny-looking eyes. And you leapt on him and you both came." He shrugged. "Seems like he got what he wanted from you in the first place and left. You think he owns that dog?"

Joe got to his feet again. He was weak from getting his ass kicked twice, and lack of caffeine. Breakfast might help. When he swayed, Trent was right there to support him. "Thanks. And maybe. I didn't ask him." He had forgotten about the dog, honestly.

"Maybe he's a werewolf," Trent suggested. "Or a weredog?"

"Trent…" Joe couldn't even think of a comeback for either of those suggestions.

Trent cackled. "Yeah, yeah, you're the one who hit your head. Shouldn't be me with the crazy-ass ideas."

"That's not an idea, that's the ramblings of a nut," Joe teased. "I need to shower." *And pick up the condom. And see if I can track Diego down. I'm not letting him go like this.*

"You're going to try to find him, aren't you?" Trent asked while watching Joe.

His brother knew him well. "Can you handle things here for a few hours?"

Trent sighed like he was the most put-upon man on earth. "I reckon, but keep the phone with you in case there's an emergency or a dozen heifers decide to calve today. Shit always happens when it's most inconvenient."

Joe didn't argue since Trent was right.

"I'll make the coffee and some eggs. Toast, too." Trent left the room, still talking as he did so. "Better take him some clothes seeing as he left here naked."

* * * *

After a quick shower and some ibuprofen, Joe almost felt human. The scratches weren't bad, the bite mark was kind of a turn-on, which he figured made him twisted, all things considered. His jaw hurt, but Joe suspected Trent had held back some of his strength since he hadn't broken it.

All in all, physically, he'd be okay. He was sore, and frustrated—but mostly he was worried. Diego had been distraught. Joe was relatively certain Diego wasn't normally a mean person.

"Stupid. Ain't like I know him," he muttered, disgusted with himself. "For all I do know, he could be unbalanced, or a criminal. Could have left behind a string of bodies from here to wherever he came from."

The idea was so ludicrous, he laughed and shook his head. He might not know Diego well, but he knew better than that.

Joe dressed, putting his worn straw cowboy hat on last. He rolled up a pair of sweats, a shirt and a pair of flip-flops he'd rarely worn into a bundle, which he secured with two rubber bands. Then took it with him when he went into the dining room where Trent was sitting at the table drinking coffee. Joe set the clothes for Diego down.

The sun was up almost fully, and the day was racing ahead before Joe was ready for it to. He wanted it to slow down so he could get a leg up on finding Diego.

"God, take the damned eggs with you. Forget the toast." Trent tossed a couple of tortillas at him. "You're mooning after that guy like a teenage girl after one of those boy bands." Trent stood up then went to the kitchen cabinet. "I'm fixing you a canteen of water, too. You'll need it if you're going to be gone for more than an hour."

"Thanks." Joe grimaced and scooped the eggs out onto the tortillas. "You spend too much time reading the gossip online."

"Gotta entertain myself somehow. Speaking of which." He cleared his throat.

Joe looked at him. "Yeah?"

Trent's cheeks pinked up. "I would like to take a weekend off once we're through the calving season."

"Go on and plan it." Like Joe would cockblock his brother. "I'm gonna head out. I'll take a four-wheeler."

"He'll hear you long before he sees you then." Trent tucked the Thermos under Joe's arm.

Joe stuffed half an egg taco in his mouth and nodded. An ATV would be faster, but a horse would be quieter, for the most part. Hooves on dirt weren't exactly quiet, though.

Still, he saddled up Oni out in the barn. It didn't take him five minutes to be out behind the house, looking for tracks. They were faint, but there. Joey followed them for a dozen yards, out past clumps of scrub and beyond some mesquite.

Then things got weird. Joe stopped Oni and got off. He walked back to the last footprint—the last human one. He walked in a circle, Oni minding and staying put like he'd been told. There were no more footprints heading away from his house.

But there were other prints, fresh ones, and they belonged to something with four legs, not two.

Trent's teasing about werewolves came back to Joe and he tried not to get creeped out. "That's just silly shit."

Another ten minutes and Joe was beginning to think he was either losing his shit or Trent's joke might not have been a joke after all. All he could find were animal tracks.

Curiosity got the better of him and despite feeling like an idiot, he used his phone to Google for differences between wolf prints and dog prints. What he found was that while there wasn't a whole lot of difference, and it was suggested not to use tracks alone to declare an animal dog or wolf, the tracks matched the description of a wolf's.

A big wolf. The rear feet weren't as large as the front ones, and they often landed in the same track as the front paws. The toes spread out pretty far, too.

It could have been coincidence, but with Trent's comment and the disappearance of the human footprints, Joe was bordering on freaking out. Even so, he wasn't going to be deterred from his pursuit.

On impulse, he tried to find images of wolves at night to see if any of them had the same kind of eyes as the dog-maybe-wolf on the ranch did. Joe found entirely too many pictures drawn, painted or created on computers. It took him a few minutes to even see an actual photograph. As before when he'd tried looking up animals' eyes, the wolves' on his phone didn't match the creature's that had been outside his home last night.

But it was very close.

Joe shivered, a chill coming over him. He tucked his phone away. It wasn't going to help him find Diego. He got back on Oni. "Follow the tracks…" *Or not.* If he did follow the wolf — if it *was* a wolf, what then?

He didn't want to think about it. Instead he told himself that a wolf on the ranch was a danger to the cattle. True enough. Red wolves were extinct in the area, had been for decades. Strange things happened, though, and Joe believed nature would always find a way to keep going.

Joe had always been a fair to middlin' tracker, as his dad used to say. Not the best, but decent enough. He followed the wolf tracks for over an hour. In his mind, he was definitely pursuing a wolf, not a dog. He'd been messed up the night he'd first encountered the beast, true enough. Still, he saw it in his head. Joe took his phone out again.

This time he looked up red wolves and Texas. What he saw, the images of the wolf itself, took his breath away. That was definitely the animal he'd seen, except the one that had leaped onto his truck had been bigger than the ones in the pictures.

Nature will find a way. That's the first time I encountered Diego, too. Maybe he's the man who was raised with wolves. Thinking about some of the scars he'd seen on Diego's body, Joe wasn't sure that was far from the truth. There'd been what looked like claw marks, and bite marks.

Of course, Diego also had unusually vibrant eyes, the color not contact lenses, as Joe had learned. Diego hadn't had to remove them in the shower, nor had Joe seen any telltale rings around his irises. No, those amber eyes were all Diego's.

Joe wondered what they would look like in the dark. It hadn't occurred to him to check when he'd woken up in the middle of the night with Diego in his arms.

After another hour, Joe decided to risk spooking the wolf. It occurred to him that the thing was wild and could hurt Diego should it encounter him first.

So he started calling out to Diego, and kept doing it every few minutes until his throat began to ache some time later, and his voice began to give out. Joe stopped Oni in a spot of shade and took a long drink from the

Thermos. It was getting hot, and he knew Diego was barefoot. He still hadn't seen any signs of the man, either. Just wolf tracks.

"Diego," he hollered after he'd drunk a little more water. "Hey, man, come on. Enough of this. I'm sorry I was an ass. Let's discuss this."

He repeated some variation of that confession and plea for another hour and a half before he lost all hope, along with the wolf's tracks. They'd just upped and vanished amongst some trees, and Joe couldn't for the life of him figure out where they picked up again. Just like Diego's earlier, the wolf tracks simply ceased.

Oni was restless, though, shying away from the trees. The horse snorted and set back, making it clear that trying to guide Oni in farther was going to result in a possible attempt at tossing Joe off. Since Oni was always so even-tempered, this both alarmed and spooked Joe.

And he figured the wolf was nearby. Oni was reacting to the scent of a predator. The hair on the back of Joe's neck stood up. He'd never had that experience before and didn't care for it at all. He refused to let himself tense up or feel fear, however. That would transmit to Oni, and likely to the wolf if it was eyeing them for a snack.

Instead Joe sat up taller in the hopes of making himself appear broader. He narrowed his eyes and tried to see everything around them. Oni still wanted to back up, so it seemed the threat was in front of them, or to their sides.

"Buck up, Oni. I won't let anything hurt you, buddy." Joe projected a calm he had to really struggle to maintain. "Diego," he said in a slightly louder voice. "You're spookin' my horse. Come on, honey. I ain't going to freak out on you."

Why he said it, Joe wasn't sure. He hoped Diego was hiding up ahead, and that was what Oni had picked up on. Didn't make a lot of sense, but it was the best he could come up with for his words.

So when Diego shimmied down a tree right by where the wolf prints stopped, Joe should have been relieved. Part of him was.

The majority of him was trying really hard not to lose his shit, because there was no way he would have missed a man's footprints out there.

And all he'd seen were a wolf's.

Chapter Ten

As stupid as he knew it made him, Diego still couldn't force himself to remain hidden. He'd run, with every intention of never seeing Joe again. There were so many reasons why staying for one minute longer was a bad idea, not the least of which was the potential to fall too far for Joe.

And Diego wasn't completely ignorant. He was aware that Joe had tracked him, tracked his wolf form, rather. Diego had shifted mid-leap at the tree's lower branch, and had morphed completely before reaching it. Sometimes he got lucky like that. So he'd scampered up the tree, hoping Joe would leave.

Hoping he would stay.

Diego had clung to the tree so tightly his arms ached. His fingers did, too, and a glance told him they were bleeding, torn from him digging them into the bark.

Yet for all his restraint, he'd failed. Joe called out to him, used that word that broke Diego's defenses down like they were nothing more than twigs snapping beneath the weight of them. *Honey.* No one had ever called Diego anything so sweet. It stripped him bare, knowing he was so embarrassingly eager and needy for even a hint of kindness.

The knowledge didn't stop him from lowering himself down to the ground.

Joe's eyes went wide and Oni's nostrils flared as the horse tried to back up.

"Nuh," Joe murmured, whether to Oni or him, Diego had no idea. Joe's tanned skin paled the longer he looked at Diego.

Diego wanted to duck his head and hide, or turn back the past sixty seconds so that he was still in the tree. He settled for averting his gaze.

"Don't."

Joe spoke the word softly yet with a commanding note in his tone that Diego couldn't ignore. He cautiously glanced up to look at Joe again.

"You aren't dirty," Joe observed. "Been running for hours, outrunning me on Oni here, and you ain't even broke a sweat."

Diego's heart beat so hard he saw black spots. He struggled for something to say, opening and closing his mouth, but nothing came to mind.

Except the truth, and that he could *not* speak.

"No footprints, either, which is kind of beside the fact that a human can't outrun a horse, usually," Joe continued. He clucked his tongue at Oni, spoke gently to the horse then dismounted. "Not a single human footprint around here, Diego. How'd you do that?"

There was a knowing glint in Joe's eyes and it scared the shit out of Diego. He'd been careless, so very careless.

"I—" He coughed, startled he'd gotten even that much out.

Joe took a Thermos off the saddle where he'd had it hanging. "Take a drink." He extended it out to Diego.

There was water in it, Diego could smell the moisture and it made him even more aware of how dry his throat and mouth were.

Joe shook the Thermos, gesturing for Diego to come closer. "I ain't going to bite you, honey."

How did he know what that did to Diego? All he could figure was that it showed in his expression, some pleasure at having earned an endearment. It warmed Diego up from the inside out.

Diego trembled from head to toe before he took a step closer. He looked from the Thermos to Joe's face, then back again once he was assured Joe wasn't up to any trickery.

"I shouldn't have tried to grab you, huh?" Joe asked quietly. "Not when it was obvious you were freaking out already. I made it worse, and I'm sorry for that. I just didn't want you to leave, which doesn't make what I did right."

Diego's knees wobbled and his stomach did an odd dip-spin combo. "I should go." He forced the words out, because it was the truth.

Joe didn't pull the Thermos back, but his hand did waver. "No. Don't go. Where you got to be?"

Diego wrinkled his nose at the way Joe asked the question. It sounded off to his ears, not that Diego was the most educated guy. He knew Joe could talk properly. "Why do you do that? Talk like a hick," Diego added.

Joe snorted. "I am a hick, Diego. Barely made it through high school, and I don't worry all the time about speaking right unless I'm doing business for the ranch and my speech reflects on me as a businessman.

Some people think you're stupid if you don't speak like you got a PhD. Ain't the truth, though."

Diego supposed he was right. Another step brought him close enough to reach for the Thermos and take it. "Thanks."

Joe dropped his hand to his hip. He studied Diego, and Diego wondered if he was waiting for him to turn into a wolf. Of course, maybe Joe didn't have the faintest suspicion. He hadn't said the wolf and Diego were one in the same being. Really, such an idea should be so insane no human would think of it.

Diego took the lid off the Thermos. His nose twitched as he caught the stronger scent of the water. He was thirstier than he'd thought. Diego raised the container to his lips before taking a long drink.

"Drink it all if you want. There's plenty at the house."

Diego choked on the water he'd been swallowing.

Joe eased forward and patted him on the back. "You okay?"

Diego gasped while he tried to form an answer.

Joe dipped his head down and tipped his hat back, giving Diego a better look into his eyes. All the fluttery nervousness inside Diego calmed as he lost himself in those eyes for a moment.

"Come back with me," Joe asked, softly touching Diego's arm. "I don't know what's going on, and maybe I'm thinking some crazy shit because—" He sighed. "Well, you might think I'm crazy, and I might, too. But there's only the one set of tracks coming out here, and I followed 'em all the way from out back from the house. Where yours ended, Diego. What do you think that means?"

Diego gulped down another mouthful of water. He couldn't breathe right, was so thrown off center by

Joe's intense gaze and question and by the fact that Joe had come after him in the first place.

"Why?" Diego found himself asking. "Why didn't you just let me go?"

Joe caressed his arm then stepped back. "I won't be like my dad, Diego. I got— I got rough, and it spooked you. Didn't like that about myself."

Diego put the lid on the Thermos while he thought that over. He handed the container to Joe. "No, I wasn't scared. I... Well, maybe I was, but it wasn't because of you. I—" Diego gave up trying to explain something he couldn't even understand. He had been such a jumbled up mix of emotions, figuring out what drove him the most was impossible. But one thing remained clear. "I should leave. Bad things follow me." *Bad people, shifters, and you can't fight them.*

Joe grimaced. "We can talk about it. I know I'm maybe coming on strong here, but can you please at least talk to me?" Joe didn't wait for an answer, instead turning and removing something from his saddlebags. He also tied the reins to a branch. "Be good, Oni. It's just Diego and me here."

Diego had scars from attacks that would have killed Joe. Proof enough that Diego was endangering anyone he was around. He clenched his fists. "I need to go."

Joe exhaled slowly, tipping his head down as if he were trying to see every speck of dirt on the ground.

Or maybe, like me, he's trying to hide. I use my hair, he uses his hat. It touched Diego to realize they had that tendency in common.

"Brought you these," Joe said, holding up a bundle. "Don't have any shoes that would fit you, but the flip-flops ought to work for now. I'll give you enough money to buy some good shoes if you don't have any. At least let me do that."

Diego blinked, but his vision wouldn't clear up. The offer of money should have offended him, would have had it come from someone other than Joe.

But Joe was speaking from a kindness that radiated out from him. He could be the rough, dominating lover Diego craved, but that wasn't who he was. Not all of him. Joe was more complex, and Diego wanted to stay and discover everything about the man. He wanted it more than he'd desired anything else, possibly.

Maybe even more than his freedom.

Diego snatched the clothing away and skittered backwards. "You don't know. You don't know!"

Oni let loose a distressed sound and pulled against the reins. Diego was afraid, of himself and the need he was developing for Joe. He shook his head.

Joe looked stricken when he snapped his head up. "Diego—"

"No. You have no idea." Diego laughed bitterly and swept a hand down his scrawny chest. "These scars are *nothing*, Joe. Nothing. What they'd do to you—" Diego almost puked even saying that. He turned to run, but Joe halted him with five words.

"I know what you are."

Diego's legs seemed to turn to concrete, and his feet were weighted to the dirt. He couldn't take another step away, couldn't move or get his lungs to work as he tried to judge whether or not Joe was telling the truth. Or more correctly, if Joe had the right truth. Diego didn't think the man was a liar. There was no way Joe could believe—

"You're a werewolf."

Okay, Joe would admit he'd said a lot of stupid things in his life, so the werewolf thing should have ranked up there around the top of the nutty stuff regardless.

But it didn't. He'd seen the tracks, hadn't he? Had seen the wolf part of Diego and the man. The eyes… He nodded more to himself than to Diego, who wasn't looking at him anyway. Diego seemed to be rooted in place.

The eyes were what did it, what cinched it. Diego's were a little darker when he was walking around on two legs. They still had the yellow tone, even had flecks of it in the irises. Same up-tilted outer edges, too.

And things just added up, even if they added up to what should have only been possible in a fantasy world.

"I saw the tracks, Diego," Joe explained, both for Diego's benefit and his own. Oni pawed at the ground and Joe had to take a few seconds to comfort him. "Calm down, Oni. It's okay. He ain't going to hurt either of us." Joe rubbed Oni's neck before continuing, "I'm a decent tracker. I didn't lose a man's tracks. They just stopped. Then there was a wolf's instead. Same wolf I've been seeing around here. Same eyes as you, Diego. Tell me I'm wrong." Joe kind of hoped he did so convincingly.

With Oni calmed somewhat, Joe eased toward Diego, who was still standing as if turned to stone, his back to Joe. "I followed that wolf's tracks, then they stopped. And you appeared right where they stopped. I told you, I saw that. Ain't a coincidence." He crept closer. "I don't know the how of it, or if maybe I'm just crazier than all get-out. Could be, I reckon. Maybe I did some damage that night you hid under the truck and scared the tar out of me."

Diego took a deep, shaky breath then. Joe felt like he'd won a round.

"You have some scars. I think when I saw them, things started coming together in my mind, or trying to." Joe chuckled, and was rewarded by Diego turning sideways, glancing at him through all that hair. "You know, people always gotta think we're the shit. Can't be anything else in this world if we can't explain it through science or religion. Anything outside of those two beliefs is just fiction."

He was close enough now to reach out and touch Diego, but he didn't. He wasn't going to risk spooking the man. "I can admit I don't know jack shit about much of anything except ranching. Even then, there's plenty of folks that could teach me a lot more. I don't understand how a space shuttle works, or how critters live miles down under the water in the oceans. I don't understand why people let hate rule their lives, and I don't get science more than I have to. I suck at geography, can't find more than a few states on the US map. So there's every likelihood that you are just what I said you are, and maybe now you're trying to think of a way to lie to me about it, 'cause that's got to be something you wouldn't want out there in the world."

Joe had to repress a shiver himself. "Don't imagine good things would come from human beings finding out there's werewolves roaming the planet with them. We got a history of freaking out and trying to kill everything that spooks us instead of trying to get along with others and understand 'em."

Diego snorted softly, just enough to rustle his hair.

It gave Joe hope and enabled him to finish what he'd wanted to say. "So that's understandable, but it don't look like your kind is any better if they did that to you."

Diego brought the bundle of clothing up to his chest and hugged it.

Joe couldn't stand it any longer. Diego looked so dejected and hurt, it was unbearable to see. He closed the distance between them, pulling Diego into his arms. It was an awkward hug—Diego didn't turn to him, so Joe had to settle for bringing Diego against his chest sideways. Still, it felt good, *no*, it felt *right* to hold him.

He wouldn't freak out over the werewolf thing. Couldn't, because he might not get all his marbles back in place if he did. "I didn't make that up. People believe there can be aliens up in outer space, or even walking among us. They believe in angels, and demons and the Devil and God. What you are isn't impossible." Diego leaned his head against Joe's chest. "Say something, please." Joe was feeling kind of foolish, like he'd babbled a bunch of bullshit, though he didn't see how he could be wrong. Crazy, yeah, but not wrong.

"We're not ever allowed to tell," Diego murmured so lightly Joe almost didn't hear him.

Joe held Diego a little tighter. "Seems like a good thing. People got a lot worse than pitchforks and torches now'days."

That got a little chuckle out of Diego. "Exactly why we aren't ever supposed to let humans find out about us."

Joe rested his chin on the top of Diego's head. "You're human too."

"Sort of," Diego admitted. "And sort of not. Would you hold me like this if I were a wolf?"

"I'd love to," Joe said promptly. "Man, you're a gorgeous fucker when you're all hairy. Sexy as sin when you aren't."

"I thought ranchers hated wolves," Diego said. He wiggled a little until Joe raised his head and Diego did too, looking at him. "All of the red wolves in Texas were murdered decades ago."

Joe nodded. "Yep. Goes back to the fear thing. Plus there's plenty of dickheads that get their jollies killing defenseless animals. Not that wolves are defenseless," he quickly added. "Just, they ain't bulletproof."

"No, they aren't," Diego agreed. "Neither are we. Doesn't take a silver bullet to kill one of us, just a bullet in the right spot, or wrong spot, depending on your point of view."

Joe had so many questions. Most of them were unnecessary, so he didn't bother. If Diego was going to stay, there'd be time to talk and get to know each other. If he wasn't, there was no point in Joe getting more attached to him.

"Come back with me," he asked again. "Don't run."

Diego shook in his arms. "You don't understand. They're coming for me. I'm endangering the whole pack."

Pack. That's what set Diego into an unholy panic earlier! A red-hot fury filled Joe. "They put all them scars on you and expect you to stay? So they can kill you?"

"I'm an omega, and the runt." Diego shrugged but didn't pull away from him. "I heard a rumor once that not all omegas are treated badly, but every one I've known has been. Usually, different wolves are omegas at different times. But in our pack, it was just me. Always just me."

"Omega means..." Joe frowned, trying to remember. "The end, don't it? Like God is the alpha and omega, the beginning and the end? That's from the Bible, I think."

Another shrug. "I don't know. Christianity isn't a shifter thing. In my pack, my former pack, I mean, the omega is everyone's bitch and punching bag. If someone is angry, and I'm near, or even if they have to send for me, it's my place to let them do what they want to me."

"Fuck that," Joe spat out. He'd never been so furious in his entire life. If his anger could have been converted into a physical power, he'd have been able to crush the whole world with one hand. "They can't do that."

"Yes, they can," Diego argued, though he sounded defeated rather than mad. "They can do what they want. Who is going to stop them?"

Joe cupped Diego's chin. He waited until Diego met his gaze. Joe looked into those unique eyes and let himself fall. Fuck being cautious. He'd just learned that the world was an amazing, brutal place full of things he'd never even thought about. "Fuck them, and fuck that. I'll stop 'em. I won't be putting bullets in them outta fear, either. I'll be paying them back for every scar they left on you."

Whether or not he could actually kill when the time came, Joe wasn't certain. If it'd been right then, at that moment, he'd have easily pulled the trigger on every asshole that had hurt Diego. Time and intellect could change that, but he wouldn't let Diego be harmed again.

Diego blinked at him with wide-eyed wonder. "Why? Why would you even—? You don't know me. I'm just... I'm just a homeless, scarred-up, maybe crazy freak—"

"Don't," Joe growled. "Don't even start talking shit about yourself. You have value, Diego. You've got plenty of value, and no one can take that away from you. The fact that you left them all behind and didn't let them keep you down when all you knew was their way of life, that proves it."

"I didn't want to die," Diego said raggedly. "I... I just wanted to be free once in my life. To not worry about where the next pain would come from."

Joe flashed back to the handprints he'd left on Diego's backside. All Diego had known was abuse and harsh treatment, and Joe'd given him more of the same. That Diego got off on it hardly mattered because Joe knew he'd been conditioned that way.

And when Joe caressed Diego, when he held him gently and soothed him, Diego melted for him more thoroughly than when Joe had been rough. Didn't that tell him something right there? If they ever played rough again, Joe would have to know one hundred percent that Diego was into it because he enjoyed it, not because it was what he'd always had.

That was a big if, too, since Diego probably wouldn't want to stay around long enough to work past any of his problems.

"Stay," Joe said, not asking, but hoping. "Stay here, with me and Trent. Don't hide from him. He saw you go out the window anyway. He knows I'm out here looking for you. He..." Joe hesitated. Should he say it? He gave a mental shrug. "Maybe he was joking—in fact, I'm sure he was, but Trent's the one who got me to thinking about the werewolf thing. A crack he made about it before I left to search for you."

Diego had gone still again.

Joe nuzzled his cheek and felt Diego loosen up. "He don't know anything for sure," Joe pointed out. "Just a joke he made."

"His instincts were guiding him," Diego explained. "It happens. It's another reason we're to stay clear of humans. Some of you still have the primitive instincts your forefathers had. It sets off warning alarms even though no one would truly believe in my kind."

"Some people do, I think. Besides me." Joe wanted to pack Diego up and keep him, he decided. If he had a few days with Diego, who knew what would happen? It was possible, if he were smooth enough and begged just right, that Diego would agree to remain there and give the thing between them a shot.

Diego pulled back a little. Joe had to let him go and immediately felt the loss of the man who'd been in his arms. Diego pulled the rubber bands off the bundle. "I should go, but I... I want to stay here." He glanced up at Joe. "It could be dangerous. It will be, if they aren't far behind me. They almost caught me in Arkansas. Did get a hold of me in Tennessee." Diego touched a fading pink set of scars on his side. "I learned to move faster and not sleep much." He laughed tonelessly. "Not that I ever have. Sleep was always dangerous."

Joe could kill them, he was positive. No one should have to live the way Diego had. "Do you have a last name?"

Diego grunted. "No. We just don't have the need. I'm Diego of the Fuerte pack."

"Strong?" Joe asked then, "The pack was called the Strong pack?"

"Yeah." Diego slipped the sweats on. "It always has been. We originated down here, I guess. I'm not real clear on our history. Education isn't important for us." He cocked his head. "I can't read."

Joe offered an arm for balance when Diego began to put on the shoes. "I can teach you. If you want to learn."

Diego stopped getting dressed, one foot up as he'd been working a flip-flop onto it. "You'd do that?"

"Sure. It'd take a while, but it'd be worth it, don't you think?" Joe would get to have Diego there for weeks if they were going to work on that. "You know, keeping the pack uneducated, that's another means of control."

Diego shrugged. "The alpha controls the pack anyway. It doesn't matter. We live very similar to our animal sides, though I believe wolves have more compassion and decency than shifters do. It's like we got the worst qualities of both species."

"Are all packs that way?" And, Jesus, how many packs of shifters were there? How many species?

"The ones I know of, pretty much." Diego got the shoes on then scowled down at his feet. "These feel weird. I have hardly ever worn clothes. Only when I had to move through towns and cities. Cities are…" Diego shuddered and grimaced. "I don't like cities."

Joe waited until Diego had the shirt on. "Yeah, me either." Man, he wanted to ask so many questions. It wasn't the time for them, and honestly, the answers might be too much for him. If he found out there were mosquito shifters, he'd consider himself a mass murderer. Same with flies.

Maybe Buddhists have the right of it. His need to protect Diego conflicted with logic and reason.

It was something he needed to think about, while at the same time he couldn't let the questions and the whole reality he'd just discovered fuck with his head. If he wasn't careful, he could freak out. *Who wouldn't, considering all I just learned?*

The best he could do was to push away the panic and sheer disbelief that kept trying to swamp him. If he gave either its head, he'd lose his.

Then he wouldn't do Diego any good. So yeah, he was going to hold it together come hell or high tide.

Chapter Eleven

Trent had been looking at him funny ever since arriving to the spot where Joe had found Diego.

Diego tried not to pay him any attention and focused more on his own thoughts. Joe and Trent were having a brotherly chat and Diego didn't want to eavesdrop or be pulled into the conversation.

There were so many things racing around in his head, worries and memories, hope and more. He wished Joe had just let him walk back to the house, but Joe had been worried about the distance and their dwindling water supply. Oni, showing more sense than most humans, refused to let Diego get close. The horse's senses told it there was a predator inside Diego, and that was true enough. Diego wouldn't have hurt Oni in his wolf form, either. Didn't change what he was, though.

Plus, he wasn't eager to get on Oni. Diego had never ridden a horse and was frankly scared to ever try. They were big, unpredictable creatures, at least they were in his opinion. Even a wolf would be cautious when faced with such a beast as a foe. A wolf his size, anyways. Then again, he was the runt. Still bigger than a full-blooded wolf, but smaller by far than the other adults, male or female, in his pack.

Former pack. I'm not ever going back to them. Hopefully, by him leaving, any future omega would see that he or she didn't have to take such abuse. Such rebellion was almost certainly the true reason he was being hunted.

Though shifters feared exposure, short of being caught in actual mid-shift, Diego doubted there was much of a chance of their existence coming to light. Who would believe him if he said what he was, other than Joe, who'd figured it out with a jest from Trent and tracks Diego couldn't hide?

Even if people saw him shift, many would think they were just seeing things. The mind wouldn't want to accept it. And once he shifted, he was, biologically, whatever he was. If he died in wolf form, that would be all he was, a wolf. Same for his human side.

At least, that's what he'd been told. It was why they didn't worry when one of their own died, naturally or unnaturally — such as by a bullet or a car hitting them. All that was left was the body of whatever beast they'd been. Of course, he'd bet on occasion people flipped out over finding a dead beast bigger than its species usually was. *If only they knew. Better that they don't.*

"You still look scrawny, even with clothes on."

"Trent, don't be an asshole," Joe snapped at his brother. "Ignore him, Diego."

Diego tipped his chin down. He'd been trying to do that, hadn't he?

"I'm just saying, he needs to hang around and eat three square meals for a month or two," Trent said reasonably. "Some fattening snacks, too. I didn't mean it bad."

"Calling someone scrawny isn't any nicer than calling them fat," Joe pointed out.

Trent snorted. "Well, I didn't call him fat, did I?"

"Trent," Joe growled.

Diego barely kept from shivering. His dick twitched, arousal threatening to make it fully erect. Diego didn't want to embarrass himself by sporting a hard-on.

"Joe," Trent mimicked. "Lighten up. You know, I didn't see any footprints coming out this way."

Joe stiffened, as did Diego. His arousal vanished as he peeked through his hair at Trent, only to find the man staring intently at him.

"No footprints, just those dog prints, which I think maybe were wolf prints, because I Googled—"

"That's enough," Joe said firmly, slashing a hand through the air. "Just take Oni back for me."

Trent took the reins from him, but kept watching Diego. "Don't like to ride?"

Diego shrugged. He didn't owe Trent any explanations.

Trent raised both eyebrows. "Are you being rude, or do you just not speak?"

Joe took a menacing step toward Trent.

"I speak," Diego answered quickly, hoping to avert a fight between the brothers. "I don't know how to ride, and horses make me nervous. They're...big."

Trent chuckled, ignoring Joe and petting Oni. "This one's a baby. He wouldn't hurt you for the world. So how'd you get out here without leaving footprints?"

Diego cast a panicked look at Joe.

"He fuckin' flew," Joe said. "Come on, Diego. Let's get home." Joe took him by the arm.

They got on the four-wheeler. Diego's stomach dipped down to about his ankles when Joe started the vehicle. This was a new experience for him.

Trent hollered that he wasn't done talking and would get answers sooner or later. Diego ignored him.

"Put your arms around me and hold on," Joe advised. "Feel free to rub all over me, honey."

Diego liked holding onto Joe. Joe was bigger, broader, harder in all the ways that turned Diego inside out with need. He started to link his hands together but couldn't quite manage it. Joe took him by one wrist and pulled his hand down until it rested right above Joe's groin.

"Can hang onto my legs, my hips, my…anything," Joe murmured. "I like you touching me."

"You two gonna make out or drive?" Trent called out.

Joe flipped his brother off. "Hold on," he said over his shoulder.

Diego held on, all right. Joe sent them rocketing off on the ATV, and Diego squeaked in alarm as he grabbed at any part of Joe he could reach.

Joe's laughter was nice and irksome at the same time. Diego didn't like being laughed at, but he didn't think Joe meant to be cruel.

They hit a bump and Diego quit worrying about anything but staying on the vehicle. He pressed himself against Joe's back, wedging right up as close as possible.

Oddly enough, as his fear began to ebb, something else increased. Diego was growing hornier by the minute. The vibrations from the engine, Joe's body, his scent and all that he'd done for Diego combined—he was ready to strip the man naked and beg to be fucked by the time they reached Joe's house.

Joe shut the vehicle off. "You got a hard-on?"

Before Diego could answer, Joe pushed his hand down so that Diego could feel Joe's erection. "'Cause I sure do, Diego."

Joe got off the ATV and helped Diego down. Diego's legs were shaky, both from the ride and from the need coursing through him.

He'd never been so forward in his life as he had with Joe. Diego flung himself at Joe, much as others had come at Diego to fuck him.

Joe caught him and kissed Diego until Diego couldn't breathe, couldn't think. Despite the controlling way he kissed, Joe still kept it tender, as if Diego were fragile or something to be handled with respect.

"Inside," Joe rasped.

Diego hesitated, wondering if he dared to ask. Then he shook his head. "Out here, in the sunlight, please." He wanted at least one good memory of being taken out in the open.

Joe studied him for a moment. When Diego's throat went dry and his heart was fluttering around like a newly hatched butterfly in the wind, Joe kissed Diego again. Diego could live forever on those kisses. They were sweet and powerful and a sign that Joe wanted him. No biting until Diego's lips bled, or until he whimpered from the pain. Joe treated him like Diego mattered, and that was something he'd never had before.

As an omega, he'd only mattered in that he was there for others' entertainment and abuse. Maybe there were omegas in packs that were fine with that, but Diego couldn't tolerate it any longer.

Or maybe other omegas were treated better.

Diego quit thinking about it when Joe growled and palmed his butt. He got the message — Joe wanted Diego there with him, in the lust that was rising between them.

Easy enough to do. The fact that Joe even wanted him after learning that Diego was different only added to Diego's infatuation with the man. The all-consuming want whirling through him was dizzying, and made Diego's knees feel gelatinous. At the same time, it made the rest of him want to breed. He pressed closer to Joe and writhed.

Then Joe startled him by spinning Diego around until his back was to Joe's chest. "Like this," Joe whispered by his ear.

Diego didn't know what he meant until Joe plunged a hand down the front of the sweats. He immediately fisted Diego's cock, slicking the pre-cum around the head of it.

Diego let his head drop back and thump against Joe's chest.

"God damn, you're something," Joe said before sucking on his neck.

Diego mewled, the sound escaping him as he clutched at Joe's legs. He got denim, but that was good enough. Diego just had to hold onto Joe somehow.

"Pretty dick." Joe stroked it, slow at first then tighter, faster, until Diego had to thrust, had to chase that warm grip again and again. Joe slipped his other hand in and fondled Diego's balls. At the same time, he went back to kissing and sucking marks up on Diego's neck.

Diego humped mindlessly, pleasure building up inside him at warp speed. He gasped and held onto Joe as the world tipped around him. Diego's release raced up from his balls to his dick, and while cum shot from the slit, ecstasy overflowed and he cried out with relief.

"Yeah, yeah," Joe whispered, pumping Diego's cock. "Look at you. God, honey."

Diego didn't know what Joe was going on about, couldn't think when he was being turned inside out with the exquisite climax. Joe worked his dick until Diego was on the verge of whimpering and pulling away then he released it and brought his hand up to Diego's mouth.

"Taste," Joe ordered.

Diego licked his lips, then one of Joe's fingers.

"That's nice to see," Joe told him. "Better than nice. Makes me ache all the way down to my balls."

Joe brought his hand up higher. Diego tipped his head up and watched Joe lick the rest of Diego's spunk from his hand. When Joe moaned, Diego's dick tried to harden again. Didn't succeed, but if Joe moaned like that a couple more times, Diego would be ready for more.

"God, you taste good," Joe said after licking away the last of the cum. "Not like me or anyone else. Very…" Joe chuckled. "Not that I'm a spunk connoisseur or anything, but you got a smoky flavor to you."

"A conn—Conn—" Gods, Diego could hardly think and Joe was over there using big words. "A what?"

Joe grunted and kissed his temple. "It's like an expert, I guess. Maybe I don't know the word like I think I do. Could be wrong."

Diego got the gist of it, though. "You haven't been with a lot of people?"

"No, I haven't," Joe replied. "Not a lot of opportunity out here for one, and I don't want women like I want men. Being gay ain't all that easy in this part of Texas." Joe huffed. "Hell, it ain't easy anywhere, I imagine, but here especially."

"There's no gay or straight in the pack," Diego said. "The stronger members fuck whoever they want. The alpha male and female can have people of either gender, in whatever form, human or wolf. Anyone can fuck the omega, however they want, as often as they want." Diego tried not to feel shame. "Shifters are a…a highly sexed species."

Joe didn't pull away from him, like Diego expected him to. Instead he began caressing Diego's stomach and chest. "They hurt you when they forced you."

"Forced?" Diego shook his head. "I'm the omega. They didn't force me. I knew my place." Eventually. When he'd been a pup, he'd been off limits for sexual things. Even shifters had some decency and morals, he supposed. But once he'd reached the age shifters considered to be that of an adult, nothing had been disallowed except outright murder of Diego. "It was that way for the omega before me, too, until she died."

"None of that makes it right."

Diego did turn then, looking up into Joe's eyes. The man was pissed off, that was clear. It took a minute, but Diego found the words he wanted, managed to put them together in a clear and concise way that he hoped explained the lifestyle of shifters. "It's a different way of life, Joe. It's not a human society, but a shifter one. You say forced, but each member has his or her place in the pack. An alpha, male or female, can and often does kill their own offspring in defense of their position once those offspring reach adulthood. It's not seen as evil, but a necessity. There's limited space on this planet for my kind, and what spurs us to act in such violent ways is a product of Nature's designs for us."

Joe was shaking his head before Diego was done speaking. "Bullshit. There's better ways. And killing their own kids—"

"They're wolves when it happens," Diego interrupted, though why he thought the distinction would matter to Joe was beyond him. "A wolf is mature at close to two human years. Shifters are the same if we've remained in animal form for the entire two years. For that reason, we don't shift into human form until we've reached many years past that. Our wolves mature long before our human forms do. It's odd, but..." Diego shrugged. He didn't know why they were the way they were. "It's just how it is."

Joe looked horrified. "So they kill babies? That's what you're saying?"

Diego bit his bottom lip. "But the wolves are adults when they try to challenge the alphas."

"I can't even conceive of that kind of fucked up- ness," Joe muttered. "Think about it. If you had a baby, how would you feel about killing him or her when they reached two years old?"

"But I can't have a baby," Diego said, confused over the whole question. "Besides being male, all omegas are sterile. Even if they grow past being an omega. It's another way for Nature to control our species and eradicate the weak. Otherwise there might be more omegas than betas or alphas."

"That's fascinating, it really is, but think about what I asked you as if you could have a child." Joe's expression was intense as he repeated his question. "Are you the kind of person who could kill like that?"

Diego gulped. Was he? He'd been raised up to view those wolves as adults when their human sides weren't matured. Like all of the pack, it was the mature wolf side Diego focused on.

Because not to meant horrific things. "No," he admitted, nausea pulsing in his stomach. "Gods, no. That's sick. We're sick! Why are we even here?" he asked with a bit of a wail. "All I thought about was my own misery—"

"Did it happen often?" Joe asked sharply.

Diego pressed a hand to his belly. "Twice in my lifetime. We don't reproduce often and most alpha-borns leave to start their own packs. Or so we're told." Now he wondered.

"Did you help with it?"

"No," Diego answered immediately. "Never. I wasn't even allowed near, and that was fine. I... I saw enough violence." Experienced enough violence. How many times had he thought he'd been born into the wrong species? Too often to count.

"So these sick bastards are going to be coming for you," Joe mused. "We know they'll kill their own kids to keep power over the pack. They're ruthless and bent to a degree most people can't understand. I'm not going to feel guilty for putting a bullet through the brain of any fucker that shows up here."

"They'd kill you without feeling bad." Diego's insides gave another icky heave. "The betas are vicious. They'd... They'd make sure it hurt you a lot, and if they knew I cared about you at all, they'd make me watch."

"Ain't gonna happen." Joe stroked his cheek. "Do you care about me?"

Diego's entire face burned, but he couldn't lie to Joe. "Yes. I would have left after the first time, or before then, even. But I'd been watching you, and you were kind, teasing, always smiling except when you were on Oni and the sunset was sprawling across the land. You were at peace with yourself, and I respected and envied that. I still do," Diego admitted. "You've fascinated me since I first saw you a few weeks ago."

"You've been hanging around here that long?" Joe asked.

"Yes. That's why I said I should run, because if I stay in one place too long —"

"No, no more running unless you just don't want to be with me," Joe argued. "They'll keep chasing you, right?"

Diego bobbed his head in agreement. "Yes. I did the unthinkable, and as the lowest ranking pack member, to break free can't be allowed."

Joe snorted. "Right. Whatever, it *is* happening. We need to tell Trent. You might have to, you know, shift and show him, if you don't think that's rude of me to ask."

"It's not. That's a part of me." Diego hated it at times, but his wolf wasn't the cause of the hatred he'd experienced. That was all the pack and the alphas' doings.

"Okay then. So Trent's probably gonna need to see that, and if he freaks out, we'll deal with that, too," Joe said. He laced the fingers of one hand with Diego's. "You know, they also might not find you."

"They will." Diego had no doubt about that. "The betas especially want me back. I was their preferred method of releasing their frustration."

Joe got this look about him that Diego had never seen before. It was much like the one the alpha wore when assigning a wolf to death. Diego didn't cringe away. That look wasn't for him, it was for anyone who now came after him.

"They show up here as men or wolves?" Joe asked in a cold voice.

Diego looked out over the land to the west. Some might not think it pretty, but its barrenness called to him. It'd be hard for several wolves to sneak up on them out there. "Either, but probably wolves. It's going to be hard for them to walk up here as humans."

"They don't have a car or anything?"

"I don't think so. We don't have one for the pack. I wouldn't think they'd know how to drive." Diego pointed to a clump of scrub. "There are few hiding places near. That's one of them I used to sit behind. Now, the betas are all bigger than me, and there're three of them that were hunting me — that I know of. Sam, Axel and Ann. They're both really strong and determined to serve their alphas well." He bit his bottom lip. For all he knew, there were more betas coming for him now, though the pack only had a total of eight of them.

Joe gently tugged his lip free with mild pressure from his thumb. "Going to make yourself bleed," Joe said. He rubbed Diego's lip.

"There could be more than those three, or it might not be them," Diego confessed. He frowned and pointed to the west. "Not far that way is another good hiding spot. Bigger, too. Maybe we should get back on the four-wheeler and I can show you the places I hid."

"I know this land, honey, but we can do that — tomorrow, if you want. How big will these wolves be?"

Diego should have thought of that. Of course Joe knew his property. Joe wasn't an inept sort of person. "Sorry."

Joe gave him a chaste kiss. "Don't apologize. You have a good idea. Maybe we can set up some sort of alarm system or surveillance."

"You have a lot of land to try to monitor. I'm not sure we could keep an eye on it all." Traps were out, what with cattle being in pastures and such. Which raised a serious issue. "They could hurt the cattle. Kill them, just out of meanness. Maybe not at first, but if they realize I'm here and not willing to leave with them." Diego thought about running again. He was scared, which he'd been all of his life, but now he was scared for someone other than himself. "Joe, I really should—"

"No, you shouldn't." This time Joe kissed him with that tenderness Diego couldn't resist. Tears slipped down his cheeks as he rested his hands on Joe's broad chest. He parted for Joe, welcoming the deeper kiss, the taste and warmth of Joe filling him. Joe cupped his big hands on Diego's back before bringing him closer.

It caused Diego to have to go up on his toes. Joe hooked an arm beneath Diego's butt and hefted him up. He pushed his tongue in deeper, rolling it over Diego's. Diego felt the desire in him starting like a small quake that rippled out in waves.

His mouth was thoroughly plundered but with a gentleness that destroyed every barrier he'd erected. Diego didn't want to run again, ever. He wanted to stay right there with Joe, and damn the consequences of that. He was tired of being afraid, tired of missing out on living and tired of no one wanting him for any reason other than to humiliate and hurt him.

Joe wasn't like that. He wasn't like anyone Diego had ever known. Even the shifters that hadn't wanted to use him as the omega had turned away from him and not given a damn when he'd been left hurt and bleeding, bruised so bad he hadn't been able to move.

Joe wouldn't ever treat him like a disposable thing to be used. Joe wouldn't let anyone else treat him badly, either.

Now Diego had to decide how he was going to repay Joe for such kindness. Leaving might be the only decent way to do it.

Chapter Twelve

Whatever Diego had been brooding about all afternoon, Joe didn't like it. Diego kept casting him sideways looks when he thought Joe wasn't looking.

Joe was always looking. Diego drew him in like porch lights drew in June bugs.

A knock on the front door surprised Joe just for a split second until the sound registered as Trent's knock. Usually his brother just waltzed right in, but Joe guessed since Diego was there, Trent was trying to use his manners and give them some privacy. That or Trent thought the door was locked again.

If that was the case, Trent figured it out on his own because he was barreling in the door before Joe even got halfway there. "Come on in, Trent," Joe drawled.

Trent beamed at him and took off his hat. "Don't mind if I do." Trent hung the hat up and headed for the living room. "Thought I'd come fix dinner. It's my turn and all."

"You just came over here to grill us both," Joe grumbled. "And I texted you that we'd fix our own dinner tonight."

Trent stopped walking long enough to take his phone out of his shirt pocket, glance at it then smirk at Joe. "Well, damn, would you lookit that. I have a text message from you. Must not have heard the sound it makes. Whoops."

"Dick." Joe made a lunge for the phone. Trent dodged. "Bet that message wasn't showing as new."

"You'll never know for sure," Trent sang as he danced aside from another swipe.

Joe quit letting his brother goad him. "I know for sure, all right. Go on, you ain't going to be giving Diego any shit, though."

It was a good thing Trent had come over anyway, since they needed to talk. Joe had wanted to put it off until tomorrow. He and Diego had agreed to do just that, though Diego had been twitchy ever since.

Joe got that the shifters didn't tell humans about their existence, but this was a special instance. Plus, if all shifters were as horrible as the ones in Diego's pack, then Joe was having a hard time feeling bad about the idea of them being found out and pretty much annihilated.

Except Diego's a shifter, and he's not a psychotic fuck like the ones in his pack. Could just be them, though he did mention other packs. But still, there might be decent ones. I shouldn't be hating on a whole species, with the exception of one member of it. That's the kind of crazy shit way of thinking that causes wars and hatred.

Telling Trent was hardly a risk, either. Diego was worried almost to the point of making himself sick about it, yet Joe knew Trent would have their backs in a flash. Sure, he'd freak out a bit—Joe was having moments where he was feeling a bit like he'd woken up to find himself in a living dream. Things didn't quite seem real, yet he knew they were. Diego was there, he was a shifter and they were all in danger.

Trent would flip his lid, then once he believed, he'd probably get drunk and high. Come tomorrow, though, he'd be on their side and ready to kick some ass.

What he wouldn't do was endanger Diego by going off and telling people what he was.

"We need to talk anyway," Joe finally said since Trent was ogling him like he'd lost all his screws. "We can eat first. I was grilling steaks for dinner."

"I'll grill, you and your boyfriend can keep me company outside." Trent looked entirely too smug and Joe thought about giving him a nougie, catching him and rubbing his knuckles over Trent's head and tangling up his hair.

"Don't even," Trent warned. "I know you, and I know that look. You're thinking about doing something mean to me."

"Joe isn't mean." Diego ducked his head down when Joe and Trent both looked at him. "He isn't," he said defiantly.

Joe hadn't even heard Diego approaching. He joined Diego and put an arm around his shoulders. "Trent's right. I was gonna go all big brother on him, but yeah, it doesn't really hurt anything more than his pride. Even that heals in a few seconds."

"Usually by the time I knock Joe on his ass and tickle him." Trent yawned as if he wasn't aware of Diego scooting closer to Joe. "Brothers can be like that. Joe knows good and well I'd break anyone that tried to hurt him. Just like he'd do for me."

"Yep, that about sums it up." Joe gave Diego a little squeeze. "So I expect you to keep that in mind when we're talking after dinner."

Trent gave a slow shake of his head. "Nah, I think we oughta talk now. Diego looks like he's about ready to break and run."

Joe knew Diego wouldn't, but he was holding himself so tense a poke in the ribs might shatter him.

"You have really unique eyes," Trent said conversationally. "Never seen any like 'em before. You know I'm not the Devil, right?"

"What?" Diego glanced from Trent to Joe. "What—? He's not making any sense." Then back to Trent. "You're not making any sense."

Trent grinned. "Yeah, sometimes my brain just goes hopping all over the place. Hard to keep track of what I'm yakking about. I just meant I'm not a bad guy, Diego. You keep eyeing me like I'm the Devil himself. I'm only a man who is concerned for his brother, that's all."

"I'm not going to hurt him," Diego said with a fair amount of sass.

Trent's expression softened at that. "Oh, boy, I think you could easier than you know it."

Joe's cheeks went hot with the knowledge that Trent saw right through him. Of course he would. They'd been each other's best friends all their lives. Since Trent had been born, anyway.

But Trent was right. Joe cared about Diego more than he should, considering the amount of time they'd known each other. He'd always been the kind of person who rooted for the underdog and raged against cruelty and unfairness. How could he have resisted falling hard and fast for Diego?

"Let me get the steaks out of the kitchen, then we can go out back and talk while you grill," Joe suggested. "Diego, you wanna help me carry out the potatoes and butter?"

"And drinks," Trent reminded him. "Oh wait. You don't have any beer. Good thing I brought my ice chest."

"Of course he brought beer." Joe was glad, too. "Cold one sounds great. You like beer, Diego?"

Diego kept his head down and didn't answer. Joe steered him into the kitchen.

"Haven't tried it?" Joe asked.

"It smells funky on you," Diego finally said. "That and the other stuff."

"Ah. Well I don't have to have any of it." He'd sure miss the beer, though.

Diego wrinkled his nose at Joe. "No, have all of it. I want to try the beer. It just smells weird."

"Y'all don't have anything that kind of makes you high?" Joe couldn't imagine that. "Or relaxed, maybe? Mellow?"

"Not that I've tried any, but yeah, okay, we do." Diego walked over the fridge. "Butter, potatoes and anything else?"

"Grab the sour cream if it's in there." He remembered that Diego couldn't read. "White container with green letters on it. Top shelf."

"Sorry," Diego said under his breath.

Joe strode to his side and rubbed his lower back. "Don't be. Ain't any shame in anything between us. You can't read, we'll fix that. The only shame about it would be refusing to even try."

"Thanks." Diego took the butter, sour cream and potatoes out of the refrigerator.

Joe left him there so he could get the steaks off the counter. "I'm going to take out a glass of water, too. Beer might be nasty to you. Some people say it's an acquired taste."

After digging around in the bottom cabinets, Joe found what he was looking for. A big tin tray that hardly ever got used, but he'd always liked it. "Mom used it for the holidays," Joe said when he pulled it out. "Ain't really had much need for it in the past, oh, twenty-odd years, but I kept it anyway."

Joe scrubbed it off then dried it with a small towel.

"It's pretty, with all the curved designs on it. Like the wind flows through the metal." Diego rolled his lips inward, and Joe knew he was embarrassed for speaking up.

Touching Diego's cheek, he nodded. "You said it better than I ever could have. It's just a cheap piece of tin to everyone else, but to me, this holds memories and magic in its own way because of it."

That seemed to ease Diego, who smiled at him shyly.

Joe was glad that Diego liked the designs on the tray. It was one of the few things that was left in the house that reminded Joe of his mom. All her personal items had disappeared with her or shortly thereafter, when his dad had hauled them off to the dump.

"Do you wonder what happened to your mom?" Diego asked. "We can not talk about her if it bothers you. I shouldn't be so nosy."

"Nah, you're fine," Joe reassured him. Of course, his stomach cramped a little when he thought about his mom. It wasn't ever easy on a kid to wake up and find him or herself without a mom all of a sudden. "I did actually try to find her. Thought maybe I was doing it for Trent, but I wanted to talk to her, too. Ask her why she left like she did." Joe shrugged as he began stacking items on the tray.

"I couldn't find anything about her. Usually there's a paper trail, divorce or marriage records, land deeds, obituary, anything." He'd looked as hard as he knew how. "Even those online people searches that cost money. Nothing came up on any of them."

The only other option was to hire a private detective, something he really couldn't afford. "There was an obituary when Dad died. If she bothered to look for it, she'd know he was dead and that she could find me and Trent here. She don't want us any more now than she did then."

"You don't know that," Diego said, his tone as solemn as his expression. "Something could have happened to her. Maybe don't judge her without knowing for sure what went down."

Joe grunted. Diego was right. "I'll keep that in mind. Easier to just be the injured party, ain't it?"

"Guess so." Diego eyed the tray.

Joe let him carry it out, hoping it'd help Diego feel like he was actually a part of the meal prep instead of just a bystander.

"Them's some good-looking steaks," Trent said, laying on a thicker accent than his usual Texas twang.

"Should be since it's from last year's beeves." Joe preened a little. "We have the best beef cattle in south Texas."

"In *all* of Texas," Trent quickly corrected. "Fuck what anyone else says. We know we aren't eating hormone and antibiotic pumped meat, and we don't sell it, either."

Diego frowned at the meat. "What do you mean?"

Joe explained quickly about how so much of today's foods were 'enhanced' with growth hormones and antibiotics that could be found in the meat after the slaughter. "They put weird shit in plants, too. I've heard stories about people eating corn and dying 'cause there was some sort of added DNA from critters they were allergic to. Don't know if it's true, but it sure makes you think. I don't want people slipping anything in my food, and I sure as hell don't want them coating my food with pesticides or even putting it in the food."

"That's crazy," Diego said a moment later. "I thought you were joking."

"Nope," Trent and Joe said at the same time.

Diego sniffed at the meat. Trent raised an eyebrow at Joe. Joe glared at his brother.

"Why would people poison their own food supply?" Diego wondered out loud.

"Money," Joe said succinctly. "It's what everything comes down to now days." He could tell Diego had more questions, but Trent was getting out beers and Joe didn't want to lose his nerve. "I'll answer any questions you have about food later, when we're alone. I can vouch for what we're going to eat. It's clean."

Diego poked at a potato. "Even these?"

Joe grinned. "Even those."

That seemed to satisfy Diego. He took the beer Trent handed him and sniffed it, too.

Trent propped a hand on one hip. "Come on, now, what's with the sniffing?"

Diego looked like he was on the verge of passing out when put in the spotlight like that.

Joe went back to glaring at Trent. "He's never had a beer before. Diego was raised up in a very secluded manner."

Trent rubbed his chin and watched Diego. "Is that so?"

And Joe knew from the look in his eyes that Trent wasn't going to hold back. "Trent—"

"Is that why you got all those scars?" Trent asked Diego. "On your arms and other places, I'd bet."

Well, Trent knew damn well he did because Joe had told him, hadn't he?

Diego cautiously brought the bottle to his lips. He stuck his tongue out and licked at a drop of beer on the rim.

Trent hissed and Joe's cock perked up watching that little pink tip chase the beer.

Diego mumbled and took a sip. Joe wasn't the only one staring at Diego, watching that Adam's apple bob as he swallowed.

"Damn," Trent mumbled.

"Yeah," Joe agreed. "We're assholes for objectifying Diego."

Diego winked at Joe, startling the daylights out of him. "I don't mind." Diego took another drink and Joe was certain the man dragged it out just to tease him.

"Mmhm, bro, you gonna have your hands full with this one," Trent observed. "I'm going to be jealous, I'm thinking."

"You should be." Joe locked gazes with Diego and took a nice, long draw off his beer. Diego's breath hitched and his pupils dilated.

"Aw, come the fuck on," Trent whined. "No eye-fucking each other around me! I haven't gotten laid in a goddamned year!"

Joe snickered and Diego's entire face turned red as he blushed.

"You're going to have to get to town like you said, Trent. Austin, maybe." Joe took another drink but kept the ogling in line.

"No shit. I might just go tomorrow." Trent picked up the potatoes and put them on the grill. "Calving's almost over with. You can have Diego lend you a hand."

He sounded so eager, and serious. Joe almost told him to go. It was on the tip of his tongue to say 'Get gone, bub', yet Joe held back. On the off chance that Diego's hunters knew he was there, had been watching from a distance perhaps, then Trent could be in danger.

Or, it could be safer for him to leave the ranch. Joe sighed as quietly as he could manage and rubbed at one temple.

"Spit it out, bro, instead of turning all drama queen on me." Trent elbowed him in the ribs. "Come on."

Diego moved to stand beside Joe. One look in those pretty amber eyes, and Joe found his resolve.

"Well, Trent, you can go if you want to. I won't mind at all."

Trent rolled his eyes and sighed a lot louder than Joe had. "Aw, shit. There's a 'but' coming, and not the kind I'm interested in fucking."

Joe almost laughed at that. "Well, I can't disagree there. See, you said something today before I went out to find Diego. You probably didn't mean anything by it, either. Before you get all up and snooty about what I'm trying to tell you, let me show you something."

"How the hell can I get snooty when you haven't told me jack shit yet? That'd take a special kinda crazy and I'm not that flavor." Trent gestured at Diego. "You like this guy?"

Diego's lip curled up in something close to a snarl.

Trent's expression lightened. "Oh, you do. Well good, then. Wouldn't want my brother to be the only dumbass falling head over heels."

"Trent," Joe growled, contemplating whether or not he could slap a hand over Trent's mouth before he blurted out anything else he shouldn't say.

"Calm down, calm down. And get to the goddamn point already." Trent's exasperation was evident in his voice.

Joe narrowed his eyes at his brother. If Trent wanted to be a dick, fine. They'd do this the quick and least likely to result in arguing way. Joe turned to Diego. "Could you?"

Diego inhaled deeply, then let it out over a period of seconds. "How will you handle it?" he finally asked.

"Just fine," *I hope. If not, I'll fake the shit out of it and freak out when I'm alone.* "It's still you."

Diego nodded and reached for his shirt.

"Hold on now. You're cute and all, but I don't do that brothers with a lover kind of thing," Trent said loudly, taking a step back. "That's just wrong, and I didn't know my brother was kinky like that!"

"I'm not," Joe told him, trying not to laugh. "Diego's going to show you why you might need to hang around a little while longer before running off for a piece of ass."

Trent blanched. "No, I don't want to share—"

"Trent!" Joe snapped. "Get your mind out of the gutter. He's got to strip to show you."

"Show me what?" Trent asked cautiously.

Diego tilted his head to one side, the movement reminding Joe of an inquisitive puppy. "What I am," Diego offered.

Trent pursed his lips but thankfully kept silent as Diego stripped.

Until he saw the scars. "What the fuck? Man I knew you had scars but…" Trent cursed and clenched his fists. "No fucking way those were consensual. You've been tortured, a lot."

"It was my place in the pack." Diego waited until Trent opened his mouth to ask.

Trent's mouth snapped shut loudly and Joe's heart just about beat out of his chest as Diego dropped to his hands and knees, hair sprouting out all over his skin.

"Holy fuck," Trent whimpered, stumbling backwards and falling onto his ass.

Joe was rooted in place, amazed and yes, freaked out as he watched Diego's body morph from man to beast. Even seeing it happen, he couldn't process it. The entire change couldn't have taken more than a few seconds, yet it seemed that time slowed down and every little alteration to Diego's body was exaggerated and emblazoned on Joe's brain.

"Joe, he's a wolf," Trent said shortly thereafter. "Oh, God damn it, I'm losing my mind!"

Joe knelt and held a hand out to Diego. He was a beautiful wolf, just the same as Joe remembered seeing him that night when Diego had leaped onto the hood of the truck.

Diego nosed his hand, then whined softly as Joe scratched his ear.

"This isn't what I meant when I said I wanted a dog," Trent said in a shaky voice. "I want my own dog!"

Diego yipped in Trent's direction and wiggled his whole back end as he wagged his tail. Joe's potential to flip out vanished. This was his reality now, and he was going to accept it because he chose to. He wanted Diego, and whatever that entailed.

"You can have your own dog, or dogs, Trent, 'cause I sure ain't sharing Diego." Joe buried his hand in Diego's scruff and marveled at how soft it was. He glanced over at Trent. "Thing is, I'm not the only one that wants him. His pack's been hunting him down. They don't want their whipping boy to be free."

Trent rolled up to his feet. "His pack? So they did that to him?" He held out his hands. "Sorry, Diego. They did that to you? Why?"

Diego pawed at the ground.

"Because they wanted to," Joe said. That was what it came down to, anyway. "Diego was their omega, and for them that meant he was there to abuse and use any way they saw fit. You saw the results of that."

"Fuck." Trent rubbed at his face. "Man, that's messed up. No one should be treated like that. Guess they want him back so they can keep tormenting him."

"Seems like. Diego was going to leave 'cause he's worried they'll show up here. Says they're all a lot bigger'n him, and that they'll definitely find him." Joe felt steadier with every word he spoke. "I won't let them have him, and I won't let anyone hurt Diego again. Once they learn that lesson well, then if Diego wants to leave, he can."

Diego gave him a startled look, and Joe's chest ached with a longing he couldn't define.

"You've never been free, Diego, and I sure won't be another person in your life who tries to tie you down." Joe didn't know why Diego whined at that, or why he tucked his head down. "You can stay, too, if you want, but the choice will be yours, not mine. Not theirs."

That was what Joe wanted for Diego. Of course, if Diego decided he didn't want to run off, that would be good. Maybe they could have something long lasting and special, something Joe hadn't dared to hope for until that moment.

"That was almost romantic." Trent touched the tip of Diego's tail. "Huh. Soft. Cool too, like temperature wise. Think maybe you can change back so we can all talk now?"

Diego licked Joe's palm. Joe wasn't certain, but he thought Diego might be asking his opinion on that.

"If you want to. If you'd rather stay like you are, Diego, that's good, too. We can talk and if I get something wrong, you just bark." Joe smirked at Trent. "And if *he* gets something wrong, bite the hell out of him. He yelps like a two-year-old girl with a skinned knee."

Trent turned his nose up at them. "I'll have you know, I've heard some two-year-old girls scream in Wal-Mart before and that kind of lung power isn't anything to be ashamed of."

If wolves could leer, Diego did just that. Trent pointed at him. "Be good or I'll put silver in your water bowl."

"Silver won't bother him any more than it would you or me." Joe enjoyed Trent's muttering over that.

Diego stood and shook all over like he was drying his coat after a swim. He shifted, the reverse order of it just as weird to watch as the first time.

Trent agreed. "I don't think I'll ever get used to that." He picked up a steak and nodded toward Diego. "Rare, I bet." When Diego agreed, Trent set the steak back down. "I'll cook yours last. Meanwhile, we need a plan for dealing with the fuckers who're after you. I'm voting for very, very bad things."

Joe grinned. Yup, his baby brother definitely had their backs.

Chapter Thirteen

Having lived almost all of his life with a pack, Diego wasn't surprised to find himself fitting into the routine at the ranch. He and Joe were up early, usually before the sun rose. Sometimes they fooled around before they got up, but other times they were still groggy from having sex for hours the night before.

Either way, it was good to wake up with Joe. Diego liked being cuddled and held while he slept, and he really liked waking up to see Joe's face, relaxed in sleep, lips parted. He looked so peaceful and, well, sweet. Joe would have laughed his head off over that description, so Diego kept it to himself. It was like his own little secret and he treasured it.

Every morning was nice, and after they'd cleaned up and eaten breakfast, it was time for their workday to really begin. Diego wasn't much help around the horses—they spooked when he go too close more often than not. He could put feed out in the pastures for the cattle, though, and check the pens and fences.

And he checked the traps they'd been setting out in various places along the property. None were the cruel metal ones that snapped bones and crippled animals. They were just sound alarms. Thin wire that ran at various heights between trees or cacti, or anything they could use. Joe had gotten these neat little alarm buttons from somewhere online. They would automatically set off computer-generated bell-tones at the house and on Joe's and Trent's phones if the wires were stretched more taut than they already were, or if they were snapped.

Diego didn't know how effective they'd be. The betas might notice the traps and skirt them, but there were a bunch of them except, of course, where the cattle could trigger them.

And that was a whole 'nother problem, as Joe would say. If the betas went after the cattle, the losses could be catastrophic. Joe and Trent were working on that today, rigging special alarms around the perimeter of the pastures, but there was more land than alarm systems and money. They'd just have to be very alert.

"Be easier on us if I had some dogs," Trent pointed out. "If they were trained cattle dogs, I mean. They'd guard the herds."

Diego hated to burst his bubble... "The betas would tear them in half in seconds. I don't think you grasp how big and violent they are."

Trent paused in his attempt to connect the battery to the post. Electrifying the top wire of the fence was another method they were trying out. "I've seen your scars, Diego. I got a damn good idea how violent they are. A couple of pit bulls—nah, I wouldn't do that. Be like dog fighting and that's some sick shit. You're right, though. Wouldn't be fair to the dogs. Been thinking maybe we ought to move all the cattle to the two east pastures and start camping out in the RV. All of us. I'm getting edgy. Even carrying my handgun and rifle ain't helping to ease the itch."

"Guns might stop them," Diego said quietly despite his unease. "If nothing else, as many as you and Joe have, y'all could bury the betas under the weapons."

"Typical Texans," Trent had joked. "We got more guns than ammo."

"Could go back to making our own," Joe suggested.

"When we have time, maybe." Trent cursed and shook his hand. "Caught my finger. Anyway, I like making ammo almost as much as I like brewing our own beer. Gotta get back to doing that."

"Beer and ammo. Sounds like a magazine for hicks," Joe mused.

Diego had seen the arsenal of guns the brothers had. There were over a dozen longer guns—rifles and shotguns, he thought but wasn't really sure. Another dozen handguns, ranging from palm-sized to ones that surely needed to be held with two hands. Diego had barely kept back a shudder. He hated weapons of any kind. Causing pain and death were things he never wanted to be a part of.

Yet he would, because he couldn't allow Trent or Joe to fight the betas. That would be even less fair than dogs taking the wolves on. Guns were all well and good, but a shifter wolf could be on a human before the human knew they were even near.

Joe and Trent couldn't be hurt. Joe especially. Diego would return to the pack if he had to, though he found a new reason to hope every day that he could stay there at the ranch.

With Joe. Diego was teetering on the brink of utter devotion to the man. Joe was gentle, funny, kind and an ardent lover. He was patiently teaching Diego to read, a task that was proving to be easier now that

Diego had let go of his fear of failing at it. Already in just a week he could read small words.

He realized he'd zoned out on the brothers when Trent shouted at Joe to fuck off.

"Grow up," Joe retorted. "Stop throwing a fit just 'cause you're not getting your way."

"It makes sense for us to hole up in the RV," Trent argued. "You and Diego can keep your dicks and other parts to yourselves for a few days. I'm telling you, something's coming."

Joe's anger slipped away, his expression calming as he canted his head and looked at his brother. "You could have said that first. You've always had that creepy prediction thing down. Like with Diego."

Diego touched Joe's elbow to get his attention. "Trent is very in touch with his animal side. All humans are animals in the first place, but most have buried their instincts so far down they don't understand what those instincts are trying to tell them. If Trent says something's coming, I believe him, too."

Trent sniffed. "See, I am better than you at some things."

"Predicting trouble *and* causing it, for example," Joe teased. "Fine, we can drag the RV up here if you want, but it's thin-walled and not much protection at all."

Diego had to agree. He'd seen what Joe called a fifth-wheel camper, one that had to be towed behind a truck. It was beat-up looking to begin with. "They could tear through it like a tornado through a house of cards."

Trent grumbled a series of bad words.

Joe ignored him for the most part, not even waiting until Trent was done to speak. "We gotta hope the cattle won't be messed with. They're important sure enough, but not more than any of our lives. The house will be the best place. Even then there're lots of windows."

"Should have built one of those safe rooms like in that movie." Trent went back to attaching the box to the post. "I think we're going to have a helluva fight on our hands however this goes down. Can't decide if it'll be easier to shoot them as humans or wolves. I like dogs a lot."

Diego caught the screwdriver that slipped from Trent's hand. "Here. It'd be better if they were wolves. Human bodies would be harder to dispose of and much harder to explain should you get caught burying them. No one will care if you kill and bury a wolf."

"Except for the animal people, the ones that are always fighting for animal rights," Trent said. "They'd be out here throwing paint and pies at us, and I can't even blame them because they wouldn't know the truth."

Joe blinked, drawing back and paling. "Jesus, I can't believe our conversations sometimes. I think we ought to try reasoning with them first." He shot Diego an apologetic look. "I know I said I'd kill them, and I will if I have to. Time makes a man think about his words, and putting those words to action, though. Not sure how I'm going to feel if I have to kill anything." He stood a little taller. "But I'll damn sure kill man or wolf before I let him hurt you."

"What about a woman?" Diego asked bluntly. "Chivalry isn't dead?"

Joe rubbed at his chest and Trent turned his head away. "That's a harder thing to do," Joe admitted. "I'll try not to, but if she's going to hurt you…"

Joe was an honest man, and the best person Diego had ever met. Killing a female would possibly break something inside him. Maybe if he'd been born and raised around a pack like Diego had, where gender made no difference in almost anything—a female could be and was every bit as powerful as a male, hence the pairings of alpha males and females—he'd have a less rosy view of the opposite sex.

Diego had never fought back against the betas or anyone else, not until he'd flipped out on Joe.

But he could do it now that he'd begun to see what his life could be like without a pack of hateful shifters trying to ruin it all.

"I can," he admitted, hoping Joe wouldn't think less of him.

Trent jerked his head around and looked at him.

Diego ignored him, instead concentrating on Joe. "You have to understand, where I'm from, females and males are equal in all things. They've never been viewed as—" He struggled to recall the term he'd heard on a TV show a few days earlier. "The weaker or fairer sex. They're just as strong and vicious as any male shifter has ever been. Seeing them as anything else will ensure they use that as a weakness on your part, and they'll kill you in an instant, without regret."

"Jesus," Trent hissed. "Your people really suck, you know that?"

Diego did, indeed. "Maybe not all shifters are like them. Probably the other types of shifters aren't as bad." He shook his head. "Well, I can't say that. Bears can be pretty pissy shifters, and surprisingly, the deer can, too. Raccoons are brutal."

"Stop," Joe pleaded. "Man, don't tell me everything's got a shifter side, or I'm gonna lose my goddamn mind."

"Not everything," Diego offered. "Some types of birds, a few more animals. I don't know about sea creatures, but I've never heard of them being shifters."

Trent shot to his feet, the box forgotten, eyes alight with excitement. "Oh! But there could have been, and that'd explain mermaids! And Atlantis, too!"

"Atlantis?" Diego hated to seem ignorant, but in so many ways, he still was.

"It's thought to be a mythical city that sank into the ocean," Joe explained. "The people living on the island were supposed to be really ahead of their time in science and medicine."

"But not in predicting they'd all sink and die," Trent said drolly. "Most people don't believe it ever existed. I do, same as I believe in aliens and shifters."

"I believe we need to get finished up out here and head home." Joe groaned and stretched. "My back is aching."

Diego wanted to go check a few of the traps and just see if he caught a whiff of anything off. If Trent thought trouble was coming, then it could already be there. "I'm going to take the ATV and check the east and south parts of the ranch."

"We should stay together," Joe said, catching a hold of Diego's arm. "Splitting up doesn't seem to be a good thing to do."

"I guess," Diego reluctantly agreed. "My senses are sharper than a human's. I wanted to see if I could scent or see, or even hear, something you and Trent couldn't pick up."

"Thought I had sharp senses." Trent finally had the box attached to the post. He wiped at his brow. "I'm not feeling so special now."

Diego chuckled at Trent. The man was a goofball most of the time. Most of the time he was fun to be around, though he could sure be an ass when he wanted to. "You're special. Just, you're human, and that can't compete with a shifter's senses."

"I can't even pick up on whatever Trent's feeling," Joe complained. "I'm out of touch with my inner animal."

"You can work on it," Diego told him. "Listen to your instincts instead of trying to reason everything out."

Joe rolled his eyes. "That's harder than it sounds."

Which was true, Diego supposed. At least it would be for someone not raised to trust their instincts. Diego should have trusted his sooner, and left the pack before things had gotten so bad. After nearly being killed three nights in a row—all by the same shifter, who got off big time on choking Diego into unconsciousness repeatedly—Diego had broken. And run.

"What're you thinking about?" Joe asked quietly.

A quick check to make sure Trent was out of hearing distance, and Diego answered. "About what finally made me leave the pack." His heart raced. This was something he hadn't shared yet with Joe, because shame was a powerful silencer. Diego believed he could tell Joe, and trust him not to bring that shame down on Diego.

"You want to do this here?" Joe gestured around them. "We can, or I can hold you in our bed while you talk."

Diego was afraid his nerves would get the better of him. Knowing he could trust Joe was one thing, but saying the words, laying out exactly what had been done to him, was still a difficult and painful step to take.

"Y'all ready to load up?" Trent called out to them from the truck. "Or am I interrupting a private moment?"

"Where are those super instincts of yours now?" Joe taunted, but he grinned at Trent while taking Diego's hand and giving it a squeeze. "Not so special now, are ya?"

Trent flipped him off. "My super power is that I detect danger. You, obviously, aren't a threat."

"Jackass." Joe laughed, proving he wasn't offended. "I think you're full of shit and just want to eavesdrop on me and Diego when we're—"

"Not even," Trent said. He groaned. "Man, now that's gonna be giving me the heebie-jeebies when I'm lying in bed tonight. Ick."

Diego listened to the brothers tease each other on the ride back to the house. The friendship between them was something to see, especially for Diego since he'd never been around it before. The shifters in the pack were pretty competitive, battling for status and placement in the pack order. Siblings were often the fiercest of enemies then. It wasn't uncommon for one to kill the other or even all of his or her littermates. There'd even been instances where it'd been encouraged by the sire and dam.

Population control, Mother Nature at her most warped. Diego had seen it in some bird shifters, too.

"I know you said we need to stick together, and we can do that, but I want to get a few things from my place," Trent said when Joe put the truck in park. "I'll be back in an hour. If I'm not, something got me."

"That's not funny," Diego muttered.

Trent patted his shoulder. "Sorry, but I joke about everything. Don't always know when to shut up."

"Just be careful," Joe told Trent. "And we'll sure enough come for you if you're not here in an hour."

"I'd be counting on it." Trent slid over into the driver's seat once Joe and Diego had gotten out.

They waved him off then Joe tucked Diego's hand in his. "All right, let's do this first."

Diego looked up at Joe just in time to part his lips for a kiss. Joe started it out slow, lapping at his mouth. After Diego moaned and pressed closer, Joe thrust his tongue in, a sure, confident claiming that set Diego's blood to pumping like he'd run a ten-mile stretch.

Joe cupped his ass and kneaded it. Diego wanted to forget about any conversation and ride Joe right there outside, in the sunlight.

In fact, he couldn't think of any reason not to. They'd dispensed with the condoms once Diego had explained that he was disease free, and Joe had showed him the results of his last test, but Diego didn't need them.

So there was nothing and no reason to stop what they were doing. Diego ran a hand down Joe's chest, rubbing over his left nipple roughly. Joe rumbled into the kiss before nibbling on Diego's bottom lip.

Joe had sensitive nipples, and Diego liked stimulating them for Joe. He also liked for Joe to take charge, which he would do shortly.

He hadn't been rough like before Diego had taken off on him. Diego missed that, in a way. The softer touches were also addictive, however, and he knew Joe was holding back from more spanking or pain because of Diego's past. What he couldn't figure out was how to get Joe to move past that. Diego had. What he and Joe did together was nothing like the abuse he'd suffered from his pack.

Diego curled his fingers, scratching his way down Joe's chest to his belly. He was careful not to hurt the man. All he was trying to do was let his need be made known.

Joe grabbed a handful of Diego's hair and pulled his head back. It broke the kiss, but Diego couldn't complain when Joe began biting a path down his neck, leaving behind little stings that made Diego's dick leak pre-cum.

Joe had a way of being aggressive that stirred Diego without scaring him. It'd been that way from the start. Diego had flipped his lid when Trent had shown up, but that had nothing to do with sex.

Electrical currents of want zinged through Diego. His skin felt hyper-sensitized, as if he could feel every particle in the air as it blew over him.

He cupped Joe's cock through his jeans. "Please," Diego begged, aching for Joe to make him feel. "Hurt me." Diego froze immediately. Joe did, too, stiffening as if he'd been turned to stone.

"I'm sorry, I didn't mean it," Diego babbled. Then he stopped himself from lying again. "I did. Joe, I did."

Joe stepped back. Diego had to fight with himself to keep his gaze on Joe's when all he wanted was to hide.

Joe's expressionless face scared Diego more than anger would have.

"I'm sorry," he began again, this time trying to keep from spewing out all his words into one giant, incomprehensible pile. "I... I liked when you spanked me. It made me feel alive all over. All over. Please." Diego dared to reach for Joe. When Joe didn't pull his hand back, Diego was able to take a deep breath. "I know the difference between that, between you whipping my ass until it aches, or you pinching and biting my nipples until they're so sore I can feel them with every heartbeat. Those are *good* kinds of pain, ones I want. Ones I think I need."

Joe ran his free hand over his face and sighed. He hid his eyes behind his hand for a few seconds and asked, "What was it you were going to tell me before we came home?"

Diego was torn. If he told Joe, there was a chance Joe wouldn't ever so much as pat his ass again.

But, if Joe listened, if he understood, then he'd know that what he gave Diego was nothing like abuse.

Joe lowered his hand and placed it over Diego's heart. "Tell me. You gotta let me decide for myself what I can handle, and trust me to know what we can handle together. If you're holding back on me, how am I supposed to be able to trust either of us fully? I'll think you're keeping stuff back because you don't trust me, and that will fuck with my head."

Just as suddenly as he'd stopped, Joe shook his head and started talking again. "No, you know what? I won't force you to tell me anything. That's bullshit, too. Jesus, this relationship shit is complicated."

Diego went warm all the way down to his toes. "Relationship?"

Joe arched a brow at him. "Well, that's what I'd call it. I'm your lover and your friend, your partner, unless you decide you don't want to be here. I won't try to stop you again, Diego, not physically. I sure don't want you to leave, though."

"Partners?" Diego repeated, his mind racing. "Like, boyfriends? Mates?"

"As much as you want us to be, or as little," Joe rasped. "I'll take what I can get with you, and I'll give you everything I can."

Diego dared to hope that meant Joe could love him, could give him his heart. "I want everything," Diego whispered, feeling more daring than ever, more open and bare to the man before him. "I don't want to leave. I should have. I've put you and Trent in danger. That's a shitty thing for me to do, but I…" Diego had to swallow or cough, his throat was going so dry on him. It seemed like everything good hung in the balance here, the outcome of this conversation setting the course for their happiness and success together. Maybe he was overthinking it, putting too much importance on it all, or else his instincts were pinging like crazy because he was right.

Diego steadied himself with a light grip on Joe's chest. "I've been selfish by staying and putting you and Trent in danger. The thing is," he said before Joe could get more than a 'no' out. "The thing is, you're the first person who's ever wanted me, and getting to see you and Trent interact has mended parts of me. It's been *good* to watch and learn that not everything is life and death, fear and pain. Not every set of siblings — littermates, for us — hate each other and are willing to kill each other to advance in rank. To hear teasing that is all in fun, not in bitterness and hatred."

"Doesn't anyone love anyone else in your pack?" Joe asked, looking stricken. "Is it all hate and shit like that?"

"Almost all, except for the few couples who are committed to each other. Even so, they can't see past themselves." Diego had seen it time and again, the brutality such pairs would commit in order to be able to focus on each other. "No one else matters to them, except their alphas, of course."

Joe reeled his head back as if he'd been slapped. "No one? Not even their kids? You said that about the alphas killing their offspring, but the other shifters, why would they?" He seemed so appalled by the notion.

Diego felt bile rise up from his belly. "We're a horrible species. No, not even their kids. I was handed over to the pack without a backwards glance. The only rule the pack has against abusing omegas is, no family can breed with them. Apparently murder is fine, but incest is unthinkable." Diego shuddered. "Actually, I'd rather have died than have any of my littermates or parents ever touch me sexually. They did take their opportunities to hit and bite me when they felt like it. That I could handle."

"Jesus Christ, honey, every time I think it can't get any worse, you tell me something about your past that—" Joe shook his head, eyes gone wide. "You gotta be the strongest person in the world, Diego. Most anyone else would have been broken in more ways than I can count off."

"Omegas are stronger than anyone else in the pack in some ways, I think." That was a sacrilegious statement he'd never dared to speak out loud before. "Some omegas even act as the upstarts, the ones who get the fun going and still take the pack's abuse. My use was only ever the latter. All of the omegas from our pack, that I know of at least, were only used as a tool for the rest of the shifters to vent on."

Joe touched his cheek, admiration shining in Joe's eyes. "You really are stronger than the rest of them, then, aren't you? Smaller, you said you were the runt, yet they couldn't break you. Maybe you're an alpha after all."

Diego giggled. "No, not that. I don't do the leading thing well at all. And I like pain, to a point. I don't like it when it's meant to hurt me and humiliate me. I don't like it when I'm an object, a thing." He scooted close and stood on his toes to brush his lips over Joe's. "But when you care about me, when you desire me because of me, not because I'm someone to be used and discarded, that makes it better, makes it amazing. That first night, you did things to me that I didn't know could make me feel that way, like I was wanted and attractive. I'd been watching you, wanting—I didn't understand the wanting, yet I couldn't leave."

He ghosted a hand down Joe's arm. "Something in you called out to me. I left the pack, was lost and so scared, Joe. I ended up here and I don't want to leave. I don't want you to handle me like you're having to hold back, or you think I'm fragile. I'm not. You said it yourself. I'm strong. I'm strong enough to not have died when Axel strangled me three nights in a row, beating me until I couldn't move then choking me until I passed out. Do you know what it's like, believing you're going to die and the last thing you'll know is the sick hatred of the man whose hands you can't escape?"

Joe was so pale, Diego was afraid he would be sick. "Let's sit on the porch swing," Diego suggested.

He and Joe walked over to it and got settled in.

"I'm back to wanting to kill them all," Joe said a moment later. "It scares me, how angry I am, but that's nothing compared to what you must feel."

Diego rested his head on Joe's shoulder. "See, that's where you're wrong. You feel what you feel, and I feel what I do. I'm angry, sure, and scared, but the pack is the way it is. Always has been. It's not right at all. Still, it's the way of the wolf shifter's nature."

"You're not like them," Joe argued. "So it can't be all wolf shifters."

"All of them I know of. I'm not like them because I'm an omega. My nature, my personality, is different because of that." Diego was glad of it, too, because the thought of being one of the higher ranking members of the pack was horrible.

Joe turned and nuzzled the top of Diego's head. "I think it's you, too. You're the only omega that left. You're special. Maybe shifters are going to evolve, and not be such fucked up bastards."

"That's a nice thought. I don't know that I believe it. I've seen too much, and been through too much." Diego closed his eyes and enjoyed the man beside him and the sway of the swing. "It could happen. Less brutality, more humanity. Maybe they'd evolve right into being fully human."

"Humans can be pretty awful too." Joe began stroking his neck and shoulder. "They do bad, bad shit." He huffed and his breath was warm and moist against Diego's head. "Get 'em in a group, and they can have a mob mentality. Be really violent and, well, inhumane."

"Maybe there are shifters who are decent. I don't care to find them. I've had enough of my kind to last the rest of my life."

Joe snuggled him closer. "I understand that. Hopefully if we send anyone back in pieces or at least beat to shit anyone that comes after you, your former pack will get the message and leave you alone."

Diego hummed in agreement. Joe thumbed his lips, and slow, sweet-heated arousal began to build in Diego again.

"As to the other," Joe said, "yeah, I been holding back. Couldn't do otherwise knowing what you've been through, honey. I'll try to let it go and give us both what we need. It's not doing you any good to be made to feel like I don't have faith in you." Then Joe kissed his brow. "Now open your eyes, because if we're gonna be doing any playing like that, even just slapping your ass, there's going to be safe words." He cackled gleefully. "Always wanted to say that, and have safe words. Read lots of stories where they were needed and damn, those stories made me hot."

Diego quirked an eyebrow at him. "Why aren't we reading those kinds of stories when you're teaching me to read instead of making me read boring newspapers? If I had those to work with, I'd be reading a lot more!"

Joe laughed again. "Oh no you wouldn't. We'd be fucking every time we cracked a book open."

Joe was likely right. Diego still wanted to read some of those books. "What's a safe word?"

Joe explained them briefly, how they ensured he'd stop doing something if Diego said red, stop doing it permanently. Yellow would mean a pause and discussion or whatever it was that Diego needed then, and green meant go, keep on doing it all.

"Sounds easy enough." Diego glanced up through his lashes at Joe. "I never got to have a say before. Thank you." He heard the sound of the truck's motor. "Trent's coming back. We didn't get to fuck."

"We talked, and that was what we needed to do," Joe informed him. "And you better believe I'll be pounding away at your ass tonight now that we got everything straightened out. Might even see how you feel about restraints."

"Restraints?" Diego's cock hardened so quickly his head spun.

"Like ropes and maybe some bandanas, too." Joe dipped his head down and whispered in Diego's ear, "Imagine me tying you to the bed, spread-eagled, on your belly. You wouldn't be able to touch your dick while I paddled your ass and fucked you. All you could do would be lie there and take it, take everything I gave you. I'd mark you up, too. Leave so many hickies on you there'd be no way to hide them all."

Diego whimpered, pressing the heel of his hand to his cock.

Joe grinned wickedly. "Just got to wait a few hours."

"Joe," Diego whined. "You did that on purpose! My dick's so hard I won't be able to walk."

As pleased as Joe looked with himself, Diego knew that had been the man's plan. It was also clear that Joe liked it when he begged and complained a little.

They were so well suited it was as if they'd been made for one another. Diego leered back at Joe. Two could play that game.

Diego spent the next few minutes working Joe up into the same needy place he was in. By the time Trent pulled up, they were both a wreck.

It was fun and sexy, and Diego never wanted his time with Joe to end.

Chapter Fourteen

"Strip. Do it slow and make sure you give me a good show."

Diego trembled before he turned to look at Joe, who was standing in the bathroom doorway, his shoulders brushing either side of the frame. Joe had his hat off, his hair swept back messily, but he looked and sounded commanding.

Their conversation from earlier whispered through Diego's mind. His cock had been half hard off and on all evening, as he'd known tonight would be more intense if Joe had truly believed him.

Joe obviously did. "Now," Joe demanded, running a hand down to ghost it over his bulging shaft.

Diego would bet the denim covering it would be heated from that thick cock. "Yes, sir," he said as he began to unbutton his shirt. Like Joe, he'd showered before dinner, though they'd done so separately. Joe and Trent had cooked part of the meal while Diego had gotten cleaned up, then Diego had helped Trent while Joe took his turn.

Trent had waited until dinner was done, grumbling that he had to wash the dishes anyway because it was his turn. Diego didn't understand the hardship there and figured Trent just liked to complain. Griping had never done Diego a bit of good and he tried not to waste time on it. There were much more important things in life.

Like living in the moment. Diego was trying not to fumble the buttons in his eagerness to get naked so Joe could do whatever he wanted with him. He could feel Joe's gaze on him like a fiery touch, singeing his skin.

Joe backed up into the bathroom while at the same time he trailed his hand up a few inches to the thick leather belt he wore. It was worn and brown, with a buckle that had a bucking bronc on it. Joe had told him he'd rodeo'd locally during his younger days, and that was one of the buckles he'd won. Joe unbuckled the belt and Diego whimpered, an eagerness for the man almost rendering him incapable of moving.

"Diego..." Joe rumbled, and it was enough.

Diego got his shirt unbuttoned and started to take it off. He entered the bathroom, needing to be closer to Joe, knowing it was why Joe had stepped back.

Joe scooted down the length of the counter until he was resting a hip at the edge of it.

Diego shivered under the hungry look Joe gave him.

"Slowly," Joe reminded him. "Seduce me into giving you what you want."

Diego had never seduced anyone in his life. He was used to men and women coming to him for sex, using him without regard for his own pleasure. He certainly wasn't used to having to work to get someone to notice him, to want him, though up until Joe, he'd never wanted that kind of attention.

Joe, however, had that look about him that let Diego know he meant what he said.

If there'd been music, it would have helped. Diego settled for letting a tune play in his head. He moved to it, face flaming with embarrassment. At least he couldn't move about too much in the small room. Regardless, he was very self-conscious. There was no doubt he'd be bright red if he glanced at himself in the mirror.

He had no idea how to dance other than the bits of it he'd seen on TV, but he could move his hips, make pretend he was being fucked slowly and deeply. Surely that would please Joe.

It did. Joe hummed, the sound carrying an obvious note of approval. His eyes narrowed and he went back to rubbing his dick before unfastening this jeans. The rasp of the zipper sent a tingling stream of anticipation down Diego's spine right to his asshole. He clenched it, moaning, wanting Joe inside him so bad he could feel it already.

Diego added that to his strip routine, flexing his ass, arching so his butt stuck out like a temptation for Joe.

Joe nodded slightly and freed his cock from his briefs.

Diego finally dropped the shirt to the floor then started on his pants. Trent had given him a couple of pairs of jeans. They were too big all over. *Beggars can't be choosers and all of that clichéd stuff.* Wearing clothes took some getting used to. Underwear in particular was annoying.

His belt was a hand me down, too, with another of Joe's buckles on it. Diego liked that, had beamed like a star about to supernova when Joe had attached it to the belt for him to wear. Joe had told him it was his favorite buckle, too, and that Diego was to keep it.

He'd never been given a gift before. Joe's present to him had resulted in Diego curling up and crying over it when Joe had gone to the barn afterwards.

So Diego was careful with it when he undid it. He pulled the belt through the loops, undulating as best as he could. He also hoped like hell he didn't look goofy. Judging by Joe's erection, Diego thought he was doing okay.

Diego slid the pants down his legs. He'd removed his shoes earlier, something else he'd had to get used to wearing. Those were new, Trent having picked him up a pair of boots from town several days ago. They were still stiff and Diego had had to slap bandages all over. He'd never had blisters like that before. They sucked.

He turned his back to Joe and shimmied his clothing down to his ankles. Diego bent, feeling idiotic but loving the gasp he got from Joe upon sticking his ass up in the air. He put a hand on the countertop to help him balance so he could get free of his clothes. Before he even raised a foot up to slip off the jeans and briefs, Joe slapped him on the ass, hard.

"Shit!" Diego hadn't been expecting *that* at all! And Joe had *not* held back. His hand had to be stinging like a bitch because Diego's butt sure was. It went right to his cock, the ache folding around his length like a warm caress. A second smack landed, this one even more forcefully. Diego moaned. The pain flared out from his backside to nerve endings throughout his body, flushing them with pleasure. Diego stood, head bent, arm braced, panting, needy.

"Get naked," Joe commanded again. He grabbed Diego's ass and squeezed the cheeks tightly then pulled them apart.

Diego's asshole was stretched until it was surely gaping.

"Nice, honey. I'm gonna fuck that hole until you can't sit for a week."

The dark threat in Joe's voice almost undid Diego. He bit his tongue until he tasted blood, using the pain to keep him in check. Hurting himself was totally different from when Joe did it. With Joe, it was sexy and fulfilling, and when Diego did it, it just fucking hurt.

Diego got one foot up and almost out of the tangle of material before Joe grunted and shoved a spit-slicked finger into his ass. The burn was bright, sharp, perfect. Joe didn't hesitate or give him time to adjust. He started finger-fucking Diego like that, pushing the single digit in, pulling it out, not being gentle at all.

He avoided Diego's prostate, not giving him that pleasure. It was probably best. Diego would have shot all over the place if he'd had much internal stimulation at that point.

Joe slapped his ass again while running his finger around the inner ring of Diego's pucker. It put a pressure there that shorted out Diego's circuits, stole his breath and jolted his heart.

Another hard swat, then more pressure, more burn as Joe worked a second finger into him. "Better hurry, before I just fuck you dry."

Diego shuddered, eyes closing. He'd like that, to have Joe mount him and force that fat dick into him. The ache would be delicious—but it'd probably last for days, and Diego wouldn't be able to take more fucking until he healed up then.

As much as he wanted to be handled roughly, he didn't want to go for days without Joe fucking him.

Diego forced his body to move, kicking the jeans and underwear aside finally while Joe kept at his hole.

The second Diego's feet were free, Joe pushed those digits in so deep Diego was surprised he couldn't taste them. At the same time, Joe used his other hand to grab Diego at the nape. He moved Diego bodily until Diego's chest was over the countertop, then he pressed Diego down onto it.

"Grab it," Joe barked.

Diego got a hold of the sides of the counter. He curled his fingers around it.

Joe ran his hand up Diego's back. "Just how rough do you want this?" he asked, getting a handful of Diego's hair. "What do you say if it's too much?"

"Red," Diego answered, amazed he could even think. "Yellow, slow it down and talk. Green, go."

"Good boy," Joe murmured, rewarding Diego then with a hard thrust of fingers. "Now answer my first question."

Diego took a few seconds to recall what it was. His body was on fire for Joe, for the release he would bring Diego and the way Joe would own him, filling him with cock and fingers.

Joe jerked on his hair. "How rough?"

Bright pain bloomed out along Diego's scalp and shot right to his dick. "Gods, please." Diego gulped, daring to ask for what he wanted. "Your marks. From your hands, and your mouth, all over me."

Joe grunted and pulled harder at his hair. "All over?"

Diego opened his eyes, staring blurrily at Joe. "My ass and legs. You could… You could slap me if —"

"No." There was a sureness in that single word that oddly enough soothed Diego. Being slapped was humiliating, but he'd have handed the power over to Joe because Joe cared about him.

"No slapping. I won't ever hit you, I won't use a closed fist and I sure won't strike you in the face. But I'll spank your ass until you're begging me to fuck you." Joe did something with his fingers that stole Diego's breath, some spacing of those digits that opened Diego's pucker up. "Your hole is already red and swollen." Joe pulled his fingers free them promptly thumped Diego's furled opening.

Diego mewled, for all the world sounding like a feline rather than a wolf. Joe chuckled and did it again.

He moved his hand down and cupped Diego's balls. "And here?" he began to squeeze slowly, giving Diego plenty of time to protest. "You like your pain here, too?"

"Yes," Diego hissed. He hadn't known until Joe began to do it, to apply pressure that made Diego's guts clench with fear. Not because of Joe, but because it felt so good, the pain more intense and centered until it began to spread to his entire groin. Diego's legs began to shake, but he didn't want Joe to stop. Joe let go of his hair and instead raked his nails over Diego's ass. "Joe!"

"Right here," Joe said, amusement in his voice. "You haven't forgotten, have you?" He increased his grip on Diego's balls.

Diego's pulse pounded in his ears and he grew dizzy. "No," he squeaked out.

Joe released his nuts. "Good boy. Stay right like this."

Diego didn't move, not to even open his eyes. He just listened, hearing Joe's footsteps retreat, probably to the bedroom for the lube. He heard the squeak of the bed springs followed by the thunk of Joe's boots coming off. There was the rustle of clothing, then Joe was walking back, his bare feet slapping on the wooden floors. He wasn't loud by any means, but Diego's exceptional hearing made him seem so.

"Now stand up and put your hands together in front of you."

Diego did as Joe ordered.

"Good boy." Joe stretched out the belt he held in his hands. Diego hadn't noticed it until that moment. "I'm going to bind your hands with this. Won't be the most secure way of keeping your hands tied, and you can slip out of it. That's part of why I'm using it." Joe moved closer and ran the tip of the belt down Diego's spine. "That, and it's leather. I like leather."

"Me too." Diego whimpered, arching into the touch. "You could use it on me."

"Stop pushing," Joe warned in his ear. "Stop trying to see where my boundaries are. I can tell you right now, they're right where your pleasure stops. You don't enjoy it and get off on it, I'm not interested, and we're not playing around tonight to see if you can take a whipping. I got no desire to hurt you, Diego. Just to make you come so hard your eyes roll back in your head."

Diego gulped and nodded. "Sorry. I won't push. I just want you to want this."

"I want you," Joe told him. "Whatever that entails. It don't mean you having to take a beating 'cause you think that's what I want. I don't."

"Okay." Diego pressed his palms together. "I understand now. You like doing this, spanking me and such, only if I'm getting off on it."

"Exactly." Joe rewarded him with a kiss that was more teeth than not, tugging Diego's chin around so they could fit their mouths together.

Diego's lips felt swollen and raw when Joe raised his head. "Going to bind your hands now."

How having a belt wound around his wrists could be so erotic he nearly came was a puzzle Diego didn't bother to try to solve. His hips seemed to move on their own, trying to get a touch to his dick.

Joe tugged on his balls after he finished with the belt. "You move and I stop," Joe warned.

Diego didn't know what he'd be stopping until Joe parted his cheeks then licked down his crack.

"Oh," Diego gasped, mind truly boggled. He wished he could see, then he didn't wish anything at all because Joe's wet tongue was lapping at his hole. Diego moaned and tried to be very still. Joe made it difficult, pushing that slick muscle into his pucker, sucking on the tender skin, fucking him in a new way.

And he added erratic spanks, differing in intensity. Diego couldn't understand all the feelings his body was experiencing. The rimming was amazing, sweet, stingy when Joe bit, and the swats were a totally different thing.

"Such a good boy," Joe said some minutes later.

Diego wanted more of that praise, craved it like he did nothing else. "Thank you," he got out.

Joe dragged the blunt tips of his nails over Diego's already sore ass.

It was so good, so hot and undeniable—Joe was touching him like that, surely leaving trails of pink behind. There was no way Diego could ever look back on this and doubt how much he was wanted. "Oh, Gods, please."

"Only a few this time," Joe warned. "I've already bruised your ass up. Next time… Next time I'm going to use a paddle. I found one from a game Trent and I had when we were younger. Think about that, me slapping this ass with it—" He popped Diego with enough force to make him jump.

"I'm going to redden your ass and thighs, then I'll fuck you until I come." He did it again.

Diego moaned, trying to spread his legs to show Joe just how eager he was.

"You know what I'll do after that?" Joe asked, whacking his right cheek firmly. "Do you?"

"No," Diego bit out.

"Ask me," Joe ordered, bringing the belt down again. "Ask me."

Diego gasped, delighted by the burn the last whack had left on his upper thigh. "What?" he got out when he could speak. "What'll you do?"

Joe landed four spanks before leaning over him and grinding against Diego's burning ass. He grabbed Diego by the hair again. "Then I'm gonna fist you and fill you with my hand." He thrust, and Diego shouted, so turned on he couldn't stand it.

He hadn't been aware of Joe lining up his dick, had been too aware instead of the picture Joe'd been painting in his mind—but that thick cock spreading him wide open was the perfect follow-up to the spanking. Diego wouldn't have been able to handle any gentleness then.

Joe didn't give him any. He bit Diego's shoulder, pulled his hair and pounded into his ass. Diego could only hold on for the ride. With his hands bound, he couldn't even hold himself up on the counter. All his hands did was provide a buffer between his sternum and the hard surface.

When Joe reached under him to twist at a nipple, more pain bloomed and Diego keened. Joe grunted, bit him again and left off the tit torture to instead fist Diego's dick.

The dry, rough grip was too much. Diego screamed, body overloaded as his orgasm slammed into him harder than Joe was slamming into his ass. He was pinned down, held, filled, overtaken by Joe, and it was the most perfect moment in Diego's life.

Until the next one, when Joe shoved in deeper, harder, and sank his teeth into Diego's shoulder, bringing up blood as he came inside Diego.

Diego felt every shot of Joe's cum warming him from the inside out, knew it marked him forever though he wasn't sure why this time it was different. Joe had been coming in him for days.

They lay there, panting, Joe's upper body weighing heavily on Diego's back. Diego liked it, felt protected and owned in a way he never had before. After several minutes, his fuzzy brain cleared enough for him to think. Joe had fucked him every day since he'd come back.

But never like this, never letting himself go and trusting me – and himself. That's the difference this time.

That, and Diego could no longer deny the truth of his feelings—he'd fallen in love with Joe, somehow, at some point. He didn't have much experience at all with the more tender emotions, but he recognized the strong ties keeping him there with Joe.

He loved the man. The realization shook him to his core.

"What's wrong?" Joe croaked near his ear.

"Nothing," Diego got out.

Joe raised up a few inches. "Breathe, honey."

Diego did, taking a moment to get past the dizziness he felt. He knew Joe was attuned to him, waiting for an explanation. "Nothing's wrong, I promise. I just— I'd like to think about what I'm, um, thinking about, before I bring it up?" Gods, he sounded like an idiot.

Joe gave his hair a tug. "Open your eyes."

Diego did.

Joe moved back, his soft cock slipping from Diego's hole. The warm wetness that followed, running down the insides of Diego's thighs, made him squirm.

Joe chuckled and helped him to stand up and turn around. "Look at your ass."

Diego craned his neck, saw his backside in the mirror. It was something to see, for sure, the skin dark red and marked up nicely.

"Now you tell me—too much?" Joe asked.

Diego could hardly drag his gaze away from those marks. His shoulder throbbed and he just about went cross-eyed trying to see where Joe had bitten him.

"Diego," Joe rumbled, grabbing his chin. He tugged Diego's head around.

Diego looked at him and shook his head, or tried to. Joe had a pretty good grip on him. "No. Not too much. I could have taken more and still came like there was no tomorrow."

Joe studied him for a moment.

Diego didn't blink for fear that Joe wouldn't believe him.

But Joe nodded finally. "Okay then. What was going on a minute ago when you were getting tense?"

Had he been? Diego hadn't realized, but he wasn't surprised that Joe did. Joe was very observant, especially when it came to him. "It had nothing to do with the physical part of what we did," Diego offered, hoping he could avoid a confession he wasn't sure Joe was ready for. "I can promise you, I've never come so hard in my entire life. Never felt anything like that before."

Joe kept up with that penetrating stare. "And the other, what I talked about? I want to put my fist inside of you, Diego. I want to feel you come apart from it and know it blew your mind."

Diego would beg for that if he needed to. "Yes, please. Please, I want that." It scared him, too, because Joe was a big guy, tall, big-boned, and his hands were no exception. "You'll fit?"

"We'll work up to it," Joe promised. "I'm not just going to throw you down and shove my hand up your ass."

Diego couldn't help it, he giggled and promptly tried to bite it off to no avail.

Joe huffed but looked amused as well. "You know what I mean. I want to take days to get you ready, maybe even weeks."

Well, that shut Diego's giggling off. "Weeks?" he squeaked out. "Weeks? Seriously?"

Joe grinned, an evil tint to the twist of his lips.

Yeah, he'd probably take a month just to make Diego suffer.

Diego grinned back at him.

Joe's amusement faded and an affectionate look settled in its place. "Come on, let me take care of you now. I have liniment for the bruising and soreness. After we rinse off, I'll dry you and put it on you." Joe started the shower. "And once that's done, I'll massage your legs and arms, doctor your blisters then top the pampering off with another slice of chocolate cake."

"With ice cream?" Diego asked hopefully. He'd become very fond of both sweets.

Joe nodded as he held his hand out to Diego. "Of course."

Diego really had never had it so good.

Chapter Fifteen

Trent paced the length of the front porch as storm clouds rolled in. They were coming fast and it made Joe nervous, almost as much as Trent's pacing did.

"Can you maybe not wear out the wood beneath you?" he asked as Trent made another turn at the left end of the porch.

"Nope, I can't not wear it out," Trent snapped. "Fuck, I really thought we'd be done with this already. My spine *itches*, I'm telling you."

"Maybe if you'd stand still long enough to scratch it, you'd feel better." Joe ignored the dark look Trent gave him. Almost a week had gone by and absolutely nothing suspicious had happened.

Every day, Trent grew crankier and more certain that today was the day it'd all go down. Diego hadn't sensed anything different, but he said he'd always felt like he was in danger anyway.

Trent stopped pacing, finally, to halt right in front of Joe. With his hands fisted on his hips, Trent looked ready for a fight—which he was. "I think we oughta go hunt them down. This sitting here waiting isn't doing us any good at all."

"It'd do us even less good to go out and get killed," Joe said pragmatically. "Calving's done, sure enough. That don't mean we can go running off and you know it. There's always work to be done here."

Trent got that stubborn look Joe knew so well. "We can ask the Pilickis to watch the place for a few days. They got plenty of older kids to help out, and we handled their ranch when the family had to go up north to that funeral. You know ranch etiquette rules. They're feeling indebted to us and will until they've gotten a chance to pay us back."

There *was* an unspoken rule about it. You did for your neighbors when they were in need, and they did for you in return. Refusing to ever accept help implied you were lording your money and smarts over everyone else. It was mightily frowned upon and exceedingly un-neighborly.

"It's been two years," Trent warned. "Much longer and they're gonna come over here and ask what they can do for us. Then we'll be put right on the spot. Or you will."

Because it was Joe's ranch, as if he needed reminding. Joe rubbed at his jaw, thinking it over.

Diego came out onto the porch. He looked back and forth at the brothers. "What's going on?"

Trent was babbling about his plan before Joe could even open his damned mouth.

Diego listened, head cocked, gaze trained mostly on Joe though occasionally he flicked it at Trent. "So you want to go hunt them down," he said when Trent finally shut up, adding, "You do realize they'll try to kill you and Joe for certain then?" His frustration showed in the way he held himself rigid, his hands curled into fists. "They will almost certainly succeed. I can't fight them and win. They're all bigger, meaner, better at killing. Heartless. The betas aren't like an omega. They're…*more*."

Trent was every bit as irritated, Joe could tell. "Did it ever occur to you that me and Joe don't need saving?" Trent said in a low, furious tone. "We aren't some helpless damsels in distress!"

Diego cringed when Trent raised his voice. Joe started to stride over and knock Trent on his ass, but a look from Diego held him in place. Diego wanted to handle the confrontation, maybe needed to, even. Joe gritted his teeth and waited.

"You may as well be. You'd be nothing but a quick kill for them." Diego bared his teeth, and Joe was startled to see that his canines had elongated until they looked much like they did when Diego was a wolf. "See these?" Diego asked with a slight lisp. "These are nothing. *Nothing.*" He licked his lips and the next thing Joe knew, those canines were back to regular size. "Theirs are a couple of inches longer because the betas are bigger. I'm an omega. I'm small. They're betas. They're not small. I've explained this before."

Which was true. This was the first time Diego had gotten quite so ardent in his description of the betas or showed his teeth like he'd done.

"I'll put a bullet between their eyes before they get near me," Trent snarled. "See how much those teeth bother me then."

Diego nodded. "That's fine, if you see them, hear them, first." He crept forward without making a sound on the wooden porch. "But what if you don't?"

Trent almost took a step back. "Won't happen. And how's it any safer for us to sit here and wait? What's that going to do, shrink their teeth and make them walk with all the grace of a herd of buffalo? They magically become loud, clumsy labradoodles?"

"They're a mixed breed dog," Joe offered when Diego's face was etched with confusion. "Kinda cute. Is that what you're going to get, Trent? Something cute and cuddly, maybe a dog you can carry around in one of those dog-purses?"

Trent scowled.

Joe snickered. The tension had been too much. They were all on edge. "Look, sniping at each other won't help any of us, and if you keep at it with Diego, I'm going to end up snatching you baldheaded."

"Snatch me bald—" Trent began but Joe waved off his budding hissy fit.

"Oh, calm down already. Let's try being logical instead of arguing, how's that for a challenge?" It applied to himself, too, because he'd been ready to go a round or two with Trent, but seeing his brother and Diego bickering had tempered that urge. "We're all getting edgy."

"I miss my trailer," Trent muttered, but the irritation drained from his expression.

Diego sighed. His shoulders rounded slightly. "I'm scared you and Trent will be hurt, even killed. I should leave."

Joe was right back to fighting form. "Bullshit. You keep running and they'll chase you down somewhere you ain't got anyone to back you up. Do you *want* to leave here?" *Do you want to leave me?* Joe couldn't ask that question out loud.

Diego turned his eyes to Joe, and the affection in them warmed something inside Joe that he hadn't even realized had frozen seconds before.

But Diego seemed to know. There was a change in his expression, a softening of his features that was subtle but unmistakable. He crossed the short distance to Joe and stood in front of him. Joe slipped his hands around Diego's hips and held him without pulling him closer.

"I don't want to leave, ever," Diego confessed, seemingly uncaring that Trent was witnessing his declaration. "This—I want this, the ranch, you, to be my home. I want…" Diego glanced over at Trent and a cute half-smile curled at his lips. "I want that stubborn brother of yours to be my brother, too."

"Aw, shit," Trent mumbled.

Joe knew the feeling. Diego had just undone them both with a few sentences that exposed his whole heart, and likely Joe's and Trent's as well.

"I don't want you to go, ever," Joe told him. His sense of humor pricked at him. "As for Trent, you can have him. No need to share."

Trent snorted and probably flipped him off, but Joe didn't spare his brother a look. There was an intensity between Joe and Diego that wasn't ebbing in the slightest.

How long they stood staring at one another, Joe had no idea. It wasn't until a violently loud clap of thunder sounded that they both were startled out of the spell that held them.

Joe tucked Diego under one arm as they both looked out from the porch. Trent joined them, not but a few inches from Diego's other side.

"Looks bad," Trent said. "Sky's getting a green tint to it."

Joe liked a good storm, but not a dangerous one. He took in the sky, which was indeed an odd yet not unfamiliar—unfortunately—shade of gray-green. The clouds were rolling in more ominously, and the wind howled in fits and starts.

"This is scary weather," Diego whispered, one hand clenching at Joe's belt in the back. "It smells like anger."

Joe sniffed the air. "Smells like a goddamned thunderstorm with the possibility of tornados to me. That's probably Mother Nature being pissed off, yeah."

"Tornados?" Diego pushed closer to him. "I've never seen a tornado."

He sounded interested, and Joe wasn't. "They're deadly. Ain't nothing you want to see."

"We see too many of them in this part of Texas," Trent added. "We need to take cover. I'm going to check the weather app. Got that radar one."

"Inside," Joe said as he turned them around. "Better to be cautious than dead."

They sure seemed to be dealing with a lot of possibilities that ended in death for them, he mused.

"We've always had a tornado plan," Joe explained while they headed for the hall between the bedrooms and bathrooms. "I wish we had a cellar, but people don't here. Ground's too hard and shifts too much. It'd be flooded or whatever more often than not."

"Maybe we should invest in one of those cement rooms," Trent offered. He plopped down in the hall, phone between his hands while he messed with it.

"What do we do?" Diego asked. Even in the short span of time since they'd come in, the wind had picked up to a steady bluster.

"Now we duck and tuck, and wait, and pray," Joe said. He placed a hand on the back of Diego's head. "Head down, arms over it."

"We got a tornado warning for another five minutes or so. I think one touched down a few miles south of us." Trent lowered his head and Joe did the same.

Joe's heart was pounding. Tornados were part and parcel of living in Texas, but Uvalde was generally spared the strongest of those destructive forces of Nature. They hadn't had a powerful tornado like the ones that could decimate entire towns.

There'd been one in 'ninety-six that had scared the shit out of him, and there'd been a few since, but almost all of them were rated F1s or F2s. Low in force, but still deadly and scary as hell.

He found one of Diego's hands and held onto it until Trent gave the all-clear. Diego's nose was twitching when he raised his head up.

"What're you doing?" Joe asked him. Trent was watching Diego, too.

Diego's cheeks pinkened with a blush. "I just wanted to see what it smells like after. It's weird. Clean, like the earth's been washed and rinsed."

Joe stood and held a hand out to help Diego up. "Yeah, well a tornado can leave a mess that don't make anything look clean. Same for the storms we get out here sometimes without the tornados. Nature gets rough and wreaks havoc. It's amazing and frightening at the same time."

"Wow, that was almost poetic," Trent said. "True, too. Nature's a scary bitch, but the most beautiful thing you'll ever see, too. Even the terrifying parts of it can be gorgeous." He brushed off his butt. "Now, let's go see if there's damage, and if there is, fix it. If there isn't, check with our neighbors, see if they need help. After that..."

Joe sighed and gave in. "After that, we can all figure out what to do. Diego, I know what you're saying about the betas and the risks we're taking. Trent gets it, too, but maybe us going after them would throw the fuckers off their game. Just something to think about."

Joe wasn't sure what he hoped the outcome of their discussion over the matter would be. He only wanted them to be successful so Diego could be free of his pack for good.

* * * *

The fact of the matter was, Diego was worried that Joe and Trent would be killed, gutted and left to die agonizing deaths no matter what the three of them decided to do.

He kept thinking, though, as he worked beside the brothers to repair the damage the winds had caused, that it might truly be to their advantage to change up this sick game he was a part of.

If he ended up being wrong, he wouldn't be able to live with himself. There were definite risks to anything they all decided no matter what. That Joe and Trent were willing to fight for him, to put their lives on the line, amazed and awed Diego. No one had thought he was worth anything in the pack. Nothing more than a way for the members to work off their tension or whatever. To have two men willing to possibly die for his sake was astounding, and scary. Diego knew he wasn't worth it.

And he knew they believed he was. The more time Diego spent with them, the more he realized how very fucked up his life had been. There was something wrong and evil about his pack. Maybe about all wolf shifter packs, for all he knew.

A thought flitted through his head, too quick for him to grasp it, something about Nature doing her cleansing thing on the animals that walked her earth.

"Neighbors are good as far as I can tell," Trent informed him and Joe a short time later. "Now we can talk, right?"

Diego still didn't know what he wanted to do, what was best. "Can I have a little more time to think about this?"

Trent looked moderately disappointed, but he relented. "Sure. What's another couple of hours? Tonight at dinner?"

It was longer than he'd expected to be granted. "Yeah." He understood Trent's ansty-ness to get the situation resolved. Diego didn't want to let that get in the way of rational thinking, so he'd take what time he could get and try to work out a plan for them all.

Chapter Sixteen

"Where is the last place you know they were at for sure?" Joe asked.

Diego bit his lip, thinking and wishing he knew more. "Arkansas. I thought I saw one of them when I was skirting a town. I was running scared. I haven't encountered them since, but I know they won't give up. None of them want to disappoint the alphas. That would mean death for the betas."

"What if they've decided to ditch the pack, too?" Joe scratched his chest. "Actually it seems like what anyone with a lick of sense would do—leave the evil empire. They'd be better off away from it, right?"

Diego didn't even hesitate to answer. "No, they wouldn't. Living in the human society isn't something they'd be able to adjust to. They carry too much of the wolf in them, too much aggression and they're used to having orders handed out for them. Taking such orders from humans, a species they consider beneath them, wouldn't work." He shrugged. "I don't think it would happen for most any shifter. Even omegas are going to feel the need to stay with what they know, but I'd say we're the most likely to jump pack and leave." He exhaled heavily. "I can't have been the only one who got sick of the abuse."

Joe was obviously inclined to agree. "No, surely not." *Then again...* "But you're pretty damned amazing, Diego. It's possible you've been the first and only."

Diego's cheeks heated as he blushed and tucked his chin to his chest. The urge to hide would probably never leave him, though he hated that he let it overcome him around Joe. "I'm nothing special. Anyone can be pushed to their breaking point. A stronger omega than I—"

"No," Joe interrupted. He gathered Diego into his arms. "No. Don't even go there. You need to realize just how strong you are. You say a stronger omega would have stayed, and I'll tell you that's bullshit. It's always easier to do what's expected of you than it is to buck the authority and be yourself. I know. I lived over half my life acting like a straight guy, dating women when I had to throw off my dad or anyone else who wanted to know why I was single. Sometimes I had sex with the women, or tried to. It was all easier than standing up and saying enough. Take me or leave me, but I'm done pretending to be someone I'm not anymore." Joe snorted softly. His eyes glistened and Diego's heart ached for him.

"I never did come out to my dad," Joe said as he pressed his cheek to Diego's. "Never had the balls to do it. I would have been disowned, would have lost the ranch. Maybe Dad would have come back around and realized I was still the same boy he'd raised and loved. I tell myself and Trent that he would have." Joe raised his head and Diego saw the pain in his expression. "But I'm pretty sure I'm lying when I say it. Dad never would have changed. He'd have burned this place to the ground rather than let a couple of queers live on it, never mind that those queers were his own sons. I think that's why he didn't leave Trent more than the trailer and the plot of land it's on. He suspected Trent wasn't straight."

Diego hadn't ever understood until that moment that he wasn't the only one who'd had their lives controlled by hatred and abuse. Joe had mentioned his dad using belts for discipline—but Diego had seen a couple of scars beneath Joe's butt cheeks that looked like switching scars. Diego had a few of his own to go by.

Joe tucked his head down until he was cheek to cheek with Diego again. "Yeah, I definitely think he had an idea, but no real proof, otherwise he'd have disowned Trent outright. Dad never treated Trent like he did me."

Diego pulled back enough to get another good look at Joe. "You mean he didn't beat him?"

Joe opened his mouth, a protest evident in the way he was already shaking his head.

"I saw the scars," Diego said before he lost his nerve and couldn't go through with it. "Beneath your butt, on the top of the backs of your thighs. I have scars like that too, and they came from a willow tree. A switch from one, I mean. I was maybe ten…" Diego frowned, trying to remember just how old he was when it'd happened the first time. He couldn't pin down an exact age. "Something like that. Because it tore my legs up so badly when the alphas switched me, that was one form of abuse reserved solely for them."

Joe's nostrils flared as anger all but rolled off him. "Dad did it to me once, when he caught me passed out in the barn after I snuck away with his bottle of medicinal whiskey. He had my pants down and that switch landing blows before I got both eyes open. I was sixteen, could have fought back, but I'd stole his booze and gotten drunk, something he despised in a man. He really did only use the whiskey when he was coughing a lot or feared he was getting the flu. I figured I had that one coming, and I still do. Somehow I doubt that's the case with those fuckers beating you."

"No one deserves to be beaten and left scarred," Diego stated firmly. "It's fair for both of us or neither of us, Joe. Think about it. Would you do that to a kid?"

"No, but I can't say I'd never pop a kid on the ass with my hand if the kid was acting like the spawn of Satan. It's part of the reason I'll never have any kids. I don't want to hit them," he admitted, his voice dropping lower. "Shit."

Diego nodded. "Yeah, you don't want to hit them like you were hit because you know it's wrong."

Joe ran a hand through his hair, ruffling the already disheveled strands. He'd left his hat hanging on the hook by the door, and Diego hadn't bothered to wear one in the first place.

"You tell me no one deserves to be abused, that goes for you and Trent, too." Diego wasn't going to let that bit go. "As for having kids, you'd be a good daddy, I think. Don't you know, they always say you should trust an animal's instincts in regards to liking a human. I like you lots." He had the biggest grin on his face and couldn't help it. Admitting that he liked Joe felt really good, even if he knew he more than liked the cowboy.

Joe cast his glance away from Diego before bringing it back. "I don't like to think about Dad being that way. He wasn't a bad man. He did some great things for people, and he loved us. Growing up, that was never a doubt even if he didn't say the words. I can remember him playing football with us, teaching us to shoot. Those times, he was patient and kind, and he rewarded us with praise when we caught the ball or made a shot. He just disciplined us the way he'd been disciplined. And thank you. That's one of the nicest things anyone's ever said, but I still don't think kids are for me."

"Most people aren't all good or all bad," Diego agreed. "Even the shifters that have abused me could be nice to their equals on occasion. It wasn't always constant fighting and killing." *Or was it?* Diego thought back to his life with the pack. It had seemed like someone was always fighting for position. "Maybe my pack had something seriously wrong with it. Well, the other packs I encountered, too. We're all pretty small, maybe ten shifters in the smallest pack. Ours had forty-two, and was one of the biggest in the state." Why was he even babbling about it? If there was something wrong with the pack, it wasn't his problem anymore.

"Inbreeding?" Joe asked hesitantly.

Diego knew he looked grossed out by the question, but he couldn't help himself. "They're wolves more often than humans. There was none of that with the omegas."

Now it was Joe who looked squicked. "That would be a yes with others?"

"It would be." Diego didn't want to talk about it anymore. While the wolf packs knew no shame, he did. "About Trent's idea. We've been dancing around it, haven't we?"

"Talking about it, yeah," Joe said. "I didn't want to push. He did say dinner was time to deal with it, so we should probably decide what to do."

Since Trent was cooking dinner, they had a few more minutes to themselves in the living room. Trent was a fair cook but a sloppy one and it slowed him down. Diego couldn't imagine what was going on in the kitchen right then since Trent had said he was making lasagna. Diego wasn't even sure what lasagna was. It smelled good so far.

"I think the element of surprise could work in our favor," Joe said. "As long as we don't reveal ourselves until we attack. If they find us here, who knows how long they'll sit around and devise ways to take us out before doing it."

"They won't plot for long or much at all. They'll use violence and force, because that's what they do. They aren't the best at thinking beyond their orders." Diego rested his head on Joe's chest. "We could try tracking them. Go back to where I last saw them, see if I can pick up their scent. Or…" An idea began to formulate, a plan that made him more than a little nervous. "Or we can make me easier to find."

"No," Joe snapped immediately, cupping Diego's nape and hip. "No way. I'd rather hunt them down."

Diego hated to argue with Joe. He was going to, regardless. "But I don't know where they are. They'll find me, I can promise that much. That's what betas do. Follow their alpha's orders unfailingly. All they have to do is ask around, see if any other packs encountered my tracks or scent anywhere, and they'll have a lead. I can't do that, Joe." He pressed closer, urgently. "Chances are I won't be able to find their trails at all, not from where I last spotted them. It's been weeks, and rain, heat, wind, other animals — they all mess with scents and tracks. Really, my idea is the best one." Even though it was a scary prospect to put himself out as bait, Diego was proud of himself for thinking of it. "I'm already bait here anyway."

Joe rumbled but didn't speak. He tightened his hold on Diego.

"It is," Diego said with a growing amount of confidence. "We don't know where they are, but we're staying in one place. Somehow, they will figure out where I am. I'd rather be prepared, have them think we aren't even aware of them but *us* be the hunters instead of the prey. Take down most of the traps that weren't taken out by the storm. If they don't think we're expecting them, then maybe they won't mess with the cattle or anything else. They'll think I'm weak, vulnerable." Diego was getting more excited about it as he spoke. "I'm not a victim anymore. I left that behind with the pack and they won't expect me to be different, but I am. I am, Joe. I'm stronger."

He looked up into Joe's eyes. "You've helped me to be. So has Trent. I didn't know things could be so good in life, that brothers could get along and love each other. I didn't think love was real." He gulped then, because words were trying to get out and he wasn't ready to let them. "I've seen obsessions, and possessions. I've been both to the pack. But I never saw love, never thought—"

Joe stopped him there with a kiss that made Diego tingle all the way down to his toes. He tasted Joe's need, his unspoken words that mingled with Diego's.

Diego knew he wasn't alone in this. Joe was falling, had fallen as fast and hard as he had. That love Diego had never believed in was real, tangible. He could feel it under his fingertips as he caressed Joe's face and neck. It was in the warmth of Joe's skin, the flutter of his pulse beneath Diego's fingers, in the shaky gust of his breath over Diego's cheek when the kiss ended, and in the awed look Joe gave him after.

"I can sell the ranch. We can move," Joe said. "Start somewhere else. Maybe move to an island they'd never think to look for you on."

Diego had never thought anyone would care about him so much. "No. This ranch is part of you, and it's part of Trent, too."

"It's not more important than your life," Joe argued. "Even Trent wouldn't argue over that."

He might, but Diego wasn't going to say so. He had a feeling Trent would be with him on the new plan. "This is—" *Gods, help me. I'm so scared to admit it.* There was so much Diego wanted to say. He wasn't going to let fear of Joe's reaction hold him back. Joe cared for him, and Diego knew it. Reminding himself of that gave Diego courage to speak up. "This is my home now, too. Isn't it?" he added the question as a sliver of doubt jabbed at him.

Joe sucked in a sharp breath, then Diego was kissed again, this one fiercer, making his lips ache and his dick harden. He held onto Joe and mewled. Joe gripped him the way Diego needed him to, bruisingly hard. Diego needed the anchor, needed to feel like Joe would always have him.

Joe bit at his lips, at his tongue, driving pain and pleasure into Diego until his whole body vibrated with the mix of them. He backed Diego up until he thumped the wall. Joe growled and bit again. At the same time, he wedged a leg against Diego's balls and pinched his left nipple.

Diego melted for the man, going boneless and offering himself to Joe. He was willing to let Joe do anything, *anything* to him.

Joe tugged on his nipple again. He pushed up with his leg, adding intense pressure to Diego's balls.

Whimpering, Diego tried to rut against Joe's thigh.

"Jesus Christ!"

The outburst was like a thunderclap in the room. Joe growled and whipped his head around to glare at Trent.

Diego just tried not to come in his sweats. Joe being all dominant and growly made it very difficult not to fuck away on the rock-hard thigh still pushing Diego's balls up so far he'd make nothing but a squeak if he tried to talk.

"Hey, don't give me any shit," Trent drawled. "I'm not the one mauling my boyfriend in the living room while my bro is cooking dinner. I don't even have a boyfriend. And dinner's ready. Wash your hands and stop having sex where I can see and hear y'all. Gonna blue ball me to death." He kept muttering about his balls after he turned and left them there.

Joe quit glaring at Trent and looked at Diego. "I want to turn you around and shove those sweats down, fuck you raw right here. Push in and hear you inhale from the stretch and burn, know it aches but you're taking it because it's me, and because you love it."

Diego clenched his ass, deeply aware of his empty hole.

"Nothing but some spit for lube," Joe went on, voice dropping lower. "I'd thrust in, not stop until I was so deep in your ass you'd never feel complete without me again. Then I'd pin your wrists up by your head. Hammer away at your ass, drive your dick against the wall every time I thrust. You'd be raw and loving it by the time I came in you. The wall would be dripping with your spunk just like your ass would be dripping with mine."

"Gods," Diego whimpered, mindlessly riding Joe's leg. "Joe, please."

Joe's smile was pure evil. "I'd lick every bit of cum out of your ass. But we can't, because Trent is right in the dining room waiting for us, and I'm not one for being his porn show."

Diego was going to burn up with sexual frustration. He closed his eyes and tried not to whine. Joe gave his nuts another nudge. At the same time, he pinched Diego's nipple harder than he'd done before. Pain zinged down to Diego's dick. Joe cupped his dick through the sweats then gave it a sloppy couple of tugs.

It was enough. Diego's head spun as he came, shaking and gasping, pleasure heating him from the inside out.

"I heard that, you pervs," Trent hollered from the other room.

Diego thought he added 'lucky bastards' under his breath but wasn't sure.

"Go get cleaned up. We'll wait on dinner for you." Joe stepped back and held onto Diego's shoulders until Diego gave him a slight nod.

"I won't fall over." *Probably.* He stood on his toes and kissed Joe lightly, only managing to land his lips on the edge of Joe's.

Joe chuckled warmly and patted Diego on the butt. "Go on. Trent's already gonna give us grief over that. Don't want him to have more ammo for picking on us if he has to wait much longer to eat."

Diego hated to risk killing the afterglow, but he needed to know. "And… And my suggestion for dealing with the betas?"

Joe's grin slipped away and tension pulled at the corners of his eyes. "We'll discuss it with Trent. I'll try to be reasonable instead of suffocatingly protective. I just want you safe, honey, but I know you've probably got a valid point about this whole deal. My instincts say keep you protected and hidden. I won't insult you by insisting on that."

Diego had never had someone listen to him like Joe did, or respect him. He fell even more in love with the man for it. "Thank you."

Chapter Seventeen

Trent wanted to actively hunt down the shifters, but he finally listened to reason. Joe was glad his brother wasn't all dense. Actually, he knew Trent was smarter than he'd ever be, but the man could be stubborn to a point of foolishness. In this instance, he conceded that Joe and Diego had the better plan.

"But I'd like to add something to it," Trent said before Joe could completely relax and let go of the topic of their conversation.

Diego hummed and Joe just asked Trent what he was wanting to babble about.

Trent narrowed his eyes at Joe. "I'm not babbling. Get your head out of your boyfriend's ass and listen to me."

Joe sat up a little taller on the couch and narrowed his eyes right back. "You need to back off on the raunchy talkin'."

"Okay. I probably do." Trent glanced at Diego. "Sorry, bud. I'm seriously just jealous that y'all get to have sex and I have to, you know." He made a jacking motion with his hand. "Anyway. You said the biggest fear shifters have is being exposed to the world and found out by humans, right? What if we could threaten them with that somehow?"

Diego went so pale Joe thought he was going to pass out. Joe pulled Diego closer to him on the couch as Diego frantically shook his head.

"They'd kill us all for sure then," Diego got out in a stripped voice.

Joe stroked Diego's back and stared at Trent. An idea was building on Trent's suggestion. Trent tipped his head to the left, a familiar, considering look on his face. Joe nodded. They were thinking along the same lines.

"They wouldn't if they thought killing us would get them, and all shifters, exposed," Joe stated firmly. "Bet they'd back the fuck off and leave you alone if they believed our deaths would result in that."

Diego shuddered in his arms and sucked in a loud breath.

Joe kept caressing him, trying to soothe away his fears and articulate a loosely formed plan at the same time. "We could have some cameras up around the house so that if they showed up, we'd be filming them. Get 'em to shift, and tell them those videos would be broadcast worldwide or something like that if they didn't get the fuck away from here. Permanently."

"Would they know we couldn't just do that?" Trent asked. "Are they tech savvy at all?"

Diego's body warmed up as if his nervousness was causing a rise in his temperature. His breathing was uneven, and Joe recognized the fight against panic that Diego was waging. "You can do this. We're right here, and ain't going to let anyone hurt you again."

It seemed to be what Diego needed to hear. Slowly, he calmed, not quite relaxing but loosening up a bit. He even wiggled, pressing closer to Joe. "I'm sorry," he offered.

Joe cupped his chin while Trent muttered, "You don't have anything to apologize for."

"You don't," Joe told him, wishing he could build Diego up faster, show him what he was really worth. In reality, Joe knew it would take time—years even—after all Diego had been through. "There's no shame in feeling anything you feel. Won't anyone here tell you any different. There's been more than one time I've cried as a man, and I don't think it makes me weak." Both times had been over the death of someone he cared about, his uncle then his father. Still counted, as far as he was concerned.

"You aren't weak. Maybe I'm not, either. It's scary, trying to be something other than what I've been told to be, but I'm trying," Diego muttered. "Just, it's hard to let go of a lifetime of fear, and I'm doing it in more than one case."

"Leaving the pack and letting me film you shifting?" Joe surmised, touched by Diego's trust. "We don't have to. I could lie about it."

Diego gave a bare shake of his head. "They'd demand to see proof if they even stopped to listen to you in the first place."

Trent cleared his throat. "Um, we could set up my laptop. I can make it so it doesn't shut off or sleep, and if those fuckers show up, hit play first then shoot. They'd see you on there, and it might give 'em pause."

"Or it might incite them to greater violence." Diego shivered, but there was a look to his eyes that showed the strength of the man's core. "I think it'll freak them out for at least a few seconds."

"That's all the time we'll need to pull the trigger," Joe said, tipping his head toward Trent, who nodded in return. They'd kill first if it looked like that was the only way to keep Diego safe.

"They probably wouldn't be coming too close to town, would they?" Trent asked Diego.

Diego leaned forward as he turned his attention to Trent. "No, I don't think so. They were skirting the cities, same as I was, as far as I know. We're not used to towns and cities, and they'd probably be too worried about standing out to risk it."

"Would they do that, get close to Uvalde but not into it?" Joe's heart thumped while he weighed his next words.

"Probably," Diego said, looking at him.

Joe didn't like what he was thinking, but it seemed like the best idea if they were going to get those other shifters onto the ranch and straighten their asses out. As much as he wanted to protect Diego, he knew he couldn't ever ensure Diego's safety until the pack was dealt with. To do that, the betas had to find them. "If we left a good scent trail, they'd find it then. A very deliberate trail they couldn't possibly miss."

Diego licked his lips. "Well yeah. We can do that. I can do that. Just me—"

"No, all of us, or at least me and you both." No way was Joe having Diego out on his own when the betas he'd heard so many horrible stories about could hurt him.

"I'm coming too," Trent piped up with. "We need to stick together anyway, ain't that why I've been staying here in the house?"

Diego looked like he wanted to argue. Joe braced himself for it, but in the end, Diego finally agreed. "Okay. It would be better if we are all together. I should be shifted, though. That way I can pick up any hint of the betas if they've been near. And I can, you know—" Diego's cheeks darkened. "Mark stuff. So they can follow my scent."

Trent perked up, smirking. "You mean like pissing on stuff?"

"Exactly like that," Diego mumbled.

Joe shot Trent a warning glare before Trent could make a crack about wanting to whip his dick out and pee on stuff too. "You do what you gotta. Me and Trent will be armed and we'll keep you safe."

"If I smell anything suspicious, we're done with this plan," Diego said fervently. "Promise me we'll call it off then."

"I promise." Joe sighed when Diego did.

"You two are so cute it's making me queasy," Trent groused. "I'm going to watch TV now. That's a hint for y'all to leave and go do your thing while I'm in the living room with the volume up all the way. Better than hearing y'all when I'm in bed."

Joe stood and held out a hand to Diego. "Okay then. If you insist." He thumped Trent on the back of the head, eliciting a yelp from him.

"I'll get you back for that," Trent promised.

"I know you will." Joe knew good and well that Trent would thump him twice as hard or twice as often in return, which was fine. Then it'd be Joe's turn again.

Diego was strung tight by the time they reached their bedroom. It was theirs, not Joe's any longer. He couldn't imagine sleeping there without Diego beside him. Diego stopped by the bed and looked over his shoulder at Joe, fear pulling his features taut.

Joe knew the reason for Diego's tension. Worry was a hindrance that could be chased away, at least temporarily, by some good ol' loving. "I know you're afraid something will happen to me and Trent, but you need to let that go for now. Won't do any of us any good to fret like it's a done deal."

Diego's shoulders drooped slightly, not so much with defeat, Joe thought, but more like acceptance or relief. He watched Diego for a moment, saw him calm himself with slow, deep breaths. Once he was settled, Joe began.

"Strip," Joe ordered, his voice cutting the silence like a whip.

Diego turned to him, eyes wide, lips parted, and it was all Joe could do not to put him on his knees and fuck his mouth. As if he knew Joe's thoughts, Diego lowered his eyelids halfway and licked his lips.

"Teasing works two ways," Joe warned.

The almost silent hiss that got him made Joe grin.

Diego pulled his shirt off over his head. Joe knew every scar on that thin chest, and knew the sound of Diego's heartbeat, the taste of his nipples, his skin. He knew how much of a bite turned Diego on, and how much pushed too close to an edge Diego didn't like. He knew the strength in Diego's arms, the grace in his movements. Diego was so much more than just a piece of ass or a creature that shouldn't have existed. He was, Joe realized in that moment, almost everything to him.

Stunned by the depth of what he felt for Diego, Joe remained silent while Diego removed the rest of his clothes. He'd gained little weight in his time at the ranch, but his ribs weren't quite so prominent, his belly no longer so concave.

Joe's entire body pulsed with emotions he'd never expected to experience. They were, like Diego, a part of him he could no longer imagine being without.

The tenderness that swept through him made his eyes burn. He'd thought to take Diego hard and rough tonight. His heart was telling him something else.

"Undress me," he said in a softer tone. He and Diego both liked it when Joe was in control, and he wasn't giving that up. Even so, he couldn't keep the truth of his love for Diego from leaking into his voice.

Diego, smart as he was, picked up on it. Joe wasn't sure he knew exactly what was going on in Joe's head and heart, but Diego knew something had changed. It was evident in the way his eyes went wide and his cheeks tinted a pretty shade of pink, in the flaring of his nostrils and the skittering of his pulse at the base of his neck.

And it showed in the way his hands shook as he reached for Joe.

Joe cupped his cheek. He waited until Diego met his gaze, then he nodded slightly. It was enough for them both. Diego's eyes glistened and Joe dipped his head to taste the berry-red lips. Warm, plump flesh that Joe dreamed of gave beneath the pressure of Joe's lips. He licked into Diego, tasting all the flavors he had memorized, drinking in the sounds of the man. Joe didn't bite or demand as much with the kiss as he usually did.

This kiss was the acknowledgment of those strong bonds Joe wanted to tie him and Diego together. It was more than sex, more than two bodies needing. It was love, strong and new, beautiful in its complexity.

Joe didn't even mock his own thoughts. His heart ached with what he felt for Diego. His body thrummed with need of the man. "Touch me," he breathed against Diego's lips. "Put your hands on me. I want—" Joe broke off, clenching his ass. "I want you in me tonight."

Diego jerked his head back looked almost panicked. "Y-you want m-me to—"

Joe hoped his smile was reassuring. The truth was, he was nervous. He'd never bottomed. It was easier to find a guy who wanted to be fucked by a cowboy than the other way around. Maybe it was the places he'd sought out sex. And maybe it was because he'd never really felt like he wanted to do it. It didn't matter. He was corny and glad that he'd never let anyone else fuck him when he saw how shocked and, buried underneath that, eager Diego was.

"I'll still be in control," Joe assured him. They both needed that. "I've never let anyone—" It was true, too, even though no one had asked, either. "Maybe I couldn't because I didn't know how to give up a part of myself like that. With you, I'd give you anything."

Diego clung to him, hands on Joe's biceps. "I want to. I haven't, ever." Then he blushed darker and glanced down. "I hope I don't come before we get that far. Just knowing you want me in you is enough to have me right there at the edge, once I got past the immediate fear of screwing it all up."

"You got past it pretty quickly," Joe teased. God, he was tingling inside, and was more aware of his asshole than he'd ever been in his life.

Diego turned that pretty gaze up to him again. "It's you. I want you, and you'll still be in control."

"I will." Though he might lose it internally, because Diego was killing him with that trust. Any barriers Joe might have had left were decimated under it. "Take my clothes off," he said. "Touch me when you do it. I want to feel you everywhere."

"You will." Diego started by running his hands up Joe's arms to his shoulders, then to his neck. He rubbed his thumbs along the side of it and Joe felt it all the way down to his dick, which hardened more than it already had.

"Rough," Diego whispered. "I like this." He rubbed Joe's stubble.

"It's a pain in the ass having to shave every day." Joe tilted his head when Diego raised one hand up to his jaw.

"I love the way it feels on my skin. You should let it grow out."

Joe arched an eyebrow at the suggestion. "Gets hotter'n hell here in the summer. I don't know if I could handle it." He'd give it a shot for Diego if it'd make him happy.

Diego wrinkled his nose. "Eh, no. This stubble is enough. The way it feels on my thighs and tits…"

Joe's breath stuttered out of him. "Yeah. That does it for me, too."

Diego moved his hands down to Joe's shirt. He unbuttoned it steadily, then spread it open. "And this. Gods, I love this." He tugged gently at Joe's chest hair. Diego caressed the planes of his chest before pushing his thumbs down on Joe's nipples. The sting of his fingernails shot through Joe, and he couldn't resist letting go of Diego's hips in favor of palming his ass.

Diego hummed while continuing to touch Joe. "You have to let me go so I can get your shirt off," he said eventually.

Joe gave Diego's ass a good squeeze, one that would ensure Diego felt it for several minutes. He traced Diego's crack down to his hole, and rubbed over the hot skin there.

Diego gasped and arched his back. "If you want me not to come, you should maybe stop."

Joe grinned and pushed a fingertip into that hot grip. "You won't come. You can't until I say so."

Diego bit his bottom lip. Joe knew how much Diego liked the orders, and how much he liked to push himself. It showed when Diego wiggled his butt in an attempt to get more of Joe's finger.

Joe didn't let him have it. Instead he pulled his finger free then popped Diego's ass twice. Diego's yelp was immediately followed by the thrust of his wet-tipped cock against Joe's thigh.

"Uh-uh," Joe warned him. "You're taking care of me right now."

"Sorry. I didn't mean to be selfish," Diego said once he'd stopped shaking. "I want you so bad I can't hardly control myself. But I will," he added before Joe could tell him to.

Joe didn't tease Diego anymore while Diego was undressing him. By the time Joe was naked, his was on the verge of saying fuck it and tossing Diego onto the bed to ravish him. Knowing how much Diego wanted to fuck him kept Joe in line.

Diego touched him everywhere, heating up Joe's skin. Everywhere but his dick, balls and ass, that was. Diego kept the caresses light, stimulating Joe to the point where he was having trouble breathing without his cock aching. There was a low burn in his groin, a tangle of want that was spreading out from there. It would consume him soon, Joe knew it would, and he wanted to fall right into it. Only the knowledge that Diego needed his guidance kept him from just flopping down and rolling onto his belly.

"Kiss me," he said, taking Diego's chin in hand. Joe didn't stoop, and Diego had to stand on his toes to do as told. He also had to press the whole length of his body to Joe's, which was the main reason Joe'd had him do it. He took the opportunity to stroke Diego from the top of his spine down to his butt. Diego pushed his tongue into Joe's mouth in sloppy, hot kiss that had Joe wrapping his arms around Diego tightly.

He lifted, bringing Diego up off the floor by a few inches. Diego held on at Joe's nape and shoulder. The kiss turned desperate, their need for each other slamming together.

Joe had to pull back before he forgot what he wanted them to do. Diego could scramble his mind like no one and nothing else could. "Get on the bed," Joe said, releasing Diego.

Diego stumbled back and sat on the mattress. "I thought—"

"I've got this." Joe took the lube out from under the pillows. He uncapped it and set it beside Diego. "I said I want you to fuck me, but that wasn't all I wanted."

Diego gave him a questioning look. Joe pressed on his shoulder, and Diego went back until he was lying on the bed. "You keep still."

Joe bent and nipped at each tit until they were both hard and wet. Diego mewled and vibrated with every sound he made. Joe knew it was hard to keep still, to not writhe and demand more. "You're so fuckin' strong, Diego."

Before Diego could reply, Joe lapped at his slit.

"Oh," Diego whimpered.

Joe took a hold of the length, sliding his hand down to the base. "Watch me."

Diego opened his eyes, though it seemed to be difficult to do. He looked at Joe.

Joe licked over the crown until Diego cried out. "Please!"

Then he took the tip into his mouth and sucked.

Diego shouted but he didn't move except for a full-body shudder.

"You can grab onto the bedding if you need to," Joe said after letting the crown slip from his mouth. "I'm gonna suck on this for a bit."

"Joe," Diego mumbled, tossing his head as he fisted the sheets. "I need to come."

Joe decided to let him. Diego would get hard again in a matter of minutes, whereas Joe took longer usually. "Okay. You tell me before you're gonna shoot, though. I got plans for your spunk."

"Oh, my Gods," Diego whined.

Joe tapped his legs. "Get these spread and up."

Diego did as ordered and Joe stopped playing around. He took Diego's dick in fast and deep, the head breaching his throat. A quick swallow and he was coming back up.

"Joe," Diego said repeatedly, each time with less sound and more air.

Joe went back down. He ran his tongue over every spot that always drove Diego wild. A hard suck, the scrape of teeth, and Diego was bucking up on him.

"Stop!"

Joe heeded Diego's warning. He left off sucking for tugging, watching the way Diego's balls pulsed right before cum spurted from his dick. Joe caught as much of it in his hand as he could, and he jacked Diego until he was sure he'd gotten all of that load.

Joe climbed up onto the bed and straddled Diego's chest. "Give me your hand."

Diego shook his head, not a no, but like he had to clear out the cobwebs. He put his right hand palm up in front of Joe.

"You're gonna take this and use it to lube my ass up first," Joe told him, turning his own hand over to pass Diego's cum back to him. "Then lube your dick up with the actual slick stuff. I'd love to have you fuck me with just your spunk for lube, but I don't think that'll work the first time you do this."

"First time? And I get to…get to prepare you with this?" Diego asked. "Gods, my dick isn't even going to get soft. I want you."

"You got me." Joe maneuvered himself around until he was facing Diego's feet. It was kind of challenging for him to present his ass like he was doing. Joe hadn't ever realized the kind of confidence it took to do such a thing.

Then he wasn't thinking about anything but the way it felt to have Diego's hand cupping his balls.

"Can I taste you?" Diego asked softly.

Joe's heartbeat tripled. "Yeah. Get up, then."

Diego did, but Joe had to move forward to give Diego room to get behind him. A long, wet lick down his crease and Joe's arms trembled. Diego murmured something Joe couldn't comprehend. Joe's entire body clenched when Diego lapped over his pucker. It was tempting to lower his shoulders down to the bed, but he didn't.

Diego licked him again, then a third time. Joe closed his eyes and struggled to get air into his lungs. He had to reach under and grab his dick, hold it tight enough to hurt to keep from coming. It felt like Diego pushed his whole face into Joe's crack, like he was trying to get into Joe.

He did, with a press of his tongue, licking into Joe's ass. Joe gripped his cock harder and slid his knees farther apart. Waves of heat washed over him with every flick of Diego's tongue. "Enough," he finally rasped before he lost it and jerked off. It'd only have taken a stroke or two, as horny as he was.

Diego gave his hole one last lick then without warning, pushed a wet finger into it. "OhmyGods," Diego whispered. "Fuck, fuck, fuck."

Joe wanted to make a smart-ass reply, but he understood what Diego meant. The finger inside him was stirring things up all the way to the top of Joe's skull. There were nerves he'd never known existed and they quivered with an electric current of need that threatened to overwhelm him. He couldn't allow such a thing to happen. Diego needed him to stay in charge.

"Another," he found the strength to say. He hissed then bit off the sound as his hole was stretched with the two digits. Diego's cock was a lot fatter than those fingers, so Joe told himself to get the fuck over the pain and fear of being fucked. Besides, it didn't really hurt so much as just spread a hot pressure around his ring.

"Move 'em."

Diego began to finger his ass slowly, easily.

Joe growled and pushed his butt back. "Harder."

The slam of Diego's knuckles against the outside of his pucker sent a shocking jolt of wantoness through Joe. "Fuck me!"

Diego touched something inside him and Joe's arms gave out. He caught himself on his elbows and panted. That was his gland, and Diego was caressing it in such a way that Joe's whole body sang with pleasure.

But he was too close to the edge. "Diego, now!" Joe demanded. If it hurt, then maybe he'd be able to keep from coming before Diego got his dick all the way in.

"Yes, sir," Diego said. "The lube..." He slipped his fingers out and in short order, far sooner than Joe was ready for despite his aroused state, Diego shuffled into place behind him.

For one split second, fear coalesced in Joe like a heavy weight pressing down on his lungs. *This is Diego. It's Diego I'm doing this with.* Joe pushed himself back up on his palms and spread his legs farther apart, thinking of their height difference.

"Joe…" Diego murmured right before pushing against Joe's pucker.

It ached more than Joe would have thought. He gritted his teeth and pushed out. The head popped in, perhaps too fast if the pain was anything to judge by.

Diego cursed. "Sorry! I didn't mean to —"

"You didn't. I did it, so stop taking credit," Joe said, not wanting Diego to feel any guilt. "Come on. Give it to me."

Despite his bravado, Joe was glad that Diego went slow, pushing in just an inch or so before backing off and trying again. By the time Diego had his shaft fully buried in Joe's ass, they were both breathless and Joe at least was covered in sweat.

"Is this still what you want?" Diego asked gruffly, his hands resting above Joe's butt.

Joe tried to glare at him but couldn't see through blurry vision, thanks to the sweat that rolled into his eyes. "You better fuck me, boy."

Diego slid his hands down to Joe's hips. "Now?"

As if Joe couldn't hear the anticipation in that single word. "Yes, now."

Diego huffed and surprised Joe by moving his hands up to Joe's chest. That was followed shortly thereafter by Diego lying on him, his chest to Joe's back.

There was no thinking after that, because Diego began to move, pulling back a little and thrusting in again. Joe couldn't do more than try to parse out what he was feeling down south. The position they were in limited Diego's movements, but that was fine with Joe. It wasn't entirely a good feeling yet, being fucked.

As suddenly as he had that thought, Diego canted his hips, wiggled, and his dick brushed over Joe's gland.

"Again," Joe demanded.

Diego tried, but the position wasn't the best and Joe wasn't patient in seeking his pleasure. He tried shoving back, then growled and reached back to slap at Diego's hip. "Out. Get out and on your back." He was taking over the show.

Diego was gone a few seconds later, Joe's ass empty and need clamoring at his gut. He got himself into position over Diego, staring him in the eyes. Diego's were almost all black pupils, the irises dilated down to a thin ring. Joe lined Diego's cock up and rubbed it over his pucker. It stung, letting him know that skin was abraded from the unusual experiences. Joe shrugged it off and lowered himself down.

There was something about the way it felt, that first push, the stretching of his hole that let him know his man was coming in. Joe closed his eyes and tipped his head back. He liked this after all, the sense of fullness and the way Diego whimpered. They both needed to come, soon.

Joe grunted. Diego's cock went deeper this way, and he'd swear it touched him all the way to his collarbone. He wiggled, rubbing his butt over the thin nest of pubic hair at Diego's groin.

"Joe, Joe, please," Diego begged while Joe clenched his buttocks.

Joe began to ride, his legs strong from years on horseback, years of working hard. He came up and went back down, speeding up until he was jostling them both and the bedsprings squeaked.

Diego gripped his thighs hard enough that Joe was aware of the hold. He didn't mind, liked that Diego was clinging to him. Joe rode him faster, harder, leaning forward and shouting when Diego's dick slid over his prostate. That was what he'd been seeking, and now that he'd found it, Joe was going to chase that pleasure until it burst in him like a ball of hot bliss.

"Jack me," Joe barked out, his throat raw though he didn't know why. Diego's hand around his dick shoved a shout right out of Joe. "Fuck! Yeah — "

Diego moaned and scratched Joe's thigh. Combined with everything else — the fucking, the jacking, Diego's scent and sounds — Joe couldn't hold back any longer. He pushed down hard and undulated as he came, his heart and thoughts racing.

He heard Diego's drawn out moan, felt the swell and throb of Diego's cock. Then there was wet heat spurting into him and his own dick gave a sympathetic dribble of spunk.

When it was over, and Joe could finally pry his eyes open to look at Diego, he could have howled with pride. Diego looked wrecked, like he'd been fucked rapturously until he couldn't fuck anymore.

There certainly wasn't any worry in the man's expression. In fact, Joe thought Diego was almost unconscious. He beamed.

Diego gave a crooked smile, his eyelids drifting shut. Joe would have handed over the rest of his heart right then if Diego hadn't already had it.

Chapter Eighteen

"Hey, Joe. Come here, will ya?"

Diego leaned out of the front door, intending on letting Trent know Joe was in the bathroom. Instead he froze, words turning to a single squeak as a chill shot down his spine.

Trent looked at him, shock turning Trent's face grayish. "This was here." Trent pointed to the bone, which looked very, very much like a human femur. "On the porch step. Just waiting there."

Diego sniffed then and cringed. "Come in. Come in!" The heavy, rank scent of the betas' urine burned his nose. "Can't you smell them?"

Trent spun around as if the wolves were behind him. "No. Fuck! What is it?"

"Piss," Diego said bluntly. "They marked this home as theirs."

"Fuck those fuckers," Joe growled from behind him. Diego had been so intent on trying to spot the shifters himself, he hadn't heard Joe.

Trent turned back to them. "Joe, look." He gulped, and Diego worried Trent was going to be ill.

"It's a femur," Joe murmured, subdued in a way Diego couldn't place. "I don't know if it's a human's or not. Looks like it, but are there other animals with similar bones? I have no idea."

"I can tell," Diego said. "I've seen plenty in the pack, when someone dies in human form or is, um, is torn apart. Sometimes the pups dig up bones, too." Gods above, they were a fucked up species. That was such a familiar refrain in his head that Diego was surprised he didn't dream it, too.

"I'm going to get the guns." Joe placed a hand on the small of Diego's back. "Y'all come inside."

"I've got to check the bone," Diego protested. "It's right there with Trent."

Trent grimaced at the bone. "I don't really wanna touch it."

"Come in," Diego and Joe said at the same time. Diego moved over to stand by Trent. "Go. I'm just getting this." He bent and picked up the bone. Diego knew without a doubt it was human. "It's a direct threat to you both, for me." Diego held it in both hands. It was older, at least a decade or more, grayed and pocked with dirt and sand stuck in cracks.

"Fuck them and their threats." Trent sniffed and cupped Diego's shoulders. "Come on."

They went in, Diego still holding the bone. He couldn't have said why he was feeling odd about it. There was something besides the threat that was pulling at him. Since he couldn't pinpoint it, he settled for talking about what he did know. "They want me to know they'll do this to you. Both of you. And yeah, they want y'all to know, too, but mainly me. Right now, they don't know if you have any idea what I am. I'm betting they haven't even considered it. They think they have all the power."

"Instead of getting the gun, I'm getting my phone." Joe locked the door. "Trent, check the back, okay?"

"Got it." Trent darted off and Joe went to get his phone.

Diego set the bone on the floor and started taking off his clothes. They hadn't filmed him yet, but they were about to. He was fine with it. Neither Trent nor Joe would let the video get into the wrong hands.

Diego kept checking out of the windows. He didn't see anything suspicious, which meant nothing. He hadn't known the betas were close, and certainly not on the property, either. What surprised him was that they didn't just attack. "Maybe because they don't want trouble with humans."

"I assume you're wondering why they didn't just come kill us all," Joe said as he came back into the living room. "That's probably the reason. Even if we're easy for them to kill, it'd arouse suspicion, and who knows what might be discovered. There's people out hunting Big Foot and the Loch Ness Monster, people hunting aliens and vampires, so ruling out people hunting werewolves wouldn't be smart."

"I don't know if they are aware of all that. Maybe." Diego shrugged and kicked off his pants. He was totally nude when Trent walked in.

"Well, you're looking less like a bag of bones," Trent said. "Nice ass. Bigger dick than I'd have thought, too. Not bad, bro. You done well."

Joe glowered at his brother. "Can you stop ogling him?"

"I could," Trent mused. "But where's the fun in that? You get so mad."

Diego rolled his eyes at Trent. "I'm right here and I don't like it. How's that?"

Trent had the decency to blush. "Yeah, okay. Sorry. I was—well, I wasn't joking, 'cause that makes it sound like what I said wasn't true, and you might get a complex—"

"Trent," Joe snapped. "Get serious."

Trent took his phone from his pocket. "Wait. Let me get the laptop. We should have done this already."

"Should have, but we didn't." Joe waited until Trent had left the room. "You really are a stud, you know that? I can't even blame him for looking."

Diego was pretty sure he was blushing all the way to his ankles. "Er, thanks. You've got me beat. All over."

Joe snorted, then chuckled, and Diego realized what he'd said. He laughed too. Joe didn't beat him, but he sure did spank Diego's ass when they both needed it.

Trent came in carrying his laptop and gave them both an exaggeratedly disgusted look. "You two. I can't leave y'all alone for one minute without y'all getting in each other's pants or making smoochy eyes at each other."

"Smoochy eyes?" Joe repeated, his eyebrows almost coming together above his nose. "Seriously?"

Trent set the laptop on the coffee table. "Sure. I'm running out of descriptors for what you and Diego look like when y'all are all—" Trent made a swirling gesture in the air. "Doing that head over heels thing."

Joe grunted. Diego debated covering his cock and balls with his hands when Trent glanced at him but didn't see the point.

"Get your phone set on video," Joe said to Trent. Joe turned the phone so that the camera lens was pointing toward Diego. "Whenever Trent's ready."

"Almost." Trent pressed a button on his phone. "Yeah, okay."

"Let me count down from three, then give it a couple seconds. Take these phones at least that long to start recording after I hit the button." Joe began counting. "Three, two, one. Go."

Diego took the 'go' to be for Trent, so he was recording too. Diego gave it a good five seconds, then he lowered himself to his hands and knees. He refused to think about the fact that he was being filmed. Hopefully what they were doing would work.

The shift came over him quickly. Diego gave a fleeting thought to wishing it took longer because it would make for better viewing, but in a few heartbeats, he was a wolf.

"Diego, shift back."

At Joe's command, Diego returned to his human form. He stood and stretched.

"Damn. That just looks painful," he heard Trent mumble.

"I'm used to it, I guess." Diego reached for his clothes. "The first few times, it's excruciating."

"Can you turn humans into werewolves?" Trent asked.

Diego was actually surprised neither brother had asked the question sooner. "No. You're either born a shifter, or you aren't. That's probably another control set by Nature to ensure we don't get overpopulated."

"Guess Nature's too busy keeping y'all in check to stop us humans from overbreeding." Trent tucked his phone away.

Joe did as well, then he offered Diego a hand getting dressed. "So that bone. You got no doubt about it?" he asked so quietly Diego had to strain to hear him even with his shifter-enhanced hearing.

Diego settled for a slight shake of his head since it seemed apparent that Joe didn't want Trent hearing them.

Joe averted his gaze. "Let me button you up."

It was the first time Joe had done such a thing. He frequently undressed Diego. This was something Diego wasn't sure how to process. He thought it was another way Joe was showing that he cared, or perhaps he was working past the worry that he must be feeling.

Diego decided it didn't matter. Joe was trying to take care of him. "Thank you."

Joe brushed a soft kiss over his lips.

"I've got my clip on the laptop now. You want to send yours, Joe?" Trent asked.

Joe gave Diego a lingering look. "Yeah. Just a sec." A second kiss, deeper, warmer, and Diego was ready to beg Joe to take him back to bed.

Trent huffed. Joe winked at Diego then walked over to join Trent. "You'll find your guy, Trent. Now where do I send this, and how?"

"You can send it via text to me. I can open texts on here." He tapped the laptop screen lightly.

"For what it cost, you oughta be able to fly on that thing."

Diego finished dressing. He squatted and picked up the bone again. What was it about it that was bothering him?

"I don't know how I feel about keeping that in the house," Trent said. "It's part of someone's body. A dead person. That's like bringing a graveyard into the house."

Joe frowned at Trent. "You're being quite the drama queen."

Trent flipped him off. "Fuck you. That's just offensive."

"Fine," Joe said. "You're being quite the drama dork."

"Better," Trent asserted. "And I don't care. It's gross."

"I wonder where they got it from," Diego murmured, touching one of the deeper breaks in it. "They wouldn't have been carrying it around."

Joe went so still after a sharp inhalation that Diego dropped the bone in alarm.

"What?" Diego asked, coming to his feet. "What is it?"

Trent looked confused. "Joe?"

Joe shook himself. "I don't know. Nothing, I bet. I'm just being stupid."

Trent narrowed his eyes at Joe.

Diego touched Joe's arm. "You're not stupid. Don't say that."

"I'm just wondering the same thing you are. Where'd the bone come from?" Joe gestured at it. "There ain't any graveyards within fifty miles or so of here. I reckon there could be remains…"

"Remains from who?" Trent asked, rubbing his biceps as if he were cold. "Could be gangs dumping bodies on people's property again. We've had that problem before, though not…not on our ranch. But it's an old bone."

"It is." Diego could tell. "It's also smaller than — well, I was going to say the average man's, but I don't know what that is for humans. It's not a very long femur, though, and it's thinner than the ones I've seen from males. That probably means nothing since I've only seen shifter bones."

But Joe had gone and done his statue imitation again and Diego wondered why. Joe was staring at the bone. Diego stepped in front of it. When he did so, Joe looked at him instead. "What is it?" Diego asked.

"He thinks it's from our mom," Trent answered in a rough voice. "That's why he's—"

"I don't," Joe interrupted. "I don't know where it's from. We need to call the police, or Sheriff Kenzie, and have her come out here. This has to be reported."

"There'll be cops all over the place searching for more, and dogs, too, maybe." Trent's smile wobbled. "What if it is her, Joe? What would that mean?"

Joe turned to Trent. "It wouldn't mean anything unless some bone doctor could prove how she'd died. It's a moot point. It ain't her."

"What if she didn't leave us?" Trent asked.

Joe lowered his head. "You saying you think Dad killed her?"

Trent shrugged. "I don't know. He was violent at times."

"Not like that, he wasn't," Joe snapped. "He spanked us when he thought we had it coming—"

"He beat the ever lovin' shit out of us both on more than one occasion because of stupid shit kids do!" Trent yelled.

Diego's gut cramped. He hated anger, hated seeing two people he cared about arguing. He slipped between them. "Please stop. There's no use to this. There isn't. This femur could be something the betas dug up and dragged with them."

"Didn't think you believed that was likely," Trent accused.

Joe rumbled and Diego tipped his chin up at Trent. "I don't *know* what they did or didn't do. That's the point. None of us know who that femur was a part of, or how it got found. Well, before we found it. Arguing and fighting is a ridiculous waste of time."

"That's the truth." Joe slid an arm around Diego's waist. "We got to call Sheriff Kenzie, though. Maybe the betas will see they screwed up with the bone stunt. Or we could wait a few days." Joe held up a hand when Trent sputtered. "Hear me out, bro. Whoever that thing belonged to is long dead and they ain't going to be any less dead if we wait. We need to put an end to this shit with these fuckers trying to get to Diego."

"Sheriff'll be mad as hell we didn't call her sooner," Trent argued.

"You gonna tell her we waited?" Joe retorted.

Trent quit giving Joe a hard time, and Diego was relieved. "What do we do now?" he asked Joe. "Are we going to try to find them?"

"I don't know that we should get far from the house. Got the video loaded to the laptop and all." Joe looked out of the nearest window. "But we gotta take care of the cattle and horses. We'll do that together, the three of us, then get back here and hope they'll approach us."

Diego frowned, confused just a little. "We can show them the video on the phone, right?"

"Yeah, we can. Still rather have them come here than catch us out in the open." Joe nodded toward the spare room where the gun cabinets were. "I never did get our weapons. Come on, y'all. Let's gear up."

"Boy, for a second I thought you were gonna say something lame like 'Let's lock and load' and I was gonna have to deck you." Trent cackled when Joe tried to thump him.

Diego smiled and felt like at least one thing was righted. Joe and Trent were arguing, so that was good.

In the spare room, they took out the guns they'd each chosen. Diego's had been picked for him since he hadn't had any experience with them. Not until Joe had started teaching him to shoot. The forty-five was heavy, solid, and Diego preferred it to the nine millimeter Trent tucked into a holster. Trent would also be carrying a three fifty-seven Magnum like Joe was. Then there were the rifles and shotgun.

All in all, they were a small militia. Diego didn't like guns, but he agreed they could be useful if whoever wielded the weapon was a good shot—and not a psychotic asshole.

They left the house after a discussion over who would take the lead. Diego and Joe ended up walking together with Trent moving to Diego's side once they were off the porch.

"They've been all over out here," Diego said quietly. "They've marked the truck and the barn as well as the house."

"I'm gonna kill them just for that," Trent muttered. "Assholes."

"We need one of them left alive to send a message back to the alphas," Joe pointed out. "Otherwise there'll just be more sent out."

"You just won't let me have any fun." Trent got the last word in before they all began on their chores. Despite there being the three of them working together, it took longer to get the tasks done. Had they been able to split up, or willing to, they'd have cut their work hours down.

It wasn't worth being separated. Diego kept his senses on high alert.

"Nothing?" Trent asked for the sixth time as they fed the last of the cattle.

Diego was tempted to tell him that yes, he'd been watching the betas all along. If he'd caught a hint of them, he'd have said so. "No," he said through gritted teeth. His nerves were as frayed as could be.

"Well, I keep expecting them to jump out and attack," Trent grumbled.

"Jump out from where?" Joe asked. "We have the cattle in the pastures with nowhere to hide around them. The horses are out of the barn, too, so we don't have to worry about that. Okay, there's the tractor that won't start until we get the part in for it, and that rust-bucket car that needs hauling off, and the shed — can't move that. But we know about those. We know they're all potential hiding spots, so we keep an eye out around them. It's not as many places as there was before, and we just can't risk tearing the tractor up. We need it. And the car, well, that'd take time and we haven't had much of that to spare. Plus, it'd just be put somewhere else on the ranch where it could be used by the betas to hide. It's best to keep 'em where they are. We are prepared for this."

"Yeah I know."

Diego let go of his frustration. It wasn't doing him any good at all. He tried to imagine what the betas might do next. Since he'd only known them to be violent instead of logical, it was a hard guess. He thought he might be close after a minute or two of concentrating on the issue. "I think maybe they're waiting until dark. There aren't any good hiding spots other than the ones Joe mentioned, we made sure of that like Joe said." They'd even stacked bags of feed and hay in the back laundry room to prevent having to go into the barn, and past the two vehicles in the yard, where many opportunities for an ambush awaited them.

"They could be in the barn," Joe said, looking off in that direction. "Or breaking into the house even now."

"We set the alarm, so I don't think they'd be in the house." Diego shivered at the idea of it. "And you put up all those alarm signs. I know at least one of the betas can read somewhat. Sam can. He wouldn't risk a call to the alarm company."

It was a good thing they had printed off signs, because there was no alarm company in all reality. The signs were legitimate, however, and Diego believed they would keep the betas at bay—at least briefly. There was an actual *alarm* that would go off if the house was broken into, though it only worked for the doors. And it only made a lot of racket. It didn't automatically send out a call to the police.

But the betas knew none of that, Diego reminded himself. He glanced back toward the house, too. "We could sit out on the porch tonight. I believe that would be enough."

"I could stay inside and shoot the fuckers when they showed up," Trent offered. "All but one, since y'all wanna send a beta back to tell the alpha to fuck off. I think killing them all and sending the alpha proof of it along with a nice note about the videos would be just as effective."

"You're a bloodthirsty sort," Diego said to Trent. "I had no idea just how much so. Plus, we'd need to leave one alive to get the stuff back to the alpha."

Trent laughed then cursed. "Well, fuck. Yeah I'm bloodthirsty, but also, these bastards are coming onto our property, making threats, and they want to hurt you."

"They have hurt you," Joe stated. "Have any of the three betas ever left a scar on you?"

Diego nodded his head. "That was their right in the pack."

"Well, you aren't in their pack anymore, and they're going to let you go." Joe dusted off his hands.

Diego figured there was symbolism in the gesture but didn't ask.

"Let's get back to the house. We need this to end so we can take care of the ranch properly. Can't keep enough food in the washroom for more than another day." Trent opened the truck door. "And I think we should have put those metal bear traps out in the barn. I found those old ones, and they're rusty as hell, but I could have cleaned 'em up. I think."

"And lopped your damned hand off doing so," Joe said. "Then I'd have had a helluva mess to clean up and you'd have been hollering and bitching like a wuss."

"Aw, fuck you," Trent drawled. "I'm driving. Gimme the keys."

"It's my —" Joe stopped and tossed the keys to Trent. "Fine, but remember, I love this truck."

Trent gave an exaggerated sigh. "Yeah, yeah, more than you love me. Whatever."

They got in, Diego sitting in the middle. The brothers were both broader then he was and there wasn't much wiggle room for him. Joe took Diego's hand in his and rested them on his thigh. Diego liked the feel of the worn denim under the back of his hand, liked knowing Joe's skin, his body, was warm and strong beneath it.

Trent started the truck then put it in drive. "You really think they'll show up tonight?"

"Hope so," Joe answered. "If not, we gotta draw them out. I still think the porch-sitting tonight is the best idea."

"They won't have guns, for sure?" Trent asked. "I know you said they wouldn't, Diego, but it'd sure suck dog balls to be on the porch swing yakking away one second and have your brains blown out the next."

"Our pack has never had a weapon, not even knives. They pride themselves on being self-sufficient in all things."

Joe made a derisive sound, something more forceful than a snort but not quite a word. "Well, like Trent says, fuck 'em. We're not going to cower in the house, and we sure as hell won't let them get the jump on us." He turned a fierce gaze on Diego. "And they ain't touching you or anything else—"

"Fuck!" Trent shouted.

Diego went flying forward as Trent stomped on the brakes.

"God damn it!" Joe shouted.

Diego hit the dashboard and his head hit the windshield. They didn't wear seatbelts when they were on the ranch property. Diego's ears rang from the impact and the yelling as Trent and Joe kept up the cursing.

"What the fuck—?" Joe gasped. "The house!"

Diego blinked and blinked. His vision was hazy but a good shake of his head made the pain swell then ebb. He looked out of the window and saw the plume of smoke reaching up to the sky. He blinked again. From where they were, they couldn't actually see the house, but he thought...

"No, it's one of the barns. The house would be to the left some." Diego stared dumbly as orange and red flames shot up on the porch.

"Mother fuckers," Joe growled.

"They're dead. All of 'em." Trent floored the pedal and the truck fish-tailed on the dirt road before shooting forward.

"Every last one of 'em," Joe agreed. "We'll send the alphas a message some other way."

"Maybe it isn't too bad," Diego mumbled, his heart in his throat. "I'm sorry. I'm sorry. I'm so sor—"

"Stop it," Joe ground out, taking Diego by one shoulder. With his other hand, he cupped Diego's chin. "You didn't do this. They did."

"Because of me." Diego couldn't look at Joe. No matter what was said, this wouldn't have happened if Diego had moved on.

"It's just a barn. It ain't more important than you or Trent, or me, for that matter."

But Diego heard the loss in Joe's voice, the anger. Shame filled him and he kept his gaze averted.

"Diego. Look at me."

Diego was saved from having to try by the bump and slide of the truck as Trent took the last turn entirely too fast. He stomped on the brakes again.

"Guns," Joe barked. They were in the truck, either on their persons or in the gun rack mounted on the back window. "Shit! Call the fire department. Trent—"

"On it."

Diego helped get the guns down, but he knew the betas wouldn't be there if they weren't already out and waiting. Not once had they seen the weapons. *Maybe.*

A part of him hoped he was wrong and the betas would attack. He wanted this over as much as Joe and Trent did. He just hoped when it was done that they were still alive, and the betas... Diego didn't care if they lived or died, just as long as they left him in peace with his lover and sort of brother-in-law.

He wondered if he'd be so lucky.

Chapter Nineteen

The barn was going to be a total loss. Joe cocked the shotgun. "Come out and face us, you gutless fuckers!"

Beside him, Trent fired off a shot toward the barn. "Yeah, come on out here." Trent leaned toward Joe. "Fire department will get here as soon as possible. We need to make sure this doesn't spread to the other buildings or the fields."

"I'll get the hose." Diego didn't wait for permission, and he ignored Joe's shout to stop.

It wasn't like Diego was going far—the water hose was attached to the spigot beside the porch, which was fifty yards or so from the barn. The hose wasn't that long, so it was a wasted attempt. Joe was more worried that the betas would pop up and take Diego away.

He'd built them up into boogey monsters in his mind, giving them more power than they surely had. The betas couldn't appear out of thin air, nor could they swoop down from the sky or burst out of the ground. Joe knew he was being unreasonable, but his fear of losing Diego was incredibly powerful.

He chased after Diego, but there was no way he could match Diego's speed.

Joe realized his mistake a second after a blur appeared in his peripheral vision. "Diego! Look out!"

Had he stood still and kept the shotgun trained in Diego's direction, he could have provided Diego with cover via the threat of being shot.

Now he was in the way should Trent need to shoot, and on top of that he couldn't stop and get a good aim quickly.

"Joe, duck!" Trent yelled.

Joe was trying to get the double-barreled shotgun steady. Loaded with double-ought buckshot, the weapon was definitely capable of killing even the huge wolf running toward Diego.

Diego leaped in the air and shifted, his clothes ripping and a snarl leaving his muzzle.

A deep, maniacal growl followed, though it didn't come from Diego. It came from one of the three wolves barreling toward him.

"We know what you are, you stupid fuckers," Joe shouted. "And we got proof of it! Leave him alone or—" The smallest of the three leaped.

Joe aimed and pulled the front trigger. The resulting explosion of sound made his ears ring even though he was expecting it. Before the echo of it ended, another shot was fired, this one from Trent.

The wolf yelped and twisted to no avail. Blood sprayed out and pieces of flesh and fur did the same.

"We'll tell everyone!" Joe bellowed. "Everyone! If you lay a hand on him, people will come after your kind and not stop until every one of you is nothing but a bad memory!"

The bigger wolf pawed the ground. Diego lowered his head, teeth bared.

"We got it all on video," Joe added, glad his voice didn't shake. Now that he was looking at the betas, he saw what Diego meant. They were huge, the biggest almost twice as broad and a good foot taller than Diego.

The other beta growled. Joe flicked a glance at the still-twitching form of the dying one. "Try me, fucker," he muttered, raising the shotgun again.

"I told you we just need to kill them and be done with it," Trent said.

"We can do that." Joe pointed his weapon at the bigger wolf. "Take the other one."

Before he could pull the second trigger, the wolf leaped onto Diego. It was so fast, Diego didn't have the chance to dodge the attack.

At the same time, the remaining beta ducked and ran to the right.

"Shoot the fucker," Trent hollered.

Joe couldn't get an aim on it, and he knew Trent wouldn't be able to because he was in between Trent on the wolf. "Save Diego!" Joe needed his brother to listen to him.

"We'll let the world see the videos! If we die, people we trust know how to release the videos to everyone with a computer." Trent sounded calm.

Joe was glad, because he was about to lose it as he tried to get the beta he was attempting to track in the crosshairs. It kept moving, and hiding behind the things they hadn't moved, like the tractor and the rusted out car that Joe needed to haul off, the shed that wasn't going anywhere without the help of a bulldozer, and the other barn.

Joe wanted desperately to look and see what was happening with Diego. That big wolf was making a lot of vicious noises. If he dared to peek, Joe feared he'd be attacked himself.

"Trent," he urged. His brother would know Joe's concern.

"Everyone in the world," Trent said. "Won't your alphas be proud?"

A loud, snarling bark was followed by a yip from the wolf Joe was tracking.

"I ain't lying about the videos. Look."

Joe knew Trent was taking his phone out and getting the video pulled up. That's what he would do.

"You watch this and see. We have more, too. Diego ain't stupid. He knows you assholes won't leave him alone."

"And he knows we won't let anyone hurt him," Joe added when Trent went silent. "We show that video to every online news source, hell we put it on YouTube and it'll be viral—which means it'll be seen by millions of people worldwide—in minutes. Then you can kiss your ass and your pack goodbye."

Joe started to look when he heard the video begin. He caught himself, then Trent gasped and an unfamiliar male spoke.

"And who will protect Diego here from the masses of humans looking to kill all of us shifters? You two, with your guns?"

"Now you're just sounding like a clichéd B-movie bad guy," Joe said, knowing he had to be speaking to the biggest beta, the one that had attacked Diego. He couldn't see him, but he'd have bet his last dollar on it being that shifter, and obviously, that beta at least had morphed into human form to be able to speak. "And fuck you. I'll take him somewhere no one will ever find us."

"We'll find you," that bastard stated.

"Since he ain't listening to reason— Shoot him, Trent."

"I can't," Trent said in a way that sent a chill down Joe's spine. "Diego's... He's got Diego."

Panic and fury flared bright and hot in Joe. He was done playing nice. He was done with Diego being bait. Joe spun around and by the time he saw that Diego was being used as a shield by the shifter, he knew he couldn't get off a shot without hitting Diego.

"You're dead," Joe promised the beta.

The edges of the man's smile showed around one side of Diego's muzzle. "No, I think that's you, fuckheads." He jerked the arm he had around Diego's throat.

Diego whined and kicked his back legs.

Joe felt a surge of anger unlike anything he'd ever experienced before. "Fight him, Diego! You don't have to take anything from him!"

The shifter laughed, a rusty, abrasive laugh that was worse than nails on a chalkboard. "But he does. He's just an omega. He's nothing, the least of us all."

"He's not just an omega," Joe growled. "And if he was nothing, your alphas wouldn't have sent you three assholes after him. Diego's stronger than any of you. I bet you couldn't put up with half of what was done to him. You'd break, you worthless—"

"Joe!"

At Trent's shout, Joe jerked his head around in time to see the other wolf shifter coming for him. Though he tried to get the shotgun aimed, there wasn't time. He saw teeth, big, sharp teeth, and he swung the weapon in the hopes of hurting the beast with it. The impact sent a shock of pain all the way up to his shoulder, but the shifter didn't so much as yelp. Joe gritted his teeth and stumbled backwards, barely avoiding claws and teeth. He brought the butt of the shotgun down on the wolf's head.

The beast yelped and skittered back. It leaped again before Joe had the chance to get his handgun out or the shotgun aimed.

He landed a glancing blow, not good enough at all and he knew it. The wolf snarled, its heated, acrid breath wafting over Joe's face an instant before Joe felt the searing pain of something tearing into his shoulder.

Behind him, he heard the sounds of other scuffles, but he had to concentrate on not getting his throat ripped out. He was twisting, moving, trying to get away from the wolf, while at the same time trying to get a grip on the three fifty-seven he'd shoved in the holster.

His fingers were going numb and they slipped over the butt of the gun. Joe dropped to the left, going down on one knee and contorting himself in ways he'd never known he could, but he had to get away from the wolf that was almost on top of him.

And it was blood on his fingers, he saw, the image of the red wetness stunning him.

"Joe!" Trent yelled.

Joe didn't know what he was supposed to do. He was saved from having to figure it out when a rifle blast nearly deafened him. Blood was everywhere, and it wasn't all his.

The wolf made a gurgling sound. Joe forced himself to his feet again, flinging the dead thing off him.

"Diego," he shouted, heart thumping as he spun to look for his lover.

"Those bastards took off with him—another came out from behind the shed when you were fighting.

They went that way." Trent pointed the rifle toward the house. "Out back!"

So there'd been four betas. At least. Joe's head spun and he shook it, hard. He wasn't going to pass out from a little dog bite. "Shoulda shot him."

Trent scowled. "The biggest one was using Diego as his shield. You're bleeding."

Like Joe cared. He put one foot in front of the other and ran after Diego.

Diego was bouncing like a rag doll on a kid-filled trampoline. He had tried fighting, but Sam was too big, too strong for him to take. Then the other beta had appeared, Marc, and Diego had been overpowered and Joe had been attacked, been bitten. Giving up seemed to be the best thing Diego could do for Joe.

"Take me. Leave them alone and just take me," Diego had rasped when he could breathe. He wouldn't endanger Joe and Trent anymore. "I won't fight."

Sam shifted and dragged him off while Marc ran along beside them. Diego thought Trent was going to shoot, and he did, but it was to kill Ann and save Joe's life.

Sam had Diego by the scruff, had sunk his teeth in deep enough that every step sent a hideous jolt of pain through Diego. It'd be worse as soon as they could stop. Sam and Marc would make him pay for running off, and for the loss of the other two betas.

He didn't care, as long as Joe lived.

Diego started to close his eyes. Sam threw him down, jarring Diego from his complacency. The snarling, barking mix from Sam were orders Diego couldn't disobey. Sam wanted him up and running on his own, so Diego struggled to his feet. Anger burned hot in his gut—he didn't want to leave Joe, didn't want to return to the life he'd known before he'd tasted freedom.

It's for Joe— The thought was ruptured by the three betas running past him, Sam and Marc in the opposite direction. *Toward Joe!*

Sam slapped him with a paw and Diego sprang at the larger wolf. Now he knew why it'd taken so long for the betas to find him—they'd been gathering their forces before coming for him.

Well, he wasn't going to let them win, not when it meant Joe's life, and Trent's, too.

Sam bared his teeth, spit and blood dripping from his muzzle. *My blood. I've let them shed enough of it.*

Gunshots rang out, and sirens rent the air. Diego was almost deafened by the ruckus, but he blocked it as best as he could while circling Sam.

Sam moved, too, making it impossible for Diego to get a good attack in. Marc flanked Sam, and Diego knew he'd be killed by the both of them but he wasn't giving in.

He also knew they wouldn't expect him to act rashly, despite having just challenged them.

So he did, leaping, snarling, snapping in a foolish move that should have ended with him being killed.

It didn't. Sam was either stunned or just distracted by all of the noise. Either way, Diego landed halfway on him, sinking his teeth into Sam's shoulder and immediately shaking his head to cause the most damage.

Sam howled and bit at Diego, but Diego was already scampering away. Marc lunged at him, and Diego thought of Joe and Trent, of all they'd done and what they'd lose. There was no way to measure the fury that pounded into him. He'd had enough, given enough already. The pack wasn't getting any more.

Diego had felt pain many times, and it didn't faze him, not like it seemed to be doing to Sam, who backed away and let Marc take over. Diego heard Sam whimper before the blare of sirens overpowered the sound. The fire department was close. Surely the betas would have enough sense to flee.

But Marc dove at him. Diego feinted right then slammed to the left, knocking Marc down. There was no hesitating as he jumped on Marc and ripped at his throat. It was messy and not entirely successful at first. Diego caused more suffering than he'd ever intended, but Marc kept fighting and every time Diego got a good bite in, Marc would literally rip his flesh from Diego's grip.

Until he didn't. Diego crunched harder, felt blood spurt into his mouth and throat. He shook his head, tearing, killing, then let go when his prey was dead.

He looked at Sam. "Come on, asshole," he growled in a series of barks. "Come get yours, too."

Sam bared his teeth again, and Diego bared his right back. He pawed at the ground and lowered his head.

Sam flattened his ears—then he shifted, holding one hand out. "Stop!"

Diego advanced a couple of steps.

"Stop, God damn it!" Sam shouted. "You win, Diego. You fucking—"

"Call him one more bad word and I blow your fucking head off."

Diego almost wept upon hearing Joe's rough voice. That, and the sound of a trigger being pulled back.

"I mean it," Joe said. "We done killed your little buddies except for the one Trent's bringing around. Don't know if that one will make it or not. Don't care.

You're going to take him or her, and help get these wolf corpses outta here except for one. Then you're going back to the pack and relaying a message — the same one I gave you before. We got proof, and we'll use it to keep Diego safe from you fuckers."

"But not the rest of the world," Sam said. "They'll want him."

Diego looked back to see Joe's steely expression. "They'll get you, and every shifter in your pack and every pack Diego can name off. I'm good with photo alterations. No one will see Diego's face in those videos. And I'll hide so deep with him no one will ever know where to find us. Or you can be smart for once in your fucked up life and take the chance to live. I don't want anything from you fuckers but Diego, and you tell your alphas to let him go. If I don't hear back from your pack in two weeks, shifters will be making their Internet debut."

"And how do we tell you if the alphas agree?"

Joe gestured with the gun. "Not by showing one of your ugly asses back here. Figure it out. Two weeks, or word gets out." He gestured to Marc's dead body. "And it'd be in your best interest to get rid of all the bodies except the one before a shit load of people get here and wonder why there's a pack of dead wolves. One I can explain as a fluke, the littlest one. The rest of you…"

Sam nodded. "Fine."

"If I see you after this, I'm killing you. No waiting for an explanation." Joe kept the weapon aimed at Sam. "Move him, and tell whoever Trent's bringing to help and why he or she better do it."

Diego shifted then and almost wept with relief when Joe caught him by the arm before pulling him to his feet. "Joe, I—"

Joe touched his lips with one finger. "It's okay, honey. This is going to work. Now let's get these wolf carcasses out of here. Judging by the sound of the sirens, the fire truck ain't but about five minutes away. They have to take it slower on the road coming in since it hasn't been graded yet after the last heavy rains. Take this." He handed Diego the three fifty-seven. "Shoot him and any other shifter if you need to. Or hell, if you want to." Joe tipped his chin toward Sam. "I won't mind at all, or think less of you."

Diego surprised himself by laughing at that. He took the weapon and leveled it at Sam. "It makes really big holes in things."

Sam gulped and grabbed Marc by the back paws. "Where do I put this?"

Joe pointed to a large metal building that housed the big tractor. "In there. You get them put away and we'll do the rest."

"I'm not leaving the bodies with you," Sam said. "No. You will have to kill me first."

Joe sighed. "Don't fucking tempt me, asshole. You're leaving one, and that's that. There'll be no way to explain all the blood if there isn't a body of something lying around. After the fire department leaves, you can dispose of them while we watch you."

Diego expected Sam to keep arguing, but maybe it was the increasingly loud wail of the sirens that made him decide to shut up. Sam ordered the other beta, Lily, to help him. Diego handed the gun back to Joe, and with Trent's help, the carcasses were hidden by the time the fire truck was parked. Diego ran in the back entry and found a pair of sweats and a T-shirt. He was back outside in thirty seconds.

"Sorry it took so long," a man said as he got out. "Third goddamned fire in a row!"

"I hope everyone's okay." Joe strode over to the man. "Jeff." They shook hands. "The barn's toast."

Jeff nodded. "Sure looks that way. It's not spreading, so you're lucky. Ain't a windy day. If it was, or if the fire was spreading, I wouldn't be talking to you now."

"Don't let me stop you from doing your thing." Joe stepped back. The man, Jeff, started handing out orders to other men and women who set about unrolling a fire hose that was attached to the large water truck. "They have to bring their own water," Joe murmured to Diego.

"Is that a...? What the hell happened here?" Jeff asked.

Joe winced. "Well, see, it's been a weird-as-fuck day here at the ranch. You know how there ain't no wolves around here anymore? That's what we're told anyway, but someone was dead wrong."

Epilogue

"It worked. I'm going home." Trent had that stubborn set to his jaw that meant there was no changing his mind.

Joe was still going to try. "You don't know that. Just because they said they were leaving doesn't mean it's the truth."

"And I'll shoot them if they lied, but I'm still going home." Trent sighed and glanced down. "None of us can live in fear, Joe. We have to go on with our lives. If they come back, then we fight. Until then, we live."

"You're right." Joe grinned at Trent. "How'd you get so smart?"

"It's that fifty thousand dollar education I got myself." Trent rolled his eyes. "All right. I'll text you when I get there, but that's it. I'm not checking in every few minutes, so deal with it."

Joe hugged his brother. "All right. Go be a grown-up if you gotta."

"I do." Trent hugged him back then pulled away. "Later."

"Hey, Trent?" Joe called out.

Trent arched a brow at him.

Joe lightly touched his shoulder. "Thanks for saving me, and helping with the rest."

"Sure thing." Trent left then, and Joe locked the door behind him. Yes, they had to get on with their lives, but he would make a few changes here and there, like locking up the house regularly.

"He left already?" Diego asked, coming into the kitchen. "How do you feel?"

"Yeah, he's gonna check in when he gets home then leave us all to ourselves." Joe opened his arms up to Diego. "I hurt like a mother, but my bite isn't as bad as yours. Still wish you'd have let me take you for stitches."

"I didn't need them, and anyway, explaining the bite would have been tricky." Diego cuddled in beside him. "I've had worse injuries."

"Not on my watch." Joe had seen the bite and wanted to kill the other shifters all over again. He was waiting for the guilt to set in. Maybe it would once the memory of Diego being taken from him faded. *So never.* "You think the alphas will listen to reason?"

Diego grimaced. "I don't know. They've never had to face anything like this, like us."

"Like you," Joe clarified. "You did this. You told them to fuck themselves, that you weren't taking their abuse anymore. It's been my experience that bullies back away quick once they know someone won't give in to their terror tactics."

"I hope you're right." Diego pressed his cheek against Joe's chest. "I've never been so scared as I was when I realized the other betas were going after you and Trent. I didn't know I could be as strong as I was then."

Joe cupped Diego's chin and gently raised it. Diego looked at him. "Love does that," Joe whispered. "Makes you strong, makes you vicious and deadly, soft and sweet. It changes you in ways that no one ever told you love would."

"It does," Diego murmured in return, his eyes glistening. "It made me a better man."

"I love you," Joe got out, and it was surprisingly easier than he'd have thought to say those words out loud. "In case you didn't get that, I love you, Diego. I don't ever want to be without you."

Diego swallowed as a tear slid down his cheek. "Oh, I know. I know, and I love you, too, Joe. I have for a while."

Joe figured they'd said enough. He dipped his head, and Diego stood on his tiptoes. The kiss was tender, slow, Joe sucking on Diego's bottom lip before slipping his tongue into Diego's mouth.

Diego put his arms around Joe's waist and leaned in closer. Joe placed a hand at Diego's nape, and the other right above Diego's butt. He pushed his tongue in deeper, twining it with Diego's, teasing, promising.

They were both injured, but not severely. Joe was more than up to some lovemaking with his partner. He massaged Diego's neck and kept plundering his mouth, taking, giving, wanting.

Diego melted against him. Joe would be careful with him, would treasure the man and make sure he had room to grow and learn about himself.

And he'd love him until the day he died. Which would hopefully be before Diego died, because Joe couldn't imagine a life without him.

"Bedroom," Joe got out when he finally ended the kiss. "Get naked for me. And get out the other lube."

Diego's eyes rounded. "R-really?"

"Unless you hurt too bad?" Joe said. He didn't think he was reading Diego wrong, though.

"No, no, I don't." Diego popped up on his toes and brushed a chaste kiss over Joe's lips. Then he turned and sprinted for the bedroom.

If Joe'd had any doubts about Diego being too hurt for fucking, he'd just been proven wrong for thinking so. Joe sauntered to the bedroom, giving Diego time to strip down and get out the lube.

Apparently he'd given Diego more than enough time, Joe thought as he lounged in the doorway and watched Diego finger his ass. "Did I say you could do that?" Joe drawled.

Diego's eyes took on that startled look again. "No, sir. No, I'm sorry. I just wanted to—"

"Finger yourself?" Joe asked. "'Cause that wasn't what I had in mind at all, but now that I see how sexy you look doing it, maybe I should bypass my original plans."

Diego had his finger out and was wiping it on the sheet before Joe finished. "Please don't! Please—I need you."

Joe frowned and wondered. "You doing that to get a spanking?" He hadn't wanted to go that way tonight, but if that was what Diego needed…

"No. I really was just trying to, er, speed things up," Diego explained, his cheeks red.

"Ah. Well, that being the case…" Joe didn't finish. Diego could wait and see what was going to happen. "Get your hands up on the headboard. Don't let go."

"Yes, sir." Diego grabbed the wooden slats.

Joe undressed, taking his time, making Diego wait. Diego's cock never softened. It remained hard and wet-tipped, the foreskin pulled back so that the fat head was exposed. Joe's mouth watered.

He strolled to the bed and took a taste. Slightly salty, kind of bland.

Diego hissed and wiggled.

Joe reached down to tease at Diego's pucker. "Be still," he warned. He pushed a thumb right into Diego's hole.

"Uhn." Diego's eyes rolled back in his head and he closed his eyes. His sphincter gripped Joe's thumb with a familiar heat that Joe craved.

"Already slicked yourself some, huh?" Joe pushed his thumb in deeper, applying pressure to the outer rim. "Not nearly enough, though."

Diego panted and raised his legs up. Joe considered putting him on his belly, but he wanted to see Diego's face, so he didn't tell him to roll over.

What he did do was grab the large container of lube. "Gonna need a bunch of this."

Diego moaned. "Oh, please. Joe, come on, I'm begging."

"I like it when you beg." Joe pulled his thumb out. "Plan on hearing you do it a lot." He patted Diego's hip. "Be right back."

Diego's eyelids snapped open. "Where—?"

"Towels," Joe answered before Diego could ask the rest of the question. "Otherwise the bed will be soaked in lube. Don't let this fall." He set the lube on Diego's belly.

Probably there were less messy ways to do it, but Joe was fine with Plan A—fist Diego tonight. They'd both been wanting, and he'd worked Diego's ass open to four fingers every night the past week. Tonight they needed the bond, and Joe was glad he'd waited. Glad they'd waited.

He got the towels and returned to the bed. "Pick your butt up."

Diego did and Joe layered two towels beneath him. "Okay."

Diego relaxed and Joe patted his leg. "Gonna have you move 'em."

"Yeah, I forgot. My brain is scrambled." Diego raised his legs, bringing his knees almost to his chest.

"Move them if you need to." Joe stuck his hand into the tub of lube and coated it thoroughly. Without preamble, he pushed two fingers into Diego's ass.

Diego's eyes closed again. "Ungh!"

Diego opened for him, those tight inner walls rippling and gripping. Joe pressed in as deep as he could get them and he spread his fingers apart. "You're such a sweet lover," he found himself saying. "So good. Mind me so good, and so tight."

He was going to be the one babbling incoherently at that rate. Joe twisted his wrist, turning his fingers inside Diego and stroking those silky muscles that rippled around his digits.

Diego huffed. "Please, I need to move. Let me hold my legs, let me—" He rocked his hips, meeting Joe's next thrust.

"Do it," Joe ordered. Usually he made Diego keep still, but tonight he wanted to see and hear everything that happened to Diego. He wanted no restraint between them. "Fuck yourself on these." Joe pushed a third finger in. "Show me you want it."

"I do." Diego undulated and moaned. "Oh, my Gods, oh, Gods. More, please."

Joe grinned. He looked down and watched the way Diego's ring stretched for him. Joe began fingering Diego harder, letting his knuckles slam against the outside of his asshole.

"Yes!" Diego shouted. "Joe, please! So good—"

Joe dipped his head down and took the tip of Diego's dick between his lips. That got him another shout from Diego.

Joe's own cock was harder than ever, but he'd get to it in time. He flicked his tongue over Diego's slit and caressed Diego's gland.

Diego yelped, not in pain, but in the familiar, alarmed, *ohmygodshelpme I'm gonna come* way that Joe recognized.

"Better not," Joe warned after he let Diego's cock slip from his mouth. "You come, and we stop. I can't fist you when you've got everything tight and sensitive."

"I won't," Diego eked out. "Please don't stop."

Joe pulled his fingers back then formed a cone-like shape with them. "Stay relaxed."

Diego panted as Joe filled him with them. Joe took his time, stopping when Diego's ass was tensed, waiting for those muscles to relax and let him in. It didn't take long, but Joe was covered in sweat and anticipation when he finally had them fully in Diego's ass.

"Breathe," he ordered, really for the both of them. He was so close to coming it wasn't funny.

Joe fingered Diego for several minutes until he was afraid that any more would be too much for Diego's hole. "Inhale, let it out on three. One, two, three." Joe pulled his fingers out. He dipped his hand in lube again. "I love you," he said, lining his hand back up, fingers coned, soaked with lube.

"Take me," Diego whispered, eyes open a fraction of an inch. Joe watched him while he pushed his fingers in slowly. Diego's cheeks went ruddy, his breathing turned choppy when Joe stopped with the widest part of his hand pushing at Diego's hole.

"Deep breath in," Joe advised, "then out for a count of three. In…and out." He repeated it two more times, and when Diego exhaled, his body relaxed, Joe pressed his hand forward.

"Gods," Diego keened, arching his back. "Please!"

Joe turned his hand a little, then it happened. His hand glided past the rim, spreading it wide, and he was inside Diego in a way he hadn't ever been before. "I'm in you, honey."

"Feel you," Diego muttered. "All the way to here." He slapped a palm to his chest.

"Yeah. I'm there, too." Joe curled his fingers into a fist. Diego mewled again. Joe opened his hand up and Diego gurgled, his cock spurting pre-cum. "Close?"

Instead of answering, Diego clenched around Joe's fist. "Move, please, please, please!"

Joe grinned and looked down at his forearm as he began to fuck Diego with his fist. He kept it slow, didn't move too deep, either. He wouldn't risk hurting Diego like that.

And the gentle movements, the slight rocking, was pushing the best sounds out of Diego—wordless ones full of breathiness and wails at the same time.

Joe turned his wrist, pushed in a little faster. At the same time, he used his other hand to pinch the underside of Diego's dick.

Diego howled and jerked all over as spunk shot from his dick. Joe held his hand still inside him and bent to lick at Diego's cock.

Diego bellowed again. Joe caught seed on his tongue and cheek. He licked Diego's shaft until it started to soften, then he nipped him on the thigh. "Need you to relax again and let me get my hand out."

"Uhn," was Diego's reply to that. Joe smirked, damned proud of himself. He lubed up his wrist and worked that lube into Diego before gently beginning the withdrawal.

It took almost as long to get his hand out as it had to get it in Diego. Once Joe had it free, he stood and lined his dick up with Diego's gaping pucker. "I want—"

"Take it," Diego said. "Gods, take it!"

Joe pressed in, filling Diego again with one hard thrust. Diego's insides were hot and looser than usual, and the reason for that was enough to push Joe to the edge.

"I had my hand in you," he muttered like a fool while thrusting. "All of it. In you."

"'Cause I'm yours," Diego slurred, reaching for him.

"You are," Joe agreed. He lowered himself onto Diego, let himself be held. "And I love you."

And nothing would ever change that.

About the Author

A native Texan, Bailey spends her days spinning stories around in her head, which has contributed to more than one incident of tripping over her own feet. Evenings are reserved for pounding away at the keyboard, as are early morning hours. Sleep? Doesn't happen much. Writing is too much fun, and there are too many characters bouncing about, tapping on Bailey's brain demanding to be let out.

Caffeine and chocolate are permanent fixtures in Bailey's office and are never far from hand at any given time. Removing either of those necessities from Bailey's presence can result in what is know as A Very, Very Scary Bailey and is not advised under any circumstances.

Bailey Bradford loves to hear from readers. You can find her contact information, website details and author profile page at http://www.totallybound.com.

Totally Bound Publishing